Praise for a Banner of Da.

'A remarkable take on the old concept of good versus evil, of mythology balanced against reality. Set in Wales in Roman times and in the modern age, the book has a wonderful sense of place, great characters and a lively and compelling plot with enough mystery to keep even the most demanding of readers content and intrigued.'

Phil Carradice Author and Broadcaster

1

A Banner of Dark Shadows
©2022 Martin Kaye

ISBN: 978-1-7399754-1-8
Printed in the UK by 4edgeLtd
First Print Run

The Baboon Press

For Nesta

Thanks to Candida for the proofreads and in loving memory
of my dad Rupert who lived for his books

To Ann and Steffan

Martin Kaye

A note regarding the fonts in this version of A Banner of Dark Shadows
The standard font is Times New Roman
THE ROMAN SD FONT IS USED FOR LATIN PLACE NAMES AND ANY
DIALOGUE THAT WOULD HAVE BEEN SPOKEN IN LATIN.

ON BADON FIELD
A BANNER OF DARK SHADOWS

Contents

Introduction

Cynric of Bernicia has brought his warriors across the mountains through the high pass at Bwlch Pen Barras and on down into the lands of Cambria. They arrive at a small Roman fort and civitas. This simple place, with recently refurbished battlements, is where they come to rest. Their guide, an ancient bitter Roman, convinces them that it is here that Arth, the last and lost leader of Britannia, would be found hiding.

Three years on from what at the time had seemed to be just a random act of callous violence, an act that had ended in the death of a young man, Anya discovers a notebook pushed in-between volumes on the library shelves, hidden and forgotten. Flicking through the pages of notes, the last days and hours of this murdered young man are illuminated, and an unusual story begins to emerge. A random murder or something far deeper and more mysterious? Anya suspects the latter and sets her mind to resolve a mystery that has had such a far-reaching impact on her own life.

Have you been called to the quest?
Is your soul prepared?

BRITANNIA

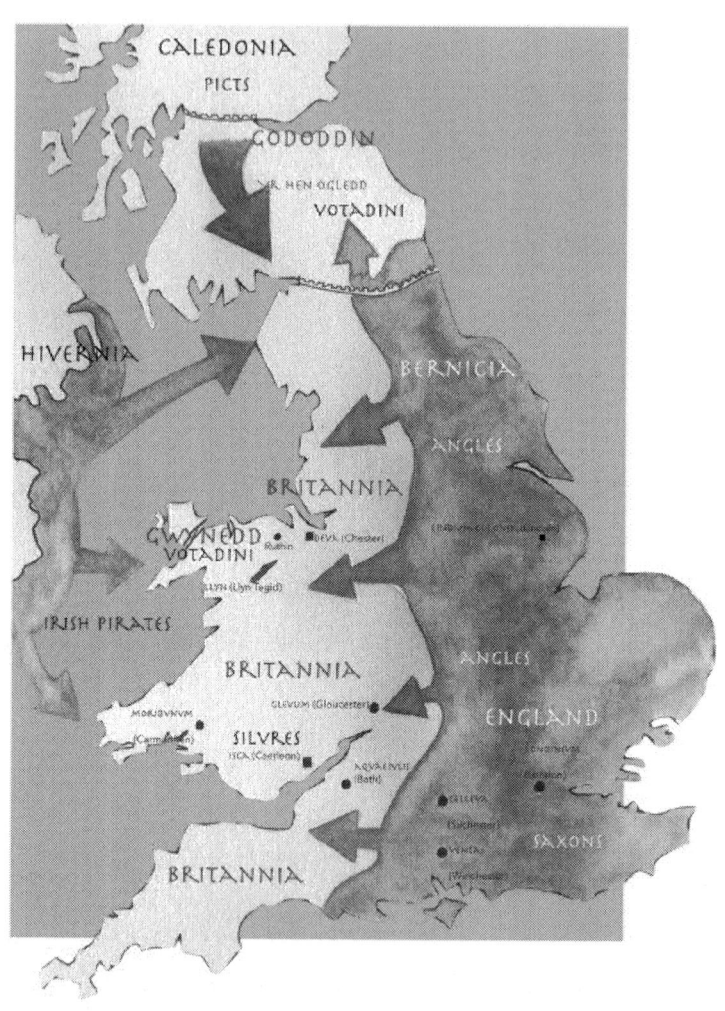

Foreword

AD 1988 Ruthin

The autumn leaves swirled about her in a vortex as Anya stamped up the steps to the main door for the reference library. Clicking the brass latch with her thumb, she turned the doorknob and pushed the old, heavy, panelled wooden door open. It caught just slightly on one of the flagstones in the corridor beyond as it swung. The wind howled and leaves pitter-pattered in the entrance way with many being blown right through and into the corridor. Anya swung the door back behind her, shutting out the tempest for the calm silence of the library beyond.

She clunked through the corridor, old boots, soiled jeans and a worn, dirty Barbour coat slung over an ill-fitting multicoloured homemade jumper. A tea cosy woollen hat was pulled over her hair, now in thick dreadlocks. Her looks were those of a woman old beyond her years. Tired, gaunt, cold, she rambled into the main library hall. Lights on, night had already approached, the windows just black reflections of the enclosed lit room.

This was a damaged young woman. A lifetime's chances lost to so many wrong choices. Recreational drugs and alcohol had shielded her from the reality and pain of a life that was passing her by. Still weak and insecure but with rehabilitation and the reality of being clean for longer than the days she could count, Anya had become a target for a rescue. Some bloody support worker had signed her up to do night classes.

'You're an intelligent young woman. You need stimulus, an intellectual challenge.' And it was in this way she had been talked into a part-time distance learning qualification.

With little enthusiasm she had gone through a list of courses that ran locally and settled on letter A – archaeology. Anya had opted for this as it was so different from economics and maths which had been her original choice for university study before she'd given everything up. She remembered her feelings for Tim, the boy keen on archaeology, and that day she had jumped down into his private dig just to get a little closer to him.

Collapsing now into one of the library chairs set out around a central table, she pulled each fingerless glove off and considered rolling one of her cigarettes. She clicked open her *bacci* tin, but under the distinct impression that she was being observed, she closed and returned the tin to the inside pocket of her shabby Barbour coat, something she'd bought in the days when she'd had money. One of the few things that had survived being sold off to feed her many addictions.

She folded her arms on the table for a moment and, resting her head on them, she considered. Then she was up and searching the shelves until, yes, local history and archaeology. Some of these books were seriously ancient. She pulled out one of the black leather-bound volumes of *Archaeologica Cambrensis*. The date on the spine put it in the 1800s and the paper within was a yellow brown.

God, what crap, she thought, pushing the book back. As she moved her eyes across the book spines, she lightly dragged a finger over each volume, squashed in as they were on the shelf. Having gone all the way from right to left with her finger she began the journey back from left to right. Her finger stopped midway.

Hello, you don't belong in this lot, do you? she thought, pulling out a much thinner school exercise book that had been covered in brown wrapping paper to protect the book's cardboard cover. Written on top was a name, Timothy James. Flicking through, she found newspaper cuttings, a teenager's handwriting, photographs.

All the while, the tempest whistled and raged outside. Was there a tapping on the window, or was it just the leaves? Holding the book in her left hand, she walked up to the nearest window. She placed the fingers of her right hand onto the glass of the windowpane, tears in her eyes. Time had gone by, a lifetime perhaps.

Looking back through the glass now, a face and images flashed through her mind's eye of her last meeting with Tim and his final words to her. Three years of lost time wiped away in an instant – the connection had been joined once again.

1. Bloody Murder

Ruthin AD 1985

August

The detective inspector had come over from Deeside. There tended to be a lot more going on there but the late night phone call from Ruthin Police Station held real promise. Murders in North Wales weren't exactly commonplace. This incident sounded like one of a type; some young hot head with a knife, too much alcohol and an argument over some girl. As murders went, it wasn't going to be all that interesting, but it was still a big deal in a back of beyond place like Ruthin.

DI John Morris arrived at the station at around two in the morning. The place was buzzing. Once inside he was met by another officer.

'Ah John, you'd better come through.' The duty sergeant beckoned him into a side office.

'It doesn't get this busy all that often here,' the sergeant said. 'I'm running out of rooms to put people in.' He motioned to a chair. '*Eisteddwch yma* John.'

'*Diolch* Tom.' The two had met more than once over the years.

'A tragic evening's events John. Our victim's a local lad, lovely family, well liked. The boy took a glancing blow, severed a main artery and he wasn't with us for long after that. Young girl out back, caught his fall; tried to hold the wound together and stop the bleed. Poor thing. We brought her in straight away. I guess with all that blood on her we needed to talk to her. I'm certain she's not implicated in any way, but you'd better have a chat. You'll want to go up to the scene too, yes?'

'Sure,' the DI responded. 'I hope there's nobody messing about with things up there?'

'No, we're checking through everyone present, taking names and addresses for witness statements. It's a big place, lots of disco goers out tonight. We've sent a fair few home.'

The DI looked up from his notebook and the duty sergeant picked up the look of concern.

'They're all local kids, nowhere near the incident most of them. They'll be easy to round up. Besides, they'll be knocking at our door first thing in the morning don't you worry about that.'

The sergeant proceeded to fill the DI in on the known facts regarding the incident before concluding with another invitation to visit the crime scene.

'You'll get a good view of events when you actually see the place and you can check that the men are following procedure – it will put your mind at rest John.'

The drive up to the Woodlands took just a few minutes. High hedges and the darkness didn't give the DI much sense of the local topography. The hall itself was a confusing ramble of a place. He worked through the officers to pull in as much information as possible. They all seemed professional – they wouldn't be missing much from here.

The villain of the peace was a different story, however. There wasn't much to go on in that department; not as yet. His initial assessment was perhaps incorrect. *A real murder then?* he thought. *Premeditated and he's gone.*

Usually with a drunken argument over some girl someone else would know those involved. The murdered boy was a local, but of his assailant there were no leads. Alcohol or drugs usually played a part and by this point, the perpetrator would typically have sobered up, would be full of remorse and hopeful that those five seconds of madness with a knife hadn't caused any serious harm.

Here tonight, however, no one knew anything. This evening was getting more exciting and the adrenaline was kicking in. Good cases, and you could keep going, stay awake for days without sleep. With murders, if you could make the breakthrough quickly, then you were away. Things would be much clearer in the morning; he could have a proper look around then. By that time, the intelligence would also be coming together too. He looked at his watch – it was already well into the early hours.

After some time, he found his way back to Sergeant Tom Llewellyn. He gave the sergeant a nod.

'*Diolch* Tom. I've got a view of things here and it will be much clearer when it gets light, I've no doubt. Are you happy to give me a lift back down to Ruthin?'

'Sure, let's head off, so long as you have all you need for now?'

12

The DI gave another nod and Tom indicated the way back to the car. From Ruthin, DI John Morris picked up his own car and headed off back home. There he slept for an hour or two but on either side his mind was working through things, playing through different scenarios. In the middle of it all he'd gone downstairs to get something to sort out a bout of acid reflux, a condition to which he was prone because the job brought with it a certain amount of stress. He'd need to contact the superintendent in the morning to see if the force wanted him to lead the case.

The little police station in Ruthin sat next to the Court House on Record Street which was quaint and convenient for policing at the turn of the century. When the DI returned sometime after mid-day the place was as it had been the previous night – full of people. No doubt Tom Llewellyn's local witnesses were turning up for their interviews. The DI considered whether the whole investigation should be shipped out to somewhere altogether far bigger, another station that had the capacity to deal with a murder case properly.

Entering the building, John headed for the little side office of the night before. He tapped the door before entering. The weary-eyed sergeant lifted his head from a bundle of report papers on the desk before him.

'Did you go home last night Tom?' he asked.

'Yes, sort of, well, more this morning really,' he replied. 'I couldn't stay away. You know, I feel guilty not being here and doing my job for the family. I don't want to miss out on anything either.'

The DI smiled; these were all things with which he was familiar, having served many years in the force. The DI briefly wondered if he'd miss it all when he retired.

The sergeant continued, 'The girl, she's still here you know, won't go home poor thing. Her dad's been in to collect her, but she won't leave with him. Richards, he's quite well known, *infamous* actually. He's got a big executive job in the council.'

The DI nodded. 'Where is she then? Might be a good place to start and then she should go home whether she likes it or not.'

The station had a grand total of just one interview room so finding Miss Richards was no real effort. Since she was the only key witness, and the only individual connected to the deceased at the scene of the incident, they'd left her pretty much where they'd started with her hours before.

Entering the room with a female officer, Morris was faced with a pathetic image, a young girl, he guessed to be in her late teens, looking tired and washed out. The DI flicked through some notes as he pulled his chair to sit down. He nodded at the constable without acknowledging the youngster sat before them.

'You do the doings constable while I just look through this lot.'

The constable nodded and ran through the introductions. 'This is Detective Inspector John Morris and I'm Constable Manon Hughes. Miss Richards are you happy to chat and go through your statement a little further?'

The DI looked up; the girl was a bit of a mess. Looking at her properly for the first time, it was clear that she really had been in the station all night; she was still in the same clothes and had possibly sat in the same seat for hours. There was a blankness in her eyes, he noted that she was shivering a little – the girl was certainly in a state of shock.

The blanket that had been placed over her shoulders was evidently doing little to comfort the girl. Perhaps the evaporation, the blood slowly drying up, had gently sapped away some warmth as energy from her body. Her hands and wrists were caked in dried blood. At some stage she may have pushed her hair back from her eyes as the right side of her face was also smeared in dried blood.

John checked his notes for her first name so as to be less intimidating. 'Anya, are you happy for me to call you by your first name?'

The girl in front of him gave a timid nod and the effort made her shiver all the more. Suddenly his parental feelings took over; she could have been his daughter.

The DI turned to face his fellow officer. 'Constable, haven't we offered Anya here the chance to go home, have a wash and a change and a big warm hug from someone who cares?'

The constable was a bit awkward with the reply. 'Yes sir, Miss Richards was brought in and at first there was some confusion about her relevance, as... a witness or... perpetrator. We were waiting for the SOCO to come and collect stuff. He got lost and somehow... but we should have at least sorted a change of clothes. I'm sorry sir.'

The DI scrunched up his nose and shot the constable a disapproving look. To Anya he said, 'I'm really sorry for the way you've been treated. I think you've been a real hero from what I've read here. You did all you could do, there really was nothing more that could be done. I've just checked your statement, and sure, there might be something we'd want to pick up later to help us catch whoever did this but there's nothing more you can do for now. You really need to go home, have a bath, get out of this awful place.'

Anya made no response.

'I think you're going to need to see someone Miss Richards, we'll arrange that. You'll need help with an experience like this in the days to come. Perhaps your dad can organise an appointment with your GP, that would be a good place to start. Your dad's been in hasn't he, is he out there waiting now?'

The DI looked at the constable for some confirmation.

Anya spoke up for the first time. 'I don't want to go with my dad. I don't want him picking me up.'

'What about your mum then?' enquired the DI.

'I don't have a mother, she died,' Anya responded in a shaky but determined whisper which forced the officers to focus and brought a sense of drama into the room. 'I think it's time to say something about my father. I want to make a statement...'

There was a loud rapping on the door which made them all jump. The door opened and Tom poked his head round, he was clearly excited.

'Sorry to disturb the interview sir, but might I have a word?'

John Morris stood and joined the duty sergeant on the other side of door.

'We've had another incident,' came Tom Llewellyn's excited whisper. 'There's been an attempted break in and robbery at Ty'n-y-celyn farm. Nasty by all accounts, some rough yob threatened to bash old Ann Ty'n-y-celyn with a shovel. Demanding money with menaces.'

'So, where's this farm then?' the DI asked.

'About a mile from the Woodlands sir, up on the Hiraethog.'

'That's him then, that's the one. We need to be getting up there.' The DI returned to the interview room and addressed Constable Manon Hughes who had remained seated. 'Can I leave this in your capable hands Constable Hughes? Young Anya here needs a break from this place, a good clean up and then perhaps someone can have a little chat with her at a later time.'

With that, the DI was through the door, already lost in the excitement of the chase. As he and the sergeant walked out into the waiting room the DI picked up on something Tom had said earlier.

'Richards, the girl's father; you said earlier that he was infamous, well known and in the council?' He motioned back towards the interview room. 'Is this the same Richards linked to the big fraud investigation?'

The sergeant nodded in response.

The DI continued, 'I'd get someone from fraud to have a chat with the girl if I were you.'

* * *

Miss Anya Richards was sitting pretty much where she had been left for most of the night. One moment the constable was saying, 'We need to sort out a lift home for you,' and the next, she had gone too.

The blood on Anya's hands and clothes had dried out from a warm sticky gore to a hard, dry, red powder. The metallic smell was still present despite the drying and evaporation over the hours. She was shivering continuously and felt cold to the core. She shouldn't have been left alone for a minute yet here she was, left for long periods, in silence. Her head dropped and her eyes closed but her restless thoughts slipped down, down to a dark, dark, place.

Anya felt utterly deserted and abandoned – the police were too busy to care. Her family – her father, stepmother and stepsister – were

18

no better. What compassion would there be for her in that house? The thought of returning home to the bleak and the cold where she would be expected to be stoic, keep up a pretence of coping, was deeply troubling. How could she put on a show as if nothing was wrong? But emotions counted for nothing in her family.

Father had been quick to try and pick her up from the station lest any home truths come out. He was looking after number one. As for the other two, they didn't want her back at all. In her mind there was no one she could turn to. No one who would hold her close, keep her safe and support her through these events. Her mind was overloaded with worries and problems of which this was just one, one demand amongst the many. Images of the night, even with her eyes closed, flashed past. The sticky liquid blood, black in the disco darkness and the voice, his voice, before the silence and stillness. In all these emotions, one was distinct – guilt. If it wasn't for her, Tim would still be alive.

* * *

Denbigh AD 1985
October
'You coming?' The girl downed the last dregs from her pint glass and made to stand.

Anya looked up. Autumn was roaring in, and she should have returned to her university course by now. Instead, she was still in North

Wales where an old school acquaintance had rediscovered her. The pair of them went way back to primary school.

'Where exactly are you living?' Anya asked. 'I mean, where am I coming to?'

'We got a squat on Love Lane. Your dad, he might know where you are, but he sure as hell ain't going to come calling.' Her *friend* was wearing a vest top, despite the autumn chill, which showed off her powerful arms and a lot more besides. 'I'm glad you looked me up. I've been thinking about you, missed you, my best mate.'

Anya rose to her feet through the smoke in this dimly lit pub, pushing herself up with a hand on the table between them, sticky from the beer. The place was crowded; it had a rough edge.

The police had been in touch again. *Miss Richards, we'd like to have a chat with you about your father.* So, she'd told them. Confiding in them had been difficult, but she'd managed to get through the ordeal. Her story, however, wasn't really what the police wanted to hear. They were interested in different lines of enquiry. Her father, it seemed, was no angel. The police wanted to talk about money and yes, as a family they'd always been well off. Her father would spend ages studying his pink weekly newspaper, the *Financial Times*. As he worked in high finance, Anya assumed he was good with his investments. Turned out he was 'playing roulette' with other people's money, and rather a lot of money at that.

The police had come to the house; they'd wanted to talk to her father about lots of things. He wasn't at home now – the social services wouldn't let him near. Her stepmother had screamed abuse at her. Donna, her stepsister, three years younger, had slinked to one side for once. She knew about everything alright; she'd been home alone this last year whilst Anya was at university – he wouldn't have been leaving her alone.

After that Anya had pulled together a few of her things and had got out of the family home. She'd stayed with some of her school friends, but this wasn't something she could do long term and the doors around her were quickly closing. How was it that Mr Richards, a pillar of society could be facing such accusations, and from his own daughter at that? The police had said it was, her word against his. They were more interested in the money – that was plain to see.

'Do you know why they call it Love Lane?' her friend asked, but at that point their conversation was disrupted by some dodgy looking bloke that the other girl seemed to know. She had a short conversation with him and then something had been passed between the two of them. When he'd disappeared, she turned back to Anya and said, 'I got some stuff, we can have a bit of fun, make us forget about life for a little while.'

'Why's it called Love Lane?' Anya followed up.

'Ah, yes, you'll find out Anya, but I'll look after you, I promise.'

2. A Letter from Gran

Oxford University AD 1985

October

Having first stopped off at the mail pigeonholes for students on the ground floor, Philomena stormed up the concrete stairwell and onto the second floor of her student digs. Third year and she'd opted to come back into university halls, to actually do some work for once.

With both hands holding a pile of books, a pencil case and other assorted junk, she arrived at her door and, balancing the pile in one hand, she retrieved her door key from the tight back pocket of her jeans. Engaging the key, she used her elbow to push down the door handle and, putting her weight into her shoulder, she shoved. The pile of books toppled and clattered to the floor as the door swung open against her weight.

'Bugger!' she hissed.

Philomena was a good fortnight into the new autumn semester. The initial nonsense of freshers dispensed with, the assignments, lectures, tutorials and reading were beginning to mass up. Retrieving some of the objects from the fallen pile she dumped them and her keys on her small work desk, depressed the play button on the 'ghetto blaster' and did a star jump backwards onto her bed.

Today had been a pain, largely because of the language seminar with Chris Stephenson, her personal tutor. Philomena had never worked harder, but Stephenson it seemed, was dishing out lower grades to her than some of the others on the course. Initially she'd been a little too trusting, too conscientious and helpful. Stephenson had been carefully reeling her in, she could see that now.

He was far too familiar with pretty undergraduates and Philomena was very much in his sights. The man was married with two beautiful children. Philomena would know, she'd babysat them more than once. Why did his wife put up with this? Perhaps she tolerated her husband's behaviour as it meant that he wouldn't be bothering her. Philomena was beginning to find his attentions threatening and he could be more than a little bit manipulative. If she gave in and let him go further, her grades would go back up she was sure of it. Stephenson was the most unpleasant individual she'd had the misfortune to deal with. Well, apart from Mod Evans; he was in a different league entirely.

Her mind wandered to the events of this summer. Had all those things really happened to her?

'Stand and Deliver', an old Adam and the Ants number, came up on the blaster. She was up and off the bed mouthing to the words, moving to the lyrics whilst she rummaged through the pile of junk she had dumped onto her desk when she'd come in, picking out several unopened letters. The song's drum sections were particularly fun and she air drummed along at the appropriate points.

Philomena had quite a wide interest in music that stretched way beyond the latest pop scene. In a past life, she'd played cello for her

23

school orchestra and had a Grade 8 ABRSM Distinction to her name. Stuff like 'Stand and Deliver' was pure commercial rubbish but it was silly and comical which was perhaps why she liked it.

The song ended and the next tune up was an altogether calmer affair. Philomena sat back down on her bed and went through her mail. She looked at the address on each envelope to see if there was anything interesting. Right at the end of the small wodge of letters – yes, Philomena hadn't checked her post in ages – there was a handwritten letter from Gran.

Good old Gran! She ripped open the envelope to access the letter inside. Unfolding the paper she began to read, noting Gran's attractive carefully formed handwriting. A newspaper cut out was attached to the letter. She put it aside to read after.

23rd September 1985

Dear Philomena,

I thought you might like a letter to read from home. I know it's always strange starting again at the beginning of a new term and it's nice to have something familiar to help settle you in. I've felt it a bit quiet here in Ruthin since your stay over the summer. It was lovely to have you dear, if only for a few days – you brought a bit of life and fun to the house!

I've had some new neighbours next door on the right, a young couple named David and Samantha. I think Samantha is a teacher in one of the local primary schools and David commutes to Liverpool and back. He has some important job in the Jaguar motor car factory. They're very nice and have started asking after me. I'm looking after Samantha's cat Nelson this week whilst she and David are away in Yorkshire. Nelson's an old tabby and a real affectionate fellow when there's food to be eaten but not much bothered at any other time. That's a cat for you but they're much less fuss and bother than a dog Philomena.

I've joined the local WI and we've had some nice talks and evenings out. There's a trip at the end of this month over to Anglesey and I'm very much looking forward to the visit, it will be nice not to be driving myself, and the ladies from the WI are a good crowd.

Your father's settling into his new job with Wrexham Council and is perhaps at last beginning to accept that North Wales is a much better place to be than Coventry. I'm seeing quite a lot of him and your mother and I'm always asking after you dear.

Oh my, it's your last year at Oxford and I can't imagine where all the time has gone. Have you any thoughts for what you might do after leaving university Philomena? Hopefully you'll get a lovely job here in beautiful North Wales where I can see lots more of you. I should look forward to that, but I guess my wishes are selfish and you must follow your own path in life my dear. I just hope it takes you to some marvellous places and that you'll meet someone special one day.

Ruthin is a quiet old place and generally not a great deal happens, but do you know, there was a murder this summer. It must have been when we were down in Carmarthen so we both missed all of the drama. It's very sad that a young lad with a bright future ahead of him has lost his life. The whole town kind of stopped for the funeral and the old church on the square wasn't big enough to take all of the mourners. The family was local and well known so I'm told. When you hear news like this it makes you realise just how lucky we are. Philomena do look after yourself – no walking down narrow lanes on your own at night. You keep yourself safe dear, that's an order from your gran! I've popped in a press cutting for you to read about the funeral. The young lad was called Timothy James.

Well dear, now that you've heard from me and that you know I'm safe I'd love to hear from you and how you're getting on in your final year. I do so look forward to hearing from you – a chat or a letter, you do both so well, you bring the world to life with your wonderful stories. Until then, take care my dear.

Love

Gran

xx

Philomena sat staring at the newspaper cutting and the letter in her hand. The print faded into a blur as tears welled up in her eyes. Her mind raced, trying to make some sense of all this, to bring calm to the disorder.

Philomena had fallen easily for Tim. She knew she would, walking back in the dark from the pub that first night. He'd quickly felt like a best friend; she was so relaxed with him, she could trust him, and once in his company she'd wanted to stay there forever. A great tear drop plopped onto the tight faded denim on her thigh. She rubbed it into her jeans with her left hand but made no effort to dry her eyes. Her hair had fallen forwards as it did when she was upset, when she lowered her head and could find no way out of a situation. What would Tim have done if it were her?

Now what? In the turmoil of feelings there was an edge of anger. She was sure that she would meet Tim again, that she was meant to be with him but that could never happen now.

Rubbing her sleeve across her eyes finally, Philomena tried to focus back on the newspaper article. Timothy James had been involved in a stabbing, the article proclaimed. Two hundred miles away she had seen the events clearly. Had he called out to her? She had left him there, all alone, even when she had sensed a danger beforehand, that something unnatural might take place. Her eyes filled up with tears once again. That summer's evening, something had been lost, and now that magic connection was truly over. Tim was dead, gone, and she would be alone forever.

* * *

Philomena went over to her cello and sat, picking up the bow in a daze, a numbness washing over her. From a set of deep tonal notes, she raced up to the high register for the instrument before dropping down and ending with several dramatic notes of termination. She stopped, the instrument's neck held in her left hand; she spun the instrument round on its floor point once, twice before halting the spin on the third turn. Then she was up on her feet again. Resting her cello against her chair, she was back at her small desk, rummaging for the second time this evening.

'Got you,' she announced. Holding the prize of her little address book in one hand she grabbed her room keys with the other and raced through the door, along the corridor and down the flight of steps, her eyes raw and stinging.

Philomena arrived at the telephone booths. All three were engaged and there were several people waiting outside. The phone booths were always busy at night.

'Dicks,' she whispered in anger as she walked up to the kiosks before pacing up and down like some demented lion in a zoo cage. One of the girls waiting gave her a dirty look – she must have heard Philomena's expletive. The temptation to give an equally dirty look back was great indeed but Philomena thought better of it. She was already worked up, tears of frustration now in her eyes. She needed to calm down, get a grip of the situation so that she could execute the appropriate action and these waiting students were just a distraction she needed to put on one side. She came to the end of the queue at last and leaned against the wall, dropping her head and closing her eyes so that no one would be tempted to engage in conversation with her.

At last, a kiosk became free, and Philomena darted in, checking her address book and dialling a number. There was a ringing tone and Gran picked up immediately – she must have been sitting on top of her phone.

Rushed and in an unsteady voice, Philomena said, 'Hi Gran, it's me, Philomena – how are you?'

'Oh, lovely to hear your voice dear, did you get my letter?' Gran replied.

'Yes Gran.' Philomena took a breath of air and closed her eyes to compose herself. 'Thanks so much, I love receiving letters, especially ones from home.' She was trying but failing to keep her voice from breaking.

'Are you all right dear? You sound a bit, well, upset. Has something happened?'

'I'm OK Gran, I'm just a little bit down tonight, about something in your letter.'

'Oh no, you knew that boy didn't you, Timothy James poor soul. I do hope he wasn't the young man that walked you home that evening. It's been such a shock to the community; I'm told he was well liked.'

'Gran... can I come and stay next weekend? I just need to say goodbye if that makes sense.'

'Well of course it does dear, but the funeral's been and gone and that was followed by the crem so, you know, there's nothing physical left to say goodbye to dear.'

'I want to say goodbye in that church Gran because... there's a special connection.'

Gran seemed to choose her next words carefully. 'I see dear, I'll let your mum and dad know too, shall I? You'll need their support. I mean, you've not had much experience of loss have you dear?'

'I'd rather you didn't Gran, I think they'd worry and really it's not like that. I'm strong and I think, well, because I only knew him briefly a quiet goodbye in the church would be the respectful thing to do.'

'All right dear but you'll have to tell them in your time – don't go keeping secrets.' Gran was as ever, the right person to talk to. She was full of wisdom born from years of experience in life.

Ending the call, Philomena emerged from the kiosk feeling slightly less helpless – *a problem shared is a problem halved* and all that. She apologised to the little queue of fellow students that had built up outside on this Friday evening for taking so long and headed back up to her room. It was now dusk, and she needed a pair of appropriate footwear on if she was to walk down to the train station.

* * *

DI John Morris was back at the Ruthin Police Station. A bit of paperwork needed to be sorted out. John was in early because it was a Saturday and he'd promised to watch his lad play football later in the morning. Making an early start and keeping a low profile meant that most people wouldn't know he was about, and he'd get much more done. The Timothy James case was pretty much sorted their end and files had gone over to the Crown Prosecution Service ahead of trial. They'd caught up with Tom Evans, the perpetrator, several days later, and he was in a sorry state having been out living rough for a couple of days with limited food or drink and no real means to escape and to affect a successful disappearance. A warm blanket and a cup of tea and the lad had confessed to the crime, led them to locate the murder weapon and gave them some psychotic reason for his actions. Things checked out with the stepmother in Prestatyn, and Tom Evans was due for a long stay at Her Majesty's pleasure. There had been no mention of anyone else's involvement. A beautiful open and shut case if ever there was one.

* * *

Gran picked Philomena up from Chester Railway Station soon after nine on the Friday evening at the start of the following weekend. Gran walked up to the main exit just before Philomena's train arrived from Crewe, but she had arrived in the car long before.

They spotted each other whilst Philomena was queuing up to show her ticket. Once through, she gave her gran a big hug.

'I'm so pleased to see you. Thanks for letting me come over this weekend.'

'You're welcome my dear. Anything to have my granddaughter with me for a few days,' Gran responded, returning the embrace and gently tapping Philomena on the back with her right hand. 'Come on, let's get in the car and out of the cold.'

On arriving at the parked car seconds later, Gran handed the keys over so that Philomena could drive back to Ruthin.

Walking into St Peter's Church on the Saturday morning, Philomena expected a special atmosphere, that she would feel Tim's presence and that there would be a connection. The place was quiet and smelt like all churches did. She looked up and noticed the fantastically carved wooden panels that made up the ceiling. In front of her was the location for Cooper's infamous ghost photo but the ghost didn't put in an appearance today, there were no creepy feelings or unexplained drops in the temperature. Philomena felt disappointed.

At the entrance was an old wooden table with a pile of information leaflets about the church and a *Please Donate Generously* box. Also resting on the table was a book. Philomena assumed it to be a visitor's book and opened it up to have a nose. It was in fact a book of condolences for Tim. Philomena flicked through, checking all the entries. She spotted three names, Daniel Jones, Andrew Cooper and

Anya Richards. They had all been present to say goodbye to Tim. Philomena added her own name and details.

Leaving through the side door Philomena walked up and round to the churchyard's elaborate wrought iron gates. On passing through these she was on St Peter's Square, the clock tower ahead of her and the Middleton Arms on her left. The glamour and excitement of the summer had gone, replaced by the grey skies and drizzle of North Wales in autumn.

Now what? In her mind there was the notion that she ought to call in to the police station to make a statement. After pausing to get her confidence up and to organise her thoughts, she was off in the direction of Record Street. Pushing the door open she stepped into the reception area and nervously approached the desk. An officer was stood behind it making notes. He didn't look up and after a couple of seconds Philomena cleared her throat.

'Excuse me, I wonder if I could speak to someone about a murder?'

Suddenly she had the officer's full and undivided attention.

'A murder you said, miss?' he asked.

'Yes, err… I think I may have some more details to add,' Philomena responded meekly.

'Your name miss?'

'It's Philomena Hutchinson.' Philomena was now considerably more nervous and no longer certain that this was the best action to be taking in the circumstances.

'And this murder miss…?' the officer probed further.

'Err… yes, I'd like to speak to someone about Timothy James.'

The officer observed her closely then said, 'Miss Hutchinson, would you like to take a seat for a minute?' He nodded towards some seats behind Philomena.

'Yes, OK.' She looked behind her and took one of the seats. With one knee crossed over the other, she nervously picked at the dry skin on the sides of her thumbnails.

Philomena watched as the officer left the room. A few moments later she heard him call out, 'Sergeant, there's a young lady out front, a Miss Philomena Hutchinson, says she has some information about the Timothy James murder!'

* * *

John Morris couldn't help overhearing from the office; he recognised the name. Over the course of the interviews, somewhere someone had mentioned the name Philomena, but they'd not tracked her down, not spoken to her, as it had seemed that she had no involvement with the events on that fateful evening.

'I'll take this one, where is she?' he called out.

'Sorry sir,' the desk officer replied, 'didn't know you were in this morning. I'd have come straight to you sir. Miss Hutchinson is in reception sir.'

Coming through to the front desk, John spotted the young woman. 'Miss Hutchinson, would you like to come through?' He indicated the way. Once she had sat down, he asked, 'Can I get you a tea or coffee?'

Philomena nodded. 'Coffee would be great please. White, no sugar.'

He left her alone to her thoughts in the small interview room.

Minutes later he was back with another female officer. He placed the polystyrene cup full of hot coffee in front of Philomena and sat down opposite her.

'OK Miss Hutchinson, I'm DI John Morris and this is Constable Manon Hughes. What can you help us with in this case?'

Philomena looked back at them both before blurting her story out like an express train with no brakes.

'Well, I don't know where you are with this investigation,' she began. 'I met Tim over the summer because I was staying here with my gran. I think you ought to know that a Mr Mod Evans, a clairvoyant in Prestatyn whom we'd consulted, threatened Tim. We'd gone up there because of a ghost photo and one of Tim's mates, Andrew Cooper, thought this Mod Evans might be able to tell us something about the ghost. It seemed a fun, exciting thing to do at the time but this Mod Evans was vile.'

John nodded. 'Were you Tim's girlfriend then?'

Philomena was silent for a while, and he felt she was holding back on something. Then she continued.

'I was in Carmarthen when Tim was murdered. My gran and I were visiting relatives.'

He nodded, noting that the young lady in front of him had made a statement that in no way answered his question.

'The young man who stabbed Tim, I kind of recognised a familiarity in him. He'd hidden his blade in the jacket sleeve of his left arm and on spotting Tim, through the lights of the disco, he made towards him. At the last minute he neatly dropped the blade handle into the palm of his hand and made one decisive punch at Tim before… before quietly walking out.'

As Philomena continued to describe Tim's assailant in detail, DI John Morris grew increasingly amazed. How was it that she could say anything at all about these events? In her story, she had shared an interesting detail. Tom was indeed left-handed and had, almost boastfully, described in his interview how he'd dropped the blade from its hiding place in his jacket sleeve into his hand. Now, how did this girl know about that? He would need to consider his line of questioning carefully before continuing.

'Miss Hutchinson, you said Mod Evans had threatened Tim. This other individual whom you have just described for us in clear detail—' he shook his head '—this individual is not Mod Evans.'

Philomena was quick to reply. 'Mod Evans was in a wheelchair, and I don't think he was able to walk. Mod didn't do the stabbing, but I know from his threats that he is somehow involved.'

John Morris sat back in his chair and observed the girl for a few seconds. 'When you visited Mod Evans in Prestatyn, can you remember the day and date Miss Hutchinson?'

Philomena nodded.

'Have you had any other contact with Mod Evans or his family?' he probed further, trying to see if she had known the family prior to the visit; whether she had met Tom Evans, thus enabling her to describe him so clearly.

'No, I'd only come across Mod Evans on that day in Prestatyn and there was a little woman who let us in. Never seen him before and never seen him since, thank God.'

'Thank you, Miss Hutchinson. Is there anything else you want to tell us?'

Philomena was again quiet for a few seconds before she responded, 'No, I don't think so.'

John Morris cleared his throat, 'Miss Hutchinson, you carefully and clearly described how Tim was attacked and who had done the attacking just a few minutes ago. How were you able to do that, if, as you say, you were in Carmarthen?'

'Err...' Philomena visibly squirmed in her seat. 'I don't know, I think I had... a vision or something. I'd had dinner and gone down into

Carmarthen town with my cousin. We'd just arrived at a pub –hadn't bought a drink or anything – but suddenly I felt dizzy and sick, so I went back outside for some fresh air. I leaned against the wall, closed my eyes and then I saw it all.'

There was a long pause when no one spoke. Constable Hughes turned to face him, eyes wide in disbelief.

'I'm so sorry; I don't know what you must think of me. Perhaps I'm wasting your time. I even doubt myself, so God knows what you think. I'll go; I've wasted enough of your time.' Philomena pushed her chair back to stand.

'Miss Hutchinson, I think before you leave, I'll need to take your contact details. We may need to come back to you and Constable Hughes here has been very busy writing notes which we'd like you to read and sign off, if you are in agreement.'

Philomena nodded. After she read and signed off her statement, the constable showed her out.

DI John Morris returned to his office with Philomena's statement. She hadn't met Tom Evans and hadn't been there at the time of the incident, yet she had described the events and the assailant perfectly. Accepting that she had met Mod Evans, as this visit had been confirmed by Jones, Cooper and Candy Gail Evans, it did not seem at all possible that she had ever met Tom Evans, who had been released from Liverpool jail and had only returned home the following day. Her gran and everyone in Carmarthen would confirm her alibi no doubt and Miss Anya Richards had not mentioned Miss Hutchinson in her statement.

There was more than enough evidence to convict Tom Evans for the murder without Philomena's statement. Not only had he confessed to doing so in his interview, but Tom had also taken them to the place where he'd hidden the knife and his jacket. This young lady's statement was only going to be a distraction. Philomena had, however, managed to share some exact details quite explicitly. There was a connection surely, but what? If she was implicated why on earth would she be coming to see them? Might she have guessed the events or was he really to believe that she had seen it all in a vision?

Manon Hughes came into the office after seeing Philomena off the premises and tapped her head with her right hand. 'That girl's bonkers.'

John returned a smile, but there was something odd here. Manon had not been in on the interview with Tom Evans. John had, and that little left-handed detail... somehow the girl knew and as far as John was concerned those details were not common knowledge.

He'd park this one for now. Perhaps it was one for his special file because he was more than a little bit interested in the occult and things that go bump in the night. This might be something to come back to one day in the future.

He looked at his watch and cursed. Half eleven; he was going to be late for that football match.

Philomena left the station somewhat deflated. *They must think I'm bonkers,* she thought and very much regretted calling in to make a statement. Walking back up towards Gran's house she deliberately chose to take the haunted pathway route. Any ghost bothering her now was likely to get a real mouthful – she wasn't scared today.

On getting to the top of the path she looked up towards Tim's house. Should she go and say how sorry she was? Would that be yet another stupid thing to do? But before she could talk herself out of it, she walked up towards the house. Well, it was too late to be turning now; Philomena stepped up to the door and pressed the doorbell.

* * *

GLEVVM **AD 516**

'Daddy, Daddy!' The little girl raced up to the top fence, a boundary between the manicured gardens and orchards of the villa and the wilderness that lay beyond. Climbing up onto the second and then third fence rung, stretching out to make herself as tall as she could be and holding onto the top rung for dear life with her left hand, she waved frantically with her right.

'Daddy, Daddy!'

A taller, distinguished aristocrat turned his great black charger away from the throng of other riders and all too briefly and half-heartedly raised a hand of goodbye before turning again to join the excited group of young men and their retainers. The little girl kept up the waving as the group moved on and over the rise. She called and called until they had long gone from sight. Until, that is, her dedicated servants had caught up with her, scalding, for she had been in their charge and the instructions from the master had been quite clear. She was not under any circumstances to see her father leave. He would not tolerate any distraction this morning. She had however, quickly slipped through their clutches earlier and now she did so once again like a wriggling eel, tears burning in her eyes.

Back down through the top orchard with its trees laden with apples, plumbs, cherries and pears, she ran, through the orchard gate and down a flight of steps that led on to the kitchen gardens before reaching the formal ornate gardens set out geometrically with sculptured bushes, paths and pools. Heading for the kitchens and the servant's quarters she entered through one of the domestic doorways. She raced down a dark unlit corridor and on into the even darker stores beyond.

Not many had much time for her in this place – the aristocratic little girl, alone, a little feared, a little strange. Father scarcely had time to devote to her, for she was of the wrong sex and rumour had it that Father had not much cared for her mother. So, for the best part she was alone. Her mother had died in the act of bringing her into this world and

41

so she had been foisted out to the care of a wet nurse and a succession of tutors and maids. None had ever shown the little girl much affection.

The great house was staffed with a mix of freed servants and slaves. Of these, there were many young pretty women selected by her father, more for their looks and carnal charms than their ability to undertake the jobs for which they were employed. The little girl likened them to cats, sly and slinky they were on the whole quite untrustworthy. There were too, a number of man servants for the house, some of whom showed significant competence in their roles but whose toil was difficult.

There was one woman, who worked in the kitchens and had the reputation for someone knowledgeable of healing and of herbal remedies, who had always shown an interest. It was to her that the little girl now ran. Servants and slaves here, though subscripted locally on the most part, had backgrounds that reached to the many parts of a once great empire. Buddug was an exception, and her lineage came from these lands back to times before Rome. The little girl understood that Buddug's family had roots in the great Brigantes tribe of the North. A proud, defiant people, Buddug was a young woman both independent of mind and of action. Buddug had told the little girl stories of a great warrior queen of the Iceni after whom she had been named. Slightly feral with wild long flowing red hair, Buddug was a little older than many of the serving girls in this place. She had borne no children despite a liking for men. On many occasions the little girl had walked in on Buddug, very naked with one of the rough farm hands from the outer fields.

'Is Daddy ever to come back home Buddug?'

Buddug knelt down from her chores and fondly pinched the girl's right cheek between finger and thumb before she responded. 'Of course he will be back little one. Your father's an aristocrat of great wealth. Be sure that at Badon he will be a long way behind the line of fighting men. Those idle youths who flunky up to him mind, boastful, bragging, they will not return.'

The little girl dropped her head. 'I will see Daddy but just once more, many years from now,' she said in a quiet, sad little voice. An emotive comment for such a young girl to make which would have been just ignored by most adults, but Buddug was in tune and considered before responding.

'They won't want you here, you know,' the kitchen maid stated, dropping her hands to hold the girl gently on each shoulder. 'In time they will wrestle this place, your inheritance, away from you little girl. Your father is not liked, despised even by everyone who is enslaved to this villa. You belong with me, I will become your mother and you will travel with me as my daughter, away from here.'

'AELIANA CORNELIUS ANTONINIA!' came a shrill call. 'Where on Earth have you got to my girl?'

Buddug gave a smile and a chuckle. 'They call for you and now you must go little one.' She gently shook her charge between her hands before tapping Aeliana lightly on the nose.

'You can see beyond the edge my dear. We both know this don't we?'

AELIANA nodded, a sincere expression on her face.

'Be patient and I will come. In the dark of night, I will come, and we will escape together little one.'

3. The Edward Gate

Denbigh 1986

Anya had spent the first few weeks of October in a large, shared house on Love Lane. The whole street was a shamble of decaying houses, tumbled one on top of another as they crawled up the twisting steep road to the castle mount. The place she'd stayed in was a den of drugs and free sex except the sex wasn't free as someone needed to pay for the drink and the drugs. There wasn't any real space that anyone could call their own and, in this atmosphere, Anya felt her life becoming more and more unstructured.

In this place were controlling influences and tortured souls, long lost to the oblivion of substance misuse and addiction. Social norms were blurred, emotions amplified. Chaotic and unpredictable, a calm safe place this was not.

With her good looks and impression of innocence Anya became the girl to have. With two other girls she'd taken money to do things that would live with the three of them forever, and she began to use drink and recreational drugs to numb her shame, to blot out the feelings of guilt and self-loathing. With the cash they moved out and up the street to a tiny mid link property – number fifteen on Love Lane. However, moving out didn't get them away from the twilight world of which they were now a part.

In Anya's mind she considered her two house mates to be more damaged by life than herself. An item, they took the larger dank back bedroom upstairs. For some weeks, the three of them kept the flat going, until one night, when one of the girls moved out without an explanation. The departure left the other inconsolable and, as winter closed in, she too decided to leave and Anya was alone in this miserable place. A space trapped in the last century, furnished from a bygone age, gloomy and threadbare.

From then on, Anya lived in a cycle of boom or bust. Her social security pay-out couldn't meet the rent alone, forcing her to rely on prostitution which brought in money, danger and self-destruction. You couldn't separate the three.

* * *

'I want you to show me some excitement, some feeling, make it real!'

'Make it feel real?' Anya responded. 'You're paying me to do something I don't want to do, least of all with you.'

Her outburst was a mistake. Volatile, unbalanced, and drunk, her punter exploded into a wild rage. He chased her down the stairs into the back kitchen. She dodged several swipes before one eventually hit her square on in the face and everything went black for a few seconds as she tumbled back into a corner and slid down the wall onto the floor. She held her arms up and crossed over her head for protection before tucking up into a tight ball in expectation of further blows. They did not come. Instead, the idiot stormed about the place yelling and throwing things around before finally settling in the front room, crashing down onto one of the moth-eaten chairs, still grumbling and swearing. Anya took the opportunity to get out of his way.

Pulling herself up and fleeing to the downstairs shower room and WC she slid the bolt to. Her heart racing with terror, she sat on the floor, her back pushed up against the door, her legs braced to withstand a determined charge from the other side. The lock wouldn't hold much, and neither would the door.

* * *

The day began like an old black and white photograph, trapped in a tragic pathetic grey drizzle. Anya was out of the house early, having hidden away cowed and shaking with fear for most of that night. In the early hours she'd heard a door slam – he'd gone.

Frozen to the core, she bolted out as soon as the coast was clear, desperate to warm up. There was an urgency in her need to keep moving.

The front door was half ajar, the lock smashed and broken. There was a large crack in the downstairs roadside window. The wind howled through on wild nights and with the lock bust the place was insecure. He could come back, or more like him. She opted to take flight and headed uphill to the great castle with its shattered ramparts. Pushing down on her upper legs she climbed up the steep incline through the

47

Burgess Gate and on up to the castle green. The Edward Gate loomed dark and ominous against the grey sky, looking sinister with its beheaded stone effigy of the once all-powerful English king.

This was an escape she'd used more than once. It was early; she wasn't sure of the time, but the castle custodian would be in promptly today. With this atmospheric weather he'd want to check the place out before opening to the public. You see, Denbigh Castle had a reputation. The great central well was a magnet for the suicidal. The railings were an easy climb for the desperate and the drop was certain. The custodian had the job of checking before the public arrived, just in case.

As Anya approached the drawbridge her mind was wrestling with choices. If the main castle visitor gate was closed, then would she climb the walls to one side and head for the well? The gate was open, the old custodian was in already. Anya experienced a feeling of relief because she didn't really want to end it all, however terrible the night before had been. The custodian would have a flask and would hide her in the museum's back-room store. She could warm up there, in quiet and safety.

'What the…?' the custodian exclaimed as she came in, shivering and dejected. She noted that he had not yet switched the kiosk lights on and guessed that her sudden, silent appearance had given him a shock. With the lights on he was able to see the deep livid bruise on her cheek. She registered the appalled look on his face.

'Right, that's it. I'm calling the police. You can't go on like this.'

She said nothing in return. She'd talk him round when they shared his flask of hot tea. She would not let the police become involved. They were too busy to care; too deaf to listen.

Anya settled in the storeroom corner. Curled up, she fell into a restless slumber. Despite the castle's great size and importance, her walls and towers today were little more than great shapeless clumps of masonry and stone. Creepy and haunted on her hilltop, the castle attracted few visitors and Anya could rely on a dry, warm, undisturbed stay. It was her place of refuge.

* * *

Anya was being shaken gently.

'Anya, Anya Gwenllian, I'm closing my queen. It's time for you to leave.'

Suddenly Anya was wide awake, and adrenaline brought her rapidly to a state of flight. Full of fear she observed the custodian. How did he know both of her Christian names? Who was he and what did he want from her?

'It's dark outside,' he said, seemingly unaware of her discomfort. 'Shall I walk you back to where you are living?'

'No!' Anya replied with much more aggression than she had intended. 'No, thank you,' she repeated, more gently this time. She found her way to the exit and the darkness outside. Anya didn't look back and once she'd cleared the threshold, she ran into the night, back to number fifteen before he could see her, before he had a chance to follow her in the dark.

Arriving at the house, everything was very much as she had left it earlier that morning. The lock was still bust but it didn't look like anyone had been in to investigate. Inside, the place was dark and silent, and Anya crept around to check it was empty, her heart beating loudly in her ears.

Anya's mind raced. She pulled one of the chairs over from the sitting area and jammed it up against the front door, stopping the handle from being pulled down. Anyone determined enough would still easily enter and she knew it.

Anya had left the house in darkness; she didn't want it to be known that she was in. Her eyes adjusted to the grey twilight of the place. Moving carefully in the darkness she made her way to the rear of the property and the back door. The sliding bolts top and bottom were engaged. Anya removed the key, placing it in her back pocket. The action gave her a sense that she had some control over the situation.

Next, she pulled out an old wooden box from under the Belfast sink, heavy with antique ironmongery and tools. Locating an old sliding bolt, she headed back to the front door to make it more secure for the night. The task took some considerable effort as she worked in greyness with only the streetlights for illumination. The hours slipped away and by the time she had finished Anya was extremely tired and hungry.

Finally, she had made what repairs she could before heading upstairs to the small front bedroom. There was nothing in this place to eat, and the bed, well, she would not be sleeping in there tonight. After last night the sheets were tainted. Tomorrow she would take the whole lot down to the laundrette but tonight she preferred the cold hard floor. Alone she curled up in one of the room's corners, clutching the patchy threadbare carpet and the exposed floorboards to see her though an endless night.

4. A Lady and the Lake

Ruthin AD 525

Late November

Cunewolfe gazed out over the rampart stockade, out across the mere and beyond, to the forests. His gaze returned to a small rise from the mere's waters which just cleared the depths; an odd, misplaced mound in what was otherwise a sheet of silent water. Carrion birds, busy on the mound summit, joined by wolves and red foxes on the periphery. They were pulling, tearing at a meal, fighting over the pieces. Some type of animal, perhaps a cow, a deer, a sheep had met it's end here. The stinking sorry spectacle was all too close to the village, but it would be over soon.

Why had they come here? For days, they had struggled against the weather, guarded and prepared for ambush on the forest and mountain paths, alert and at the ready both day and night, never knowing when the wild animal of Britannia might pounce. At last, they had arrived in this mean, empty place. The old Roman, flecks of spittle in his silver beard, had pushed Cynric ever onwards, bullied him towards the prize.

'Finish off the Votadini prince and the war will be over!' the crazed Roman had wheedled in his broken command of the English tongue. The prize would be worth the chase, for the death of Arth would mean the end of Britannia. Then Cynric would turn on this old Roman and remove his head for the act of sedition against his own people. What had driven this vindictive clown of a man to make such a betrayal against his own kind?

This place, where a small group of fighting men had given but brief resistance before withdrawing into the rising forests beyond seemed of little consequence. The villagers, mainly old men and women, they were different again – tribes from the old times. They knew nothing, would say nothing to help the Angles in their quest.

Standing on the rampart hording, grasping the stockade, he noticed it was sound, freshly repaired. Someone had been here. Had Arth been here? Whoever, they were no more, vanished and illusive. Cunewolfe looked once more out to the forests, vast and unknown, a suitable hiding place for Arth and the last warriors of Britannia.

Cunewolfe, with his eyes focused on the far distance, registered a closer movement and his attention was once again drawn to the mound in the mere. Squinting now, he noticed two figures stopped on the water's edge. With the click of his fingers, other warriors joined him on the parapet and followed his gaze.

* * *

The bolt, when it came, was swift and pitiless. Approaching Gwenllian and her escort on the pathway ahead were armed men but this was a distraction, for the true menace came from one side. The knight brought them both to a stop, his shield placed protectively in front of her. The dull thud, when it arrived, brought him senseless and blinking, falling backward, the point hitting true to his temples.

As he fell, he pulled Gwenllian down with him; she was on top of him, disorientated and attempting, without success, to get back to her feet. The approaching warriors arrived and the lead, holding out an arm, pulled her away from the stricken wreck beneath her. The twitching from the body on the floor increased and from the edge of her sight she was aware of an axe being lifted. Turned so the blade would not connect, this instrument of murder was brought down with sickening speed, smashing her escort's head like a pumpkin, the keen blade spared so that it would remain sharp. The twitching stopped.

* * *

Cunewolfe observed the woman whose arm he now held firmly above the wrist. Deep brown eyes observed him back; tiny flecks of blood bejewelled her right cheek, neck and the shoulder of her cape.

Pulling the young woman up to her feet, Cunewolfe caught a look of defiance in her eyes. This was no peasant girl he held; there was an edge of quality to her. In just one look he gauged her to be a woman of education, of refinement and class. Had that mad Roman indeed brought them to the right place? Fruitless days, weeks, months and now at last, was the great prize within their grasp?

Course twine held both hands together at the wrists, her arms hoisted high above her head, the twine lashed on a cross beam which held up the roof. Every few hours the hoist had been released and she had, albeit with difficulty and little dignity, been able to get relief from her bodily functions.

The hours of daylight had passed by and the darkness of night had descended. There was no sense of warmth in her corner of captivity, for here the hall had lost much of its thatch roofing. Gwen was afforded a fine view of the night sky above. The rain and drizzle had cleared, the air now cool and fresh. Winter, she suspected, was about to roar back with vengeance.

'Arth,' she whispered, looking up at the stars. 'Are you up there already? Have you passed over to the next world and left me behind?' Her teeth chattered loudly with the cold.

Despite, or perhaps because of, the desperate circumstance she found herself in, her thoughts became vivid and rested on those intimate moments she had shared with Arth earlier in the year when she had first joined him here in this place. Time and again she replayed the images in her mind's eye; it brought relief from the discomfort and an escape from those negative ideas about what might happen to her next.

Desperate for rescue and for this ordeal to end, the true reality of her position was one of dark hopelessness. Despair, seeping ever closer had begun to touch her consciousness. The hours to follow would be brutish and horrific.

'This should be our place.' His voice had been clear, breaking the long silence that had settled between them as they sat just off the path under a young oak tree. When she had not replied, he'd continued, 'This is our special place where we can be together.'

Gwenllian had always known that he had liked her, even as a young boy. Her memories reached back to her childhood and to the visits taken with her father to the court at Cynedda's remote mountain kingdom. Arth, his brother and the mix of highborn sons were a capable, energetic and educated group. Fair haired and dreamy, she had liked Arth, but not in a serious way. The boys had always showed off and tried to attract her attention which had made her giggle. His older brother was the one that had made her heart beat faster. He was dark haired, handsome and quick of mind, but he had been too old for her.

In her later teenage years, when she had been at court, Arth was shy and remote. Even now, a respected leader of men, he was not a confident man and especially not so with women. She had imagined then that he saw her as a princess just beyond his reach, but this was not the case, and in the years since Badon Field she had grown to love him.

She remembered agreeing with him. 'Y dderwen ifanc, this young oak tree, it will grow forever, so yes, let's make it our special place.'

Then he had turned to face her, and she'd known he was searching for something more in her words.

Gwenllian visualised again how on that afternoon she had been absently twisting and twiddling a teasel head that she had snapped off from the dry brown skeleton, all that was left now after the summer's heat. She had been enjoying the calm closeness of his company and the teasel had been something to occupy her, to control her desire as she had willed him to come closer so that she could look deep into his eyes.

'Arth…' she had begun, before looking away and breathing in to catch her composure, to order her thoughts before once again meeting his gaze. 'If we get too close, then there will be children and where will their futures be in all of this?'

His head had dropped at this.

'Come on,' she'd continued, getting up onto her feet.

There was the pathway, clear now in her memories, a cutting through tall grass with the young oak trees lining one side. At this point the track climbed upward and the slight elevation afforded a view down through pastures to woodland which marked the edge of a great marsh. To follow the track onwards would lead out of this collection of small hamlets to the bald hills beyond. The gift of oysters came to her mind and their sea salt slipperiness. It was a meal that had made her gag, much to Arth's amusement.

'Let us walk down to the wetlands,' she had said. 'We could swim.' She noticed the positive impact her suggestion had made to his mood. They had swum together before and the act of being naked in cold water had a strong meaning for her. She saw it as an act of purification.

She set off towards the marsh. Behind her, Arth was up and on her tail. She waited on the path for him to catch up. In the tall grass the trackway was neither clear nor obvious from where they had started off. Eventually, the meadow gave way to blackthorn and then woodland before suddenly they were at the water's edge.

'It's where some of the women come down to bathe. You can swim out to the other side. Its perhaps the one place where the waters are deep.' She reached for his hand. 'Come on. Let's swim across.'

He watched her as she untied the cords of her garment before pulling it off and over her head, leaving her quite naked.

Nervous now under his gaze she fumbled to untangle the plaits of her hair. He stood silent, seemingly dazed, watching her. With both hands she loosened the braids and her hair fell free to her shoulders.

'Meet you on the other side,' she said shyly, and with that she quickly glided into the dark waters. He joined her a little after, swimming powerfully to beat her, but there was no catching her, for in the water she was king.

Arriving first at the wooden landing stage at the other side she pushed herself up to sit on the deck. With both hands she pushed her wet hair back between her fingers, stretching her torso as she did so.

Reaching the landing stage, Arth pushed up to sit beside her and tenderly placed his right hand on her knee. Leaning in, he gently kissed her on the lips, and their noses rubbed softly together. She pushed the fingers of her right hand through his hair and softly ran the fingers of her other through the hairs that ran along his thigh.

She stood up, hesitant about continuing, but knew that she could no longer stop, and he was up and onto his feet too, gently pulling her back to him. She looked deep into his eyes, and they kissed once more before she dropped her head to look down, her eyes now closed. Then she moved and bent her right leg, her inner thigh brushing against his side. His fingers traced down her buttocks to touch her most private place. She gasped as her body tensed and she brought her head up again.

'Go on then,' she said, 'make us one.'

Without warning, the partition fencing was pushed aside, and Gwenllian was dragged out of her dreams and back to reality. She could hear noise from the main hall – more people had arrived for a gathering. The open bangor brought some welcome warmth with it as her tethers were unleashed from above. Her arms, stiff and aching, dropped hard against her body.

She was led into the hall proper, and a wall of warmth from the great central hearths greeted her. The fires, stoked up, roared fiercely and she considered how different these unwelcome guests were behaving in comparison to Arth and her own party of visitors. These Angles were literally burning and eating away the village resources. She noted how little they cared for the villagers; they were not equals but were here to serve. This was in direct contrast to how Arth had directed his war band, who were not to be a burden on this community.

Tethered, her entrance into the hall attracted stares and looks of both dismay and shock from the villagers. They regarded her in silence, with eyes of pity.

* * *

Cunewolfe was pleased with his catch as he entered the great hall. He would not seem so foolish now on presenting her. This woman, she counted for something, she was somebody of note. Of that he was quite sure.

61

'My Lord Cynric if I may be so bold.' Cunewolfe addressed the tall, slim but powerfully muscular warrior who stood with his back to him and Gwenllian. A warrior group had just come in from the cold, but there were other new arrivals too. Women of child baring age, richly dressed, adorned with broaches of twisted gold legend and sporting long blonde hair in matching plaits. The lord turned slowly in response to Cunewolfe's address and stared directly at Gwen. Unlike the other young women in this hall, her dress was plain, her hair dark; just one Roman style broach and some speckles of blood adorned her cape. The woman's brown eyes looked straight back at the lord. She held herself with dignity.

* * *

Cynric had never met this woman, but he well knew who she was from the descriptions he had heard of her, the stories, the legends that had come to his ears.

He addressed her in Latin. 'GWENLLIAN OF THE ORDOVICES, WELCOME.' Then, in her native tongue, he added, 'Croeso.' The woman in front of him offered no words in return, but her eyes widened slightly when he spoke her name. Anyone who had not been observing closely would perhaps have missed this involuntary response which gave her identity away.

Cynric stepped towards her; he had no need for speculation, he was sure of who she was but had chosen not to name her in his native tongue. Not yet. There was every chance that by doing so her life would end quite shortly and now that he looked upon her, this was not something he wished. Indeed, for the first time, Cynric found himself a little nervous in the presence of a lady. Yes, he'd been with women, women who looked the same and behaved as was appropriate. Lords up and down the country were always keen to place their daughters before him. None, however, could hold his interest for long.

This pursuit after Arth and the last dying embers of Britannia had devoured his life for more years now than he dared count. Driven ever on by the stories of this other leader, a man who had matched him, a man he had met once, years before. Now here he was at last, at journey's end with Gwenllian, consort to the British leader and the last, lost queen of Britannia, standing in silence before him. Cynric let this silence run too long in the hall whilst he observed, no, admired the woman presented to him. Here in the flesh, she did not diminish his expectations.

* * *

Arth had described the leader of the Angles. Gwen looked without emotion at the English lord before her. So, this was the great Cynric.

* * *

'I HAVE NOT FOUND HIM.' Cynric addressed her once again, speaking to her in good Latin. The Angles in the hall had no words of the Roman tongue. They had, however, fallen silent, spectators to this confrontation. To them this woman was someone indeed and they were caught up in the drama that unfolded before them.

Cynric came right up to her, face now against face, and whispered, 'I HAVE FOUND MY PRIZE GWENLLIAN, AND NOW, I, CYNRIC, WILL SEARCH NO MORE FOR ARTH. FOR WITH YOU IN MY HANDS, ARTH MUST SURELY COME TO ME.'

5. Night-Time Caller

Ruthin AD 1988

Life was looking up for Dan Jones. He had a job in which he was excelling, his parents had supported him with a loan for a house and at the moment he wasn't alone. Hannah had become a serious girlfriend. She was a few years younger but the two worked well together as a couple.

Tonight, he had lots to do with work. Record keeping, which was easy enough but very tedious. Dan Jones didn't do tedious. Hannah had come around. She wouldn't be staying the night but had come to keep him company and that's why he liked her. Other girls would be kicking off, would be demanding his undivided attention. At least that had been his experience until now. Hannah, however, was quite happy, he had things to do and so had she.

Hannah was a bit like him, always busy on projects. One project in particular was costing her a lot of money – diving. Hannah was working her way to a professional qualification status. This was an expensive aim, and she was always keen to earn enough to pay for her ambition.

So, things between the two of them were kind of running along nicely. He was happy to give her space for whatever she wanted too and like tonight, he hadn't asked her round she'd just volunteered. Dan considered Hannah to be independently minded, good company, easy going and of course, he found her more than a little bit attractive. He wondered what her Achilles heel might be. Then he shook his head to wake himself up a bit. Daydreaming wasn't going to sort all these records out and he set about getting his job done in earnest.

The house was brand new, a kind of starter home, and Dan hadn't really got much in it as yet. Some of the windows had curtains, the kitchen was equipped and there were a few pieces of furniture, borrowed from home, gracing the living area. He hadn't gotten around to carpeting downstairs and the grey fleck Marley tiles ensured that the place was echoey.

Hannah picked up on the sound first.

'Psst, Dan, I think you've got a visitor on the way,' she whispered over to him from the living area.

The downstairs was open plan, kitchen leading out into a dining area with an arch through to the living room up front. Dan had settled himself at the black IKEA folding table in the dining area. He lifted his head up from the books when Hannah spoke. There was a silence.

The rapping on the door made them both jump even though they were expecting it.

'Oh, I'll go,' Hannah said. She padded over, clicking on the outside light before opening the front door.

Dan could hear some of the conversation from where he was sitting. It seemed Hannah knew their visitor, but her responses were cautious. He came from the kitchen table to join his girlfriend at the front door.

Looking back at him from the threshold was a girl he recognised as she'd been in his year at school. The clothes and the visitor's attire, however, came as a bit of a shock. Long tangled hair and clothing that suggested a lifestyle akin to someone who lived on the streets. Dan was taken aback because the image before him didn't fit the girl he had remembered.

'Christ, Anya Richards, isn't it? What the Hell happened to you?' Dan was not shy about mincing his words. The girl looked a mess.

'Hello Daniel.' She greeted him in a calm, silky soft voice which very much confirmed his identification.

He hadn't seen Anya since the funeral. In that time, he hadn't considered her much. They had lost touch because, well, truth be told, he was disappointed in her. His best friend had died going to meet her and that, to Dan, seemed the most important thing. Soon after the murder, around the time of the trial, Anya had brought up all sorts of allegations against her father and this kind of muddied events, created a distraction to what Dan felt was most important. He had become quite unsure of Miss Richards, questioned her sincerity. When the trial had come to an end Dan guessed she had just gone back to her very privileged life, her university course and what would most likely be a charmed future.

More recently he'd heard some rumours that Anya was living in a squat and doing drugs. From the image he saw in front of him now, the stylish society girl had, it seemed, very much fallen from grace into another life. Anya looked like drugs and trouble.

'Would you like to come in?' Hannah offered.

'No, no, I can see it isn't convenient and I should have left it until morning. I'd like to meet up for a chat though—' she fixed her gaze on Dan '—talk through something from the past.' Then she handed Dan an exercise book covered in brown paper. 'Would you look at this for me?'

Dan took the book; he recognised the handwriting on the cover. 'What's this about?'

'Perhaps you'll get back to me Daniel. Take a look and then we'll talk.' Anya was already turning to go, to disappear back into the dark night.

Dan and Hannah watched her for a minute before Hannah shivered in the cold, holding her arms and hopping back indoors across the threshold. Dan closed the door and clicked the outside light off.

'You're going to need a coffee,' Hannah said, having already retreated into the kitchen. She filled the kettle and opened Dan's fridge.

'Daniel Jones, you haven't got any milk!' she exclaimed.

'I just drink neat tea,' he responded. 'There's plenty of sugar.' He sat on the bright orange IKEA settee in the living area and began to flick through the book that Anya had handed to him.

'Oh God, I can't drink tea or coffee without milk.' Hannah was rattling around in cupboards in what he knew was a hopeless search for anything that might make the evening drink a bit more palatable.

A short while later, defeated, she joined him in the living area and placed a steaming hot mug of dark brown liquid on the coffee table in front of him. Dan absent-mindedly motioned a gesture of thanks.

'So, what's the late great Anya Richards brought for you then?' Hannah asked, taking a sip from her own mug, and pulling a face at the taste.

Dan handed her a note that had dropped from the front of the notebook as he'd opened it. Hannah read it.

'I'll be in Siop Nain at eleven o'clock on Saturday if you want to talk. If not, you can just return the book to me then.'

'Are you going to meet her?' Hannah enquired.

Dan took his first swig from the mug. 'Yuck it's coffee. I don't drink coffee!'

'You do now. You're going to need to stay up all night if you're going to get your work done 'cos I bet you haven't done much yet and you'll be looking at that notebook for hours I can tell.'

Dan pulled a face by way of an answer and put the mug back down on the table. The notebook, towards the end, was just like a diary. The dates indicated the notes had been written by Tim on the days just before his murder.

'You're not really going to meet up with her, are you?' Hannah asked again. 'I've got that catering function for the Sheridans on Saturday. I want to be with you when you meet up with her.'

The Achilles heel. Dan lifted his eyes from the notebook and observed Hannah who had settled on the one and only other chair across from the coffee table.

'Used to fancy Miss Richards, we all did.' Then he placed the open notebook down. 'I lost my best mate because he went to meet up with her.'

'Tim?'

'It wasn't her fault, she went through a lot that night, must have. Still, I kind of don't know what I think about her now. And this—' he motioned towards the notebook '—I think this might upset me.'

Hannah nodded. 'Don't read it then; just give it back to her. Don't get involved.'

6. The Paths That Cross

Oxford University AD 1985

October

The train journey back to Oxford on the Sunday evening was an overly long and empty experience for Philomena. Staring out of the window from her seat, the night was pitch black, interspersed only by each station's lights when the train passed through. The old carriages wobbled to the monotonous click clack of the lines, a noise that sped up and slowed down in an alternate rhythm making the experience otherworldly and surreal. There was no one else in the carriage to bother her, no one ignoring, staring at or talking to her.

When the train finally pulled into Oxford it was truly dark outside and she was the only one who stepped out onto the platform. Slamming the door behind her, the cold damp of an autumn evening hit and she shuddered, pulling up her coat collar and half running, half walking, she headed for the exit, ticket clutched in her right hand ready to show. There was no one at the gate and she walked straight out into the darkness beyond the station's lights. From here she headed quickly back up to the university and her digs.

Turning the door lock once, twice, God three times before the bloody thing unlocked Philomena finally pushed her way back into her room, clicking on the light switch and pushing the door to as she entered. She pulled off her damp coat and located the peg behind her door before sitting on her bed to tug off her squash shoes. She made no attempt to undo the laces, she was too tired to fiddle, and she threw them one at a time into the corner of her room that had claimed the right to her shoes and boots. Then she fell back onto her small single bed, legs from her knees down hanging off the end. She stretched out her arms above her head before breathing out. The rigours of the weekend were quickly catching up to her and on closing her eyes the minutes slipped away as she drifted into a long, tired sleep.

With a jolt she woke up sometime after midnight, stiff, cold and irritated by the fact that she was still fully clothed and that the main room lights were full on and glaring down at her. She forced herself up to a sitting position and blinked a few times before standing to unbutton and unzip her jeans and pull off her navy woollen jumper and the white T-shirt underneath. She dumped her clothing on the chair by her desk without folding them before rummaging in her wardrobe for a fresh pair of pyjamas.

Having located her night clothes and having pulled them on, she was at her sink for a quick face and hands wash before brushing her teeth. It was a quick job, she was shattered. She clicked off the room lights and snuggled under the duvet, out of the chill within the room.

The following morning, her alarm clock jingled its bells, which she silenced with the overwhelming desire to throttle the damn thing. Although she fancied very much the idea of staying in her warm bed, she was now awake and her mind, as ever, was busy. On the one hand she thought about just giving up, but the positive drive was stronger. She'd decided to get on with this year, do a good job so that one of them at least would succeed and achieve their life's goals. She owed it to herself, and she was going to do it for Tim too.

On entering the department later that morning, she nearly walked straight into Dr Chris Stephenson who seemed to be all over one of the first-year undergraduates. Short in stature, yet slim with slick combed back black hair, Stephenson sported stylish clothes. Today he wore a loud pink shirt against a neat black waist coat. He opted for expensive Italian leather shoes and all this was laced with a strong aftershave. With no shortage of self-conviction, the man was a Masai predator in a field full of gazelles.

Typical, thought Philomena. Dr Stephenson, as ever, had a roving eye and a strong interest in any attractive undergraduate in a skirt or tight jeans. Stephenson, Philomena had decided, was a reptile. He'd taken a strong interest in her from the off, used her sloppy Greek and Latin as an excuse to spend more time with her, get her on her own and weasel his way into her personal space. Philomena could see straight through him and had done nothing to encourage the man. She had considered telling him to get stuffed in no uncertain terms but as her personal tutor this seemed difficult, and the man was quite sneaky and manipulative.

Stephenson, Dr Chris Stephenson, had identified an odd quirk with Philomena's grasp of the classic languages; he'd picked up that she had neither O or A Level Greek or Latin and was switched on enough to know that had she learnt these languages on her own from textbooks or language tapes she sure as Hell wouldn't speak them the way she did. His professional curiosity, however, went no further, because his main interest, well, that was obvious to see.

On spotting Stephenson, Philomena made a swerve to avoid him.

'Ah, Philomena,' he called after her. 'I was hoping I'd catch you today. Don't forget our tutorial after lunch. We'll meet in my office, OK?'

Philomena turned and nodded before continuing on her way. She didn't want to engage in conversation. By 'tutorial' she guessed he meant her tutorial group. Not so bad then, as there were a few of them, most reading modern foreign languages. As ever, Philomena was the only one with her big toe in archaeology.

Stephenson didn't fit Philomena's idea of what a classics lecturer should look or act like. Go into the office of any lecturer for archaeology and their rooms were a mess. Piles and shelves of books, artefacts on tables, finds trays, cardboard boxes, rolls of maps and tracing paper. Stephenson's room, in contrast, had the air of being regularly jet washed with bleach. All pale wood office furniture and not a bloody book in sight. No, Philomena was convinced the man was a fraud with his two-tone leather brogue shoes, his C&A suits and his overpowering aftershave. The good doctor had been christened 'Spicy

Steve' by the young male undergraduates because of his overpowering stink.

The last time Philomena was in Stephenson's room on her own had been an unsettling experience. She'd joined him at his request, but the encounter challenged the appropriateness of the lecturer-student relationship.

Outwardly, Philomena may have had a rock chick image, but in reality, she was more of a paper tiger. No way was she going to be sleeping with anyone other than Mr Right. The thought had occurred to her so many times that she might perhaps be missing out on some very pleasurable experiences. She well knew that boys found her attractive, and she was happy and confident in their company. Some of her friends had experienced full on relationships but sex made things serious and the upsets when everything broke down – well, she couldn't be bothered with that, not yet at any rate.

Here she was again, entering Stephenson's office for the tutorial. Once in the room she noticed a distinct lack of others from her group.

'Take a seat Philomena.' Stephenson gestured to the only other chair apart from his own. She cautiously sat pretty much where she had sat by his desk the last time and half expected him to play the same trick again. She was on guard this time and after recent events was in no mood for any of his inappropriate nonsense.

She opened up the conversation. 'No pornographic comics today then Chris?'

Stephenson smiled, ignoring the quip. 'I'm so glad you could make it, I've an exciting opportunity for you Philomena.'

Her heart sank and she made no effort to respond.

'I've arranged a post graduate research project for you to join,' he continued.

'Right... but I've not graduated yet Doctor,' she replied after a moment.

'Ah, a minor impediment, there'll be no problem with that. No this isn't an opportunity to miss Philomena, the work's out on the island of Crete in the Med.'

Philomena regarded him; archaeology jobs were like finding four-leaf clovers – few and far between. Chances were, you'd be very lucky to actually do anything with the discipline once you'd finished your degree and even post grad work was a rarity.

'Who's it with and what's it about?' she questioned.

'Well, I'm looking to be joint director on this project. It's linguistic work based on the Greek and Roman site at Gortyn. I'm going to need a good researcher to support me with the field work.'

You mean you need a flunky to do all the work for you and there'll be more strings attached for me, Philomena thought. Out loud, she said, 'I'd need to know more, like how many others my age are taking part and what the on-site living arrangements would be.'

'Oh, I'll only need the one researcher and the dig's workforce will be locals from the island. You're a really lucky girl,' he continued, smiling.

'Is your wife OK with this? Does she know?' Philomena looked him straight in the eye. For the first time in the exchange, for just a fraction of a second, he was caught off guard and unprepared with his answer. When he did respond he deflected her question.

'Don't be so frosty Philomena – this is a chance of a lifetime.'

'I'd have to think about it,' she responded, showing little obvious interest in his proposition. Philomena pushed her chair back and made for the office door. Stephenson watched her go.

Relieved she was out of the room in one piece, Philomena made her way down the staircase and along to the department's library, thinking as she went. The plan was and always had been to work in archaeology if she could, despite the odds being stacked against her. Here was an opportunity, but at what personal cost? There was a word for his behaviour, the reptile. No, perhaps it was now time to take control of her own future.

The library was quiet, with shelves stacked high with books. She made her way to the study area where all the archaeology periodicals and magazines were kept. Turning a corner, she came upon a fellow student who was sat at one end of a long, old oak table. She lifted her eyebrows by way of recognition. He responded with a slight nod of his head. She didn't say hi; Giles wouldn't have coped with a girl saying hello to him.

There was something a little different about Giles – not too sociable and he tended to wear slightly old-fashioned formal clothing. He was tall and thin, something of a throwback to the 1920s. Somehow, he'd survived his private school to get here; Philomena sure as Hell didn't think he'd have lasted in a comprehensive.

She began to rifle through the periodicals. There was a file box for the Council for British Archaeology quarterly bulletins – what she was looking for. There was a new edition. Quite why she was interested in these was a good question because the general content was as dull as dishwater – discussions about the Council's activities and some Government stuff. At the rear, however, were the dig opportunities for both here in the UK and abroad. She flicked through the latest edition to get to the back. Occasionally, very occasionally, proper jobs in archaeology were advertised here too.

'Bingo,' she whispered, and Giles took his nose out of the monograph on Roman pottery he was devouring and gave her a disapproving look. *Jesus Christ, a whole book on Roman pottery*, she thought and ignored his look.

There were two adverts. One was for a job in Pembrokeshire, which required an archaeologist for the Coastal Path National Park. The job specification asked for significant experience and preferred postgraduate qualifications plus knowledge of the Welsh language and the area as a whole. They didn't want much for a job that paid so very little. Surprisingly, the other job was also for a position in Wales. It was for a Presentation Officer for the Roman Legionary Fortress Museum at Caerleon. Applicants would need to be enthusiastic, fit and knowledgeable, preferably to degree level. A good communicator, able to form excellent relationships with all visitors and especially school children were amongst some of the other requirements.

The Gods are looking down on me today, thought Philomena, and, taking out a notebook from her small backpack she wrote down the details on how to apply. She looked up at Giles again. When she had first arrived in Oxford, Giles had been the first person on her course that she had met. She remembered thinking that if everyone else on the course was the same, she would never fit in.

She returned the CBA quarterly to its box and, standing, she returned the box to its shelf. There were other magazines here too. Rows of the highbrow *Antiquity* and files for the more populist *Current Archaeology*. The latter had some competition from a new title, *Popular Archaeology*, something edited by Magnus Magnusson. It had some nice pictures but tended to be more of a traveller's guide than a serious archaeology magazine. Philomena put her notebook back into her backpack and left quietly.

* * *

A letter offering her an interview came back quickly. Standing outside Dr Grant's office door, she knocked twice. She'd be missing his seminar on Thursday to attend the interview in Caerleon. Philomena respected Dr Grant and wanted to explain her absence in advance.

Dr Grant wasn't that much older than she was. He was tall with a light peppered beard and thick short hair. He sported thin woollen jumpers, sleeves pushed up to the elbows, with faded drainpipe jeans and walking boots, always walking boots. Mike Grant was what an archaeologist should be, absolutely dedicated and passionate about his subject. Polite, quiet and thoughtful, he was everything Stephenson wasn't.

'Hi Philomena,' he said in greeting as she entered his office. 'How are you doing?'

'OK. Actually, great I guess,' she replied.

'You guess?' He looked up from a large, unrolled sheet of paper.

'Yes, I need to explain that I'm not going to be here on Thursday – sorry.'

'Oh, you off doing something nice?'

'I've got an interview.'

On hearing this, he took off his glasses and considered before responding. 'Well, I suppose congratulations are in order. What's the job?'

She gave him the details.

Mike Grant scratched his beard – he was considering again. 'So, you're not keen to take up Dr Stephenson on his Crete offer?'

Philomena pulled a face and shrugged.

'You don't like Dr Stephenson much do you?'

'No, he makes my skin crawl,' she said forcefully. There, she'd said it, shared the fact that her personal tutor made her feel uncomfortable.

'Thought so, but I know your name has gone forward for the project – accepted too.'

'What, with my grades?' Philomena was astounded.

'What's wrong with your grades? A straight First Class Honours all the way through, from where I'm sitting.'

Philomena shook her head. 'No, no, Stephenson has hauled me in several times; my grades are well down in the low forties. I haven't got a chance, but he keeps emphasising how he'll look after me.'

There was a silence. 'I've been concerned about him for a while, how he is with young undergraduate girls. Now you've confirmed my thinking. Has he abused his position of trust with you? I know your grades, you're at the top of the tree. You could really make a name for yourself one day, so you mustn't sell yourself short here.'

'Thanks Dr Grant, for believing in me. I kind of needed a boost with all the things that have happened recently,' she replied, eyes down at her sneakers, her long hair falling in front of her face.

'Has he done something to you – what's happened?'

'Oh no, Stephenson hasn't touched me. He makes me feel proper uncomfortable, but he hasn't physically touched me. Not yet anyway.'

'I bet you're not alone. It's time to alert the university authorities I think.'

Philomena looked up at Dr Grant. 'That's not what's upset me, but I reckon you're right.'

'Err… do you want to talk to me about it, or better still, with one of the women in the faculty?' Mike Grant offered. Philomena was aware of his embarrassment, that he thought this might be women's stuff, which it seemed he was hopelessly unprepared to deal with.

Philomena smiled at him. Mike Grant was as honest and straight as they came, would do anything to help, but he'd be out of his depth sorting out a young woman's relationship problems.

'It's not sex and relationships, if that's what you're worried about.'

'Thank God,' he chipped in.

'Well, it's not the sex bit at any rate, but the relationship bit, well that's a small part of the thing that's upsetting me.' She paused before continuing. 'Can you handle something really strange – like a kind of ghost story?'

He observed her closely, no doubt wondering if she was being serious. 'Now I'm intrigued, you'd better sit down.'

'Well, for me it all starts in secondary school,' she began, and she told him all about her wild dreams at Rhyn Park. She described how she had met Tim for the first time and how she had met him once again this summer. She shared the whole story with Mike Grant, everything that she knew. The different languages, the visions and the adventure that she and Tim had shared.

Philomena could see how Mike now considered her quietly. She knew that he held her in high regard so just what was he making of all this?

'So, speed this up Philomena, what are you getting to? What's the punch line?'

'He's dead. Tim's dead, stabbed, and I knew, knew something was coming.' She looked him in the eye. 'There's a lot more to the story Dr Grant, but now, now all I'm left with is a load of bloody useless ancient languages. My dissertation on ancient graffiti – I don't speak from any textbook; I speak these languages like they were spoken.'

There was a knock on the door.

'I'm happy to listen, any time,' Dr Grant said, 'I don't understand but I'll listen, talk it through.'

Philomena nodded.

The door opened and one of the second-year classics students entered. Philomena gave the student a nod of acknowledgment as she stood, pushing her chair back to leave.

* * *

Caerleon AD 1985

October

The bus wheezed and grunted up the hill, black smoke belching out from the exhaust. Having cleared the commercial district and estate after estate of poor social housing, the journey uphill was now going through what Philomena deduced from the look of the large Victorian and Edwardian houses to be a posher part of Newport – destination Caerleon. At least it was warm on the bus and for the first time this morning she had peeled off her coat, which had attracted some cat calls from some rough young yobs at the back.

After weeks of relentless drizzle, Jack Frost had arrived, bringing vast pale blue skies and a bitter chill that hadn't much warmed since she'd caught the train at Oxford early this morning.

The road dropped down and ran through a wooded area before running alongside the River Usk and at an old stone bridge the bus crossed into the small town of Caerleon. Philomena hopped off at the first stop, hoping the yobs had better things to do than follow her. There were more catcalls as she got up to leave and they were gesticulating rudely through the window at her as the bus pulled off, but she paid them no attention as she pulled her coat back on.

She'd dressed smartly, white blouse, black trousers and posh black high-heeled shoes – she looked like a fast lawyer on some TV show. It occurred to her now that perhaps she had overdressed – perhaps they were expecting a girl in faded threadbare jeans with big boots and an archaeologist's trowel tucked into her back pocket. *Oh well,* she thought, *this is an interview after all, and if I've made the wrong call the posh clothes will do OK for a job with the bank or something like that later on.*

Walking round and into the town centre she was aware that the pavements weren't exactly continuous and arriving at the National Roman Legionary Museum she looked back down Broadway to see a column of primary school children all in red who were being marched up this former Roman road. Ahead and leading the group was a young male teacher who was doing his best to keep all the children going, having introduced sin dex sin dex (left right left right marching Roman style) to them hoping that everyone would keep up. Some of them were joining in with gusto but there was the odd one who'd turn around to talk to someone behind and the column would break up. Philomena didn't fancy his chances of getting them all across the road in one go. An older lady brought up the rear, she guessed this might be a teacher helper and from what she could see there were two parents some way behind having a good chat. They'd been brought along to balance up the numbers but were clearly of no bloody use at all.

It was when the young man called for all the children to stop at the crossing that Philomena experienced a slight giddiness. She held onto the wall behind her to keep her balance. *Should have had breakfast this morning,* she thought, before looking back in the direction of the children.

She heard a voice. 'ILLAM E PLAUSTRO ITINERIBUS.'

The children were no longer children; the road ahead was now jammed with people, wagons, carts and the whole lot had come to a stop because one of the wagons had lost its wheel, tipping its contents and blocking the road behind and in front. Smoke poured out from lines of chimneys mounted on the rooves of long single story buildings that were placed on either side of the road.

Philomena blinked and pinched herself but the sights, sounds and smells of this very Roman scene refused to evaporate. The road was full of people as far as she could see, way beyond the walls, which were some six metres in height, and on into the countryside beyond. They seemed to be a people on the move, crowding, pushing, arguing, but all packed, carrying everything they could. These people, these refugees, were fleeing, in search of safety and the conversations, the anxiety and the distress of the travellers penetrated her.

'Sir, that young woman's not very well,' one of the boys from the school group called out. It was enough to snap Philomena out of this illusion and bring her back with a sliding focus into normality. She took in some long deep breaths and let go of the wall behind her. She was a little shaken, she'd thought the days of déjà vu had passed. This was just like the experience she'd had that summer outside the pub.

'Come on children don't bother the young woman,' the teacher responded. The children filed past her as they mounted the steps to enter the museum. They all looked – she was an added side show for the visit.

* * *

AD 1985 Oxford University

November

She was more serious this year, less carefree and with a certain vulnerability, which was pushing her confidence aside. Dr Grant was relieved to see Philomena attending the session. Their recent conversation had concerned him and he hoped his news for her today would begin to turn her fortunes around.

She had barely interacted in the group and was quiet, deep in her own thoughts. At the end of the seminar, he asked her to hold back so they could catch up and when the other students had filed out, she walked up to him, meeting his eyes.

'How did you get on?' he enquired.

'OK, said they had more people to see and would be in touch soon.'

Dr Grant nodded. 'Don't rush into this will you Philomena, I think you're worth a lot more. The work in Crete, your offer of a place has been confirmed. Things have changed; the team are keen to welcome two graduates from our department.'

'OK, I'll think about it.'

'Please do Philomena; there'll be no Stephenson. It's an experience abroad and it's paid.'

Philomena's eyes widened at the mention of Stephenson, but she didn't ask why he wasn't now involved. 'When do you want an answer from me?'

'Well, it's not me that needs a reply,' Grant said. 'You'll need to write and let the Greek team know in Athens and I wouldn't leave it too long.'

'Have you any contact details?' she asked.

'Yes, I'll get them for you now.' Mike Grant retreated to his desk to retrieve a large A4 manila envelope, which he handed on to her. 'Here you go, all the information for the project is in here for you.'

She took the envelope from him and started for the door before turning to look back. 'Thanks Mike, I'll send my conformation to them this evening,' she said, and she was gone.

Mike Grant smiled. *Thank God,* he thought. She really needed to achieve something in life and of all his students he wanted Philomena to win through.

* * *

HMP Long Lartin AD 1987

Tom sat on the top bunk bed, legs dangling down off the edge. His cell mate 'Dosser' had buggered off sharpish this morning having sensed an atmosphere. Being more than a bit frightened of Tom, he'd got out of the way. Dosser was in for something quite undesirable; a thin spotty creep wot the Nik had put up with Tom as some kind of a joke. Two nasty undesirables together.

Tom was indeed irritable today, had been since last night on hearing he'd got a visitor. Nobody bloody cared about Tom so who was coming now? He'd been going over the possibilities in 'is head see. Couldn't be Da' 'cos Mod was dead, sure he was. Wouldn't be the old crone neither 'cos he'd bashed Candy up proper; no way would she be coming over. Ain't no girlfriends to visit, he didn't treat women all that well so any he'd been with sure as Hell wouldn't come near. Women were a let-down. Hadn't his mother buggered off and left him with Mod? Sure, she'd kept well away, and you couldn't blame her suppose, 'cos Mod was a dark piece of work. The only person he, Tom, had ever respected, though not through love mind, no, fear would have been a better way to describe it.

Now he was here and bloody miles away from anywhere you might call home. A familiar landscape mind, just a different jail. Tom had a reputation that came before him, an impulsive tendency to become suddenly vicious, an explosive young thug whose violence didn't have much in the way of boundaries. He was therefore not bothered by most of the petty scum in this place, who had fear built in as a survival trait. There were of course the real hardened mobsters, but Tom was too thick to be of much interest or use to this type of criminal.

He'd ended up in this place because he couldn't plan further ahead than the end of his nose. Everything he'd ever done was impulsive and he got a real kick out of hurting people – it made him feel powerful. That was why he was on the top bunk, looking down on the lesser pond life like Dosser who needed to know his place.

Tom had gone off after some youngsters when his dad had died. It was their fault and they'd be paying for it. The murder was a smooth piece of work, in and out and nobody gave him a second look. The road up to that night club place had been single-track and plod were up and down and all over the place. The night had been bloody cold and by morning he needed some money, needed to get out of that dead-end backwater place. He'd spent some time watching over a farm, waiting for the farmers and labourers go out so it was quiet. He'd picked up a shovel from the yard, was going to get some money out of the wife like and bash her up too if there was time at hand. He hadn't, however, watched well enough and from nowhere some dog had got him, wouldn't let go. Next thing some strapping big farmer had come up from behind and knocked him senseless. He'd made a dash for it but with knocks like that he wouldn't be going far. He'd crashed out for another night in some hedge, but the game was up. He was going nowhere and was kind of glad to see plod the following morning. Swarming the place, they were, with dogs and choppers and God knows what!

Now who the Hell was coming today? There was a thought, an itch in the back of his head, but no, there was no reason for it, yet she could make it work for her well enough. Da's favourite – he'd always put her first. As children they'd fought like cat and dog and in the beginning, he'd always win 'cos he was older, stronger. Yet she was clever, never let things go and would stop at nothing to get even. Now he could just see her, a knowing smirk on her face, come to gloat, make him feel like dog muck on the floor. He could throttle her, but she'd be several steps ahead, calculating, weaselling a way to completely discredit and destroy him. So, could he just say no? Tell her to bugger off? An anger was building from inside because yes, he could refuse but she would get at him, someday, somehow, if she wanted.

Tom dropped to the floor from the top bunk and paced around the pokey cell like a demented caged animal. *Perhaps it's plod or someone from the court come visiting*, he thought. They wanted some information about some other case, something else nasty that he'd done, or some lowlife associate of his. No, it would be plod, sure to be. The anger subsided but the pan was still simmering on the fire. There came the clunk click of the cell door unlocking and he was out like a tiger onto the balcony, still caged but loose with the others for the day's activities and routines.

7. Love Lane

Denbigh AD 1988

October

Her back ached after bending over for such a long time, washing and washing the tangles out of her long unkempt hair. Straightening up, she was stiff, pushing herself into place, hands on hips, thumbs kneading the sore rigid centre above the coccyx.

She caught sight of herself in the mirror on the front of the old wardrobe door. Brown walnut or rosewood with swirly patterns, an item of furniture that would have been high fashion for the 1890s but today it smelt of old ladies and antique shops. One thing Anya considered as she stretched her arms up above her head to further straighten out her stiff bunched up spine was that she hadn't put on any weight over the past few years. There had in fact been times when the mirror image had reminded her of the bony sickly cattle of famines – skin draped and hanging off pointy frames; such things had compared favourably with her own body state.

She pushed her long dark hair back from her face. Cuts of self - harm ran up the insides of both arms from her wrists to the hair of her armpits. While no longer livid, puss infected sores, these marks would perhaps be there forever, a reminder of the countless attempts at self-destruction. She picked out a long-sleeved top.

It was time that she crawled out of this twilight existence for good. A change to her life view had dawned and she did not clearly know the reason why. Her father's funeral months back had helped but she did not attend, had not witnessed his coffin being slowly lowered down to Hell. Her father's demise was a positive step forward but the light at the end of the tunnel had gradually began to shine brighter before his passing.

Running her tongue over her teeth she remembered the agonising misery of her drug induced gingivitis – a devastation that gradually devoured at her gums, teeth and jaws. She had finally pulled herself out of the narcotic numbness to confront a dentist for help. Anya wouldn't forget Dorota the Polish dentist whose English was perhaps better than her own, whose compassion and devotion to duty went far beyond what could be expected for the service. Saint Dorota of Denbigh she would be to Anya forever more. Dorota had bullied Anya into seeing through the treatment, had demanded no payment and had sorted her out good and proper.

So here she was, naked in front of an ancient fading mirror. Looking now, there was tone back in her leg muscles. That was the walking. No money meant no transport, so Anya walked miles.

Today, she was going to spend significantly more than she could afford on a haircut. The transaction would leave her dangerously short for the rest of the month, but this was now a priority. Damned woman had insisted on a down payment from Anya before even giving an appointment. A sign of Anya's improving mental health was that she'd noticed the look of disapproval, the sneer of distrust in the other woman's eyes – snobby tart. Anya was now aware that people generally walked around her, crossed the road before her, because to society, she was an untouchable. A year ago, they'd have been justified – aggressive begging, abusive language, she displayed all the vicious desperation needed for drugs and survival. Times were that she couldn't give a fuck for herself or anyone else.

After today, no one would be looking at her in that way again.

Anya walked through the shambles that was her bedsit to the bathroom and its shower cubicle. There was no bath and she had been using the Belfast sink in what was loosely set aside as the kitchen area, to wash the living daylights out of her hair. This shower, for most people, would have been a formidable challenge. The water was going to be at best tepid, on account that no money was going into Anya's electric meter. However, her bedsit's water pipes seemed at least for part of their journey to run alongside those of the flat next door. Perhaps, there was the odd chance that the neighbours had put some money in their meter, but you couldn't rely on it.

Anya turned the dial, and let the water run briefly, before stepping in. It shouldn't have run at all with no electricity, but it did – there was something more than dodgy about both plumbing and electrics in this miserable box of a bedsit. It wasn't yet late autumn, but the cold water had long since lost any of the summer warmth. The shower was like walking into a frigid ice spray, forcing her to breathe in hard and fast at first, heart pounding beneath her ribs, her skin tight with the initial shock.

Stepping out after some minutes, Anya located a still damp puggy towel that had been tossed over the back of a decaying chair some days ago after her last wash – it would have to do. After taking off the excess damp from her body she bundled up her soaking hair into the towel. Still naked she put on her wristwatch. This was an act of habit, for the watch had told no time for years.

Anya stepped up to the windows on the roadside of the flat and pushed the dirty, old, stained sheets that acted as curtains to one side. Looking down on Love Lane she was able to see a clock which protruded from one of the old shops like a pub billboard. This was the only way Anya could get an indication of time when in her flat. She pulled out the knob on the side of her wristwatch so that she could adjust the hands to show the current time. Outside, the sun was just rising and there was no one abroad on Love Lane below. Anya let the window covers fall back as she stepped down and away from the window.

Tim's notebook had first brought floods of tears and then, after the initial contact, she felt his spirit was with her, close and she was empowered. Now, stronger than ever before, she had a reason, a goal and a purpose in life. Pages and pages were just newspaper cuttings going way back; local discoveries, digs, talks or activities he'd joined. There was the odd sentence or date, quite bland, sterile stuff really.

Then towards the end of the notebook, covering a great many pages, Tim had come alive through his writing. Events, comments, thoughts, he had shared them all. The spelling was atrocious but, for his perhaps last five days on this Earth, he told an animated and fascinating story.

He had written about her, too. He had liked her, more than liked her – she was his impossible dream. A deep feeling of pride, of being appreciated and loved swelled from within. Some words she went over and over again in her thoughts as she wandered round and round her pokey little bedsit. Anya felt treasured and for all the right reasons – she was worth something after all. She squeezed her eyes shut to stop the tears again, as a wave of emotions broke through into her thoughts.

Although a key player in this, Tim's story, she recognised that that there were other players too, that something dark had transpired. She felt keenly that Tim's random murder was perhaps, anything but. Now there was justice to be found, a crusade to be fought.

* * *

Ruthin

Dan Jones pushed the door open to Siop Nain and looked over the tables. It was nearing lunchtime and the place was full. Siop Nain attracted all comers from society: youngsters, teenagers in love, the retired out for a coffee with family and young mums with pushchairs grabbing a quick cigarette whilst juggling toddlers, buggies and the pet dog. Cheap, but just a little better than the greasy spoon biker's café at the other end of town, the place served a loyal clientele from opening in the morning until the whole town shut up for the evening.

As far as Hannah was concerned, he was just handing the notebook back. That's what he'd told her, but he fully intended on speaking to Anya, he'd decided on that. There were some things he wanted to clear up, some questions that needed asking. The notebook for one, this was hers to keep was it? How had she come by it? Sure, Tim was a bit bonkers on times and seriously inept socially when it came to girls, but Dan really couldn't see Tim taking this up to the Woodlands as a gift for her on a first date. He wasn't that mad, so how had Miss Richards come to be the owner of Tim's private notes? Then there were the events of that night, Dan wanted the story clear in his mind, her version of events if she'd share them with him.

Some things had continued to bother Dan over the three years since Tim's death. Only the other month he had woken up very early one morning. It had been well lit outside and he'd found himself looking out through the window, thinking of the time he'd watched Tim wandering round that old burial mound. He hadn't been to the grave since the funeral and that morning he'd felt guilty. After work, he'd walked there, feeling that he'd been called. Now how daft was that!

Having arrived, he couldn't on his first scan spy who he was looking for and suddenly he was thinking better of the whole confab. He began to retreat back through the entrance door which he still held.

It was almost a relief to be backing out; she wasn't there and there'd be no explanations due for Hannah later.

'Looking for someone?'

Dan looked down to see Anya with a bemused expression on her face. She had been sat at a table for two, right under his nose just to the right of the open door. There was no escape, no turning back now.

'Sorry, I didn't spot you there,' Dan said, pulling out the other chair to sit opposite Anya at the table. Dan peered at her; when they had met earlier in the week, he could have sworn she had long tangled hair, a stud through her nose, perhaps something through her lip and tongue to boot. She'd looked grubby. On inspection now, in the light of day, he wasn't ticking any of the boxes from the previous encounter.

'You done something to your hair since I saw you last Miss Richards?'

'Sure,' she replied. 'I wasn't convinced you'd turn up Daniel Jones, 'cos you're a little late, but it's good to see you.'

The waitress descended on their table, order pad in hand.

'What can I get for you both?' she enquired in a broad Welsh accent.

'Err... *paned*? Tea, Miss Richards, or are you a coffee girl?' Jones said.

'A black coffee would be good.' Anya looked at him with her sad brown eyes.

'Can I get you something to eat too?' Dan enquired.

'Fantastic,' she replied, a little too enthusiastically, and Dan eyed her closely.

'You eaten anything today?'

'A lady of my circumstance doesn't get to eat much, and I've had a long walk to get here.'

Dan pulled out a twenty-pound note from his wallet and passed it to the waitress.

'Put that to the drinks and whatever the lady here wants to eat.'

The waitress took the note, looking a little relieved, and asked, 'What are you having then?'

'Oh, chips, fried egg, two of those please, tomatoes, beans and, and some bread?'

'Go for it, Miss Richards!' Dan interjected enthusiastically and the waitress was off to sort out the order. Once she was out of earshot, he asked, 'So, what's this all about?'

'You had a chance to look through that school book? You know who made all those notes don't you?'

'Sure, he was a big friend of mine. Seem to remember he came to a sudden and unpleasant end on his first date with you.'

'So, you think I was responsible for that?'

'No, just don't go repeating history when it comes to me today.'

'Your other half, she happy you're out with me today?'

Jones nodded and looked around the room. He was uneasy hiding things from Hannah.

'I take it that's a no. I guess she wouldn't approve – don't think I would if I was her. What's her name? She looks young.'

'Hannah,' he replied, without offering any more detail.

Anya smiled and nodded. 'I know the face.'

'I read some stuff about you in the newspaper Anya. Was all that true?'

It was Anya's turn to nod. 'That and probably a load worse.'

'Never liked your dad,' Jones continued. 'Something about him just wasn't right. I can believe it; I can accept what you said about him…' He looked directly at her. 'I can see you've had to climb some high mountains to try and get your story across.'

She was shaking her head now. 'I don't want to talk about me now. I want to talk about Tim's book and what he says.'

'What he says?'

'Yes, in those last few pages at the end – like, could that all be connected to the stabbing?'

'I don't know Anya. There is a link, the clairvoyant's son; he somehow managed to trace and kill Tim. He blamed Tim for the death of his father – that much we all know because it came out in the trial. But do I believe there was more to it? Do I believe these notes have any relevance?'

'The girl, that girl with the ancient languages. Philomena.' Anya pressed on. 'Could she really speak Latin? Don't you think her departure that day was a little sudden and convenient?'

'There was no sign of her in the hearing. There's been nothing from her ever since,' Dan confirmed.

'Odd. Did you ever hear her speak Latin?'

'Yes, I did,' Dan confirmed. 'On at least two separate occasions.' The waitress placed a plate full of food in front of Anya, together with her cutlery.

'I'll bring the drinks over now,' the waitress announced before heading back towards the kitchen.

Anya dived in like some half-starved lioness.

'Christ, when did you eat last?'

'Couple of days ago,' Anya replied though a mouthful of egg, beans, bacon and chips.

Jones watched her wolfing down the food and on the waitress' return he ordered Anya some chocolate cake. He was beginning to feel very guilty about his comfortable life and very sorry about hers. What the Hell had happened here?

Anya cleared the plate clean, using her bread to wipe round so there were no traces of the either egg or beans left. She then used the paper towel to wipe her mouth before scrunching it up and placing it on top of her plate with the cutlery.

'Before you demolish that cake Miss Richards, what happened to you? I mean, where are you living? How are you living?'

'You really want to know?'

He nodded.

101

'I've got this room on Love Lane, you know, in Denbigh. Got to get by on handouts from the social.' She was quiet for a few seconds. 'I'm afraid the prostitution bit, that's real. Needed to pay for the drugs.' She pulled up one of her sleeves to confirm her situation.

Jones, ever squeamish, shook his head and said, 'I'll take your word for it.'

'Once a druggie, always a druggie they say but that isn't true for me. I've been clean now for months and yes, I know they all always say that too. But I know I don't need them anymore. I don't know why, it's like some power, or someone, has lifted me out of all that.'

'Tim,' Jones replied. There had been that sense of guilt, that early morning presence, his own recent thoughts for his lost friend and now Anya turning up out of the blue.

She shrugged her shoulders.

'So, this book of Tim's, what do you want me to do?' Dan asked.

'Well,' Anya replied, swallowing a great lump of cake, 'I think there are some interesting things in there, if not a bit bizarre. This ghost photo. It must have been good because you all went off to see this Mod Evans bloke. Philomena and Tim took another photo too. Tim talks about a path, about the photos and about Philomena. Like Tim was certain she could speak ancient languages and read people's minds, yours included Daniel Jones. Normally, when I read stuff like that I think, being the sceptical person that I am, what crap. But, in this case no, it just doesn't feel like a scam. It feels real and as we know, Tim's dead because of it.'

Dan observed her a minute before responding. 'Well, we've got these notes of Tim's but not much more. What are you trying to say? Do you think Philomena knows more?'

'Bloody sure she does. You were there though; you know, at Mod's place. You saw what happened that afternoon. How did Philomena react? Had she been there before, and did she know this Mod Evans? Tim clearly states in his notes that she warned him, told him to be careful – beware of the ghosts and all that. She's a bit like a clairvoyant herself if you ask me. That's if you believe in all that nonsense.' Anya looked at him questioningly.

'She was all for going at first. Philomena was a feisty, confident girl. Could handle herself or at least gave that impression to me. When we got to Mod's house, she had become very quiet, very nervous. Mod liked her, mind. He was much more interested in her than anyone else – dirty old man. She didn't like the attention and that's when Tim stood up, got in his way. It all happened very quickly.' Dan shook his head. 'No, I don't think Philomena was involved with Mod, she hadn't met him. I wouldn't have said she was into the mystic side of things either.'

'Well, Tim's notes state that she was,' Anya responded.

Dan observed her again before stating, 'We need to find Philomena then.'

'I'll make a start with that,' Anya said. 'I've got plenty of time on my hands.'

'Loads of time and no resources,' Dan countered. 'Have you got any money for this investigation? And don't be going down to the police for help – they'll laugh you back out through the door.'

Anya looked thoughtful and twitched her nose.

'Your old man was worth a bit surely. Did you get anything from the will?'

Anya shrugged her shoulders. 'I've been excommunicated, and nobody even talks to me so there's no chance anyone's going to actually hand out money in my direction. I'd never go to the house now anyway, even to collect what's rightfully mine.'

Dan nodded. 'After what you've said about them, I guess going back round there might not be recommended. So, how are you going to find Philomena then? You might need to do some travelling around, write letters and stuff. There are bound to be some costs, but you can't even feed yourself. Have you thought of a job Anya?'

Anya looked at him and shrugged her shoulders again. She blew out air from her cheeks and, shaking her head, she said, 'Who's going to give me a job?'

Dan observed her closely, there was a sadness about her, always had been somehow. 'Is it worth chasing after? I mean, you didn't really ever know Tim, did you? You'd be better trying to sort yourself out

Anya. Perhaps that's what this book can do, push you to getting your life back on track.'

She returned his gaze. 'He spoke to me right at the end you know.'

'Who did?'

'Tim,' Anya responded. 'There were some last words. I had to bend over, get really close and he gently held my head pushing his fingers into my hair.' She became visibly upset but continued. "I will wait for you. In the darkness I will always be close to you, together, forever." Oh Dan, I tried, I tried to stop the blood. I so wanted to keep him with us…'

Dan listened quietly. He had never heard any of this before and he was glad that he had come here.

There was silence between them for a while and then Anya pushed back her chair making ready to stand and leave. Dan reached out to catch her hand, bringing her back down to sit. 'You're off? You're just going to walk away?'

Anya shrugged. 'I'll have to find my own way through this.'

'I think you should have the notebook back,' Dan said. 'I don't know how you've come by it but perhaps you should keep hold of it, that is unless you want me to look after it for you.'

'It was in the reference library, waiting for me to find it. Almost like I was being guided, it was hidden between some seriously old stuff.' She looked at Dan, her gaze sad and distant.

'We'll keep in touch, perhaps I can help. I could loan you some money. You have an address surely?'

'If you've got a bit of paper and a pen, I'll scribble my address down for you. Mind, I don't want you coming around to my place; I couldn't bear it. I couldn't bear for you to see what I've become. I don't want any money either, perhaps I shouldn't be dragging you into this.'

'OK, if you say, but the offer's there for you' Dan responded. 'Just jot your details down on there for me.' He pulled out a pack of post it notes from his jacket pocket and peeled one off for Anya to use. Taking his pen, she put her details on the note and handed it, together with the pen, back to Dan.

'OK, it's time we were both off I think,' Anya announced, pushing her chair back for a second time.

Jones nodded and made to leave. 'Thank you, *diolch yn fawr!*' he called out to the waitress as he stepped up to pull open the outside door, allowing Anya through before him.

'One thing, before you go.' Dan caught Anya's arm once again. 'Those notes tell us that Philomena could read the minds of four people. Tim, myself and Cooper. She never disclosed the fourth name to Tim.' With that, Dan handed Tim's notebook back to Anya and nodded at her. 'I know the fourth person. It's you Anya.'

He left her to it, to ponder the ramifications of his last statement as he walked down Well Street's steep hill.

* * *

The Wrekin Shropshire AD 1987

Kelly had borrowed the boyfriend's XR2. An older Mk1 model, bright red with a flat grill, two extra-large front spots and larger wheels with wider tyres. She was the only one in the family who drove, but she'd never passed any driving test. Her driving was at best erratic, crashing the gears and with a heavy foot on the accelerator. Kelly had got some money and aimed to have lunch in one of the Little Chefs or a motorway service on the M5.

Driving out of Shrewsbury, she was confronted by the great lump of rock that was The Wrekin, an ill-placed anomaly in an otherwise serene flat Shropshire landscape. Was it her imagination now, her bored mind making up fantasies, but she could see a young woman with wild long red hair? There was a screaming in her ears; an image of someone falling away into darkness; the woman, wide open terror in her eyes, falling, falling away into a tunnel of darkness.

The A5 gradually brought her car closer before taking her away once again. There was something in this place; a feeling of great betrayal, the restless dead calling to be heard.

From Telford she followed the M54 before taking the M5 south. The motor way was clear today and she made rapid progress to Worcester leaving the M5 at Junction 6 to take the A422 on to Alcester and then down on to South Littleton and HMP Long Lartin.

8. Matala

Matala Crete AD 1986

Giles Everard had kept a low profile since they'd arrived early in the morning. Philomena expected that he'd spend most of the day sleeping and the other half hiding out of the sun, poring through technical guides about archaeological sites on Crete. Giles could spend months studying thousands of pieces of broken pottery, making detailed drawings and enthusing wildly over the tiniest of details. Dull, all so dull in Philomena's mind; Giles was the ultimate armchair archaeologist and really, she felt he was missing the point, the adventure, the romance. Giles needed to get his hands dirty and do some proper digging; she was determined to introduce him to the art of excavation.

Philomena stepped up to the door and rapped hard on the wood. 'Giles Everard, are you hiding? I want to go exploring and I'm not going alone.'

There were some muffled bumps from within and Giles responded, 'Err… just a moment Philomena, I'll be with you now.' There was a turning of the key and the door to Giles' studio was opened halfway. Giles peered out, dazzled by the brilliant bright light now flooding into his room.

'Are you going to let me in Giles or am I to be left out here on the threshold?' Philomena enquired.

'Oh, oh sorry. Do come in Philomena,' he responded.

'Thank you.' Philomena entered Giles' studio flat. 'You OK in here Giles?'

'Oh yes, all tip top and Bristol fashion,' Giles replied and then continued, averting his eyes, 'I can see you've been out and about but it's too hot in the day for me Philomena.'

Philomena noticed that he didn't quite know where to look. She was still wearing her one-piece swimsuit after her swim in the sea. She'd tied a wrap around her middle so it would only be her top half that was presenting a problem for poor Giles. She'd never really considered that Giles was remotely interested in girls or boys or even registered sex at all as he was such a geek. Clearly, however, he was very aware of her now, perhaps even found himself embarrassed and intimidated.

'Giles, its five o'clock now and the sun's going down. You'll be OK I promise. Get something on your feet, pop your sunnies on and let's go. There are caves in the cliffs at the end of the beach and they're just calling out to be explored.'

'OK, if you're sure you want me to tag along.'

'Course I want you to tag along – its adventure time Giles and you've got to make the most of it!'

Giles was wearing a pair of long cream trousers and a white long-sleeved shirt with a collar. He began searching in his luggage.

'What are you looking for Giles?' enquired a bemused Philomena. 'You're not dressing for a dinner party – we're walking across the beach.'

'Ah got them,' said Giles ignoring Philomena. He began to pull on some long socks. He then retrieved a pair of stylish brown leather shoes, fine for an interview but God, not for the beach.

'Right, let's go,' he announced. 'You lead on.'

They both headed back out the door.

'Stop, one moment.' Giles went back into his room and retrieved a wide brimmed straw hat, which he promptly placed on his head to protect his thin blond hair.

'Very Howard Carter,' Philomena commented. 'Come on, you'll do.'

They left the studio flat, closing the door behind them, and clip clapped down the marble white steps of the apartment block and out into the blazing sun and cooker hot air beyond. Giles quickly fell behind. She slowed down to match his pace, but when she did so, Giles slowed further. Being several steps ahead, Philomena swivelled round and on doing so recalled doing the same thing with Tim. In Tim's case he'd fallen behind because he was shy. In the case of present company, she guessed he was just trying to stay cool.

'You look like you've seen a ghost Philomena,' Giles said, catching up.

'Hmm, I've perhaps remembered one Giles.'

'Remembered a ghost Philomena? You'll have to explain what you mean.'

'Let's just say… he was someone I was attracted to. Now, are we going to explore these caves or not?'

'Oh God, its blisteringly hot out here Philomena – I'll get sunstroke.' Giles pulled out a handkerchief from his shirt's top pocket and, removing his straw hat, he wiped the sweat from his forehead. He reminded her of the Nazi Gestapo interrogator from an Indiana Jones movie she'd once seen.

'This ghost, Philomena, was he a past boyfriend of yours then?' Giles added.

'My, you are being a nosey sod Giles. Didn't think you were into finding out about relationships. I thought pottery was more your thing.'

They started to move slowly on once again.

'Well Philomena, you see, I'm not very good with people, not good at all, never have been. So, I could do with finding out a bit about how I'm supposed to act socially. Up to now everyone has just kind of kept a distance. I've never cared less but perhaps there's something to being sociable, having friends and relationships.'

'You think you're going to find out about relationships from me Giles? You'll be lucky.'

'You're popular – you get on well with people. You seem confident, perhaps you could be a good mentor for me.'

'Maybe. Look, let's just enjoy this once in a lifetime adventure, OK?'

'Yes Philomena.'

'Shake on it then Giles and no more awkward conversations, alright?'

They shook hands and Philomena led the way to Matala's beach.

Philomena kept her sandals on until she got to the wet sand, where she pulled them off and held them together in her right hand. She was suddenly aware of a fumbling behind her and, turning, she was just in time to catch a glimpse of a distressed Giles balancing on one foot whilst he tried to remove one of his long socks. Tall, thin and ungainly, he tilted like the leaning tower of Pisa before losing control of his balance altogether, falling face first into the grit and sand of Matala's beach.

Oh my God, thought Philomena. *Is my life to be one of just looking after socially awkward incompetent men?*

'Stupid thing!' Giles spat out in anger and Philomena wandered on, leaving him to sort himself out.

She stopped to watch the breakers crash and her mind strayed away back to her dreams and her few snatched hours with Tim the year before.

'Hello, hello.' Giles was waving in her face.

'Oh, sorry I was daydreaming.'

Giles had sorted himself out and had rolled up his trousers up above the knees. He looked like a proper English twit on the grand tour.

'You've seen that ghost again.'

* * *

Gortyn

They'd both been asked to get the very first bus out of Matala the next morning. Waiting at the bus stop, it was difficult to believe how powerful the afternoon sun had been the day before. At 5.45 a.m. it was still dark and although the bus timetable started at 6:00 a.m., neither Philomena nor Giles were confident that a bus would actually turn up. The place was silent, the skies were open and star lit, and the early morning air was bitterly cold.

The bus stop, a simple board with a printed timetable tied onto a telegraph post with wire was on the opposite side of the road to Taverna Paradise. They had picked this taverna for their evening meal the night before. It was one of the few still open this late in the season and they'd been looking for the bus stop.

Suddenly, a light flicked on downstairs in the taverna. The door was opened, and Philomena caught the end to a conversation that was taking place within.

'You can't let our visitors to Crete stand out there in the cold.'

One of the waiters, whom she recognised from the evening before, came out through the open front door, holding a chair in each hand. A blanket was thrown over his shoulder. He came over and placed the chairs off the road underneath the telegraph pole. He handed the blanket to Philomena. 'For you,' he indicated, 'while you wait for the first bus. I hope it won't be too long for you.'

'Thank you, that's really kind,' Philomena responded for the first time in Greek. It came out quite naturally. She hadn't intended to use the language as everyone here in Matala spoke very good English for the tourists. Come to think of it, Philomena considered, the conversation from within the taverna had been in Greek.

Giles looked on somewhat stupefied. He had studied Latin and Greek at his private school, but he wasn't someone who was all that conversational in English let alone Greek.

There was the toot of a horn and then the clattering sound of a large approaching diesel engine. The first bus of the day had arrived in excellent time and the waiter collected back his blanket and chairs. They hadn't in eventuality had the opportunity to use them.

The bus was an old job in a light blue and white livery, jacked up on its wheels with a roof rack for baggage up top. Philomena noted the make – Magirus Deutz – not something you'd ever see back home. The bus was high off the road and they had to pull themselves up and in. Philomena boarded effortlessly. Giles however, made an absolute meal of it.

It seemed no distance at all on the map, but Crete was a deceptively large and mountainous island. The trip from the airport in

Heraklion over to Matala had taken hours on the coach. The journey up from Matala to Gortyn also took longer than Philomena expected. Hopping off at the entrance to the archaeological site, the place felt dark, empty and silent. There was a light in one of the entrance buildings – perhaps one that had been left on overnight.

* * *

Dr Nicos Sakellarakis had watched the lights of the bus as it had crawled up the approach road to the site. The bus had come to a halt at the entrance gates. Sakellarakis was surprised; the two English students had actually caught the first bus. He felt that they'd been foisted on him, an unwanted extra that came with the grant funding from Oxford. What was wrong with Greeks excavating their own history? There were plenty of talented young men in Athens who were more than eager to pick up from where the English, the Germans and the Italians had left off. Perhaps he was misjudging them – they had at least turned up at this hour, out of bed early and ready to do some constructive work.

By the time he'd made his way down to the gates to greet them, the bus had pulled off and was on its way. Standing at the layby, shivering, were the two, pasty-looking English students. He'd read their CVs way back, together with their references. The young man was regarded as a serious expert in Roman ceramics, but his reference also indicated that he was distant and awkward in social company. The girl was well regarded for her field and excavation experience. Her real talent, however, lay in her understanding of ancient languages. There was a lot of fanciful nonsense about this in her reference from Dr Stephenson whom he had met and disliked. A more level-headed account was provided by Mike Grant from the archaeology department at Oxford. Mike had gained some post graduate experience with the British School in Athens and their paths had crossed. Sakellarakis had liked Mike Grant and felt he could trust what he had to say.

Walking up to welcome the pair, Sakellarakis made a point of doing so in Greek. However, he made his welcome in a more archaic form of the language. Anyone of quality would have at least come across such variations in their reading. Was the girl going to be of use?

The young man looked on with a somewhat blank expression; the girl was perhaps following what he had to say. Sakellarakis decided to test her out and directed some questions to her in order to see how she might respond. Expecting very little, he got back far more than he'd bargained for. Suddenly he was intrigued. The girl spoke in generally the same archaic form but there was something more, like some sort of accent or dialect.

'Mr Giles and Miss Philomena,' he continued now in English, parking the Greek for another time. 'You've both done very well to get up here on the first bus. We have some time as the rest of the team are travelling in from Chania this morning. There's been a delay, a problem with their coach. Perhaps you'd like a little tour of the site and then we could have a warm up over a Greek coffee?'

The pair nodded in agreement. He led them through the site gates. After passing the light at the main entrance building, he clicked on the torch he was carrying. Its beam illuminated the path before them.

'So, let's start with the first building, the early Christian Basilica of St Titus. It's one of the later standing buildings. There has been continuous worship here since the late Roman period. Come.' He beckoned them forwards, unlocking a metal security gate. On entering, Sakellarakis clicked on the lights. A towering cathedral this was not, but the minimal lighting gave the ruinous place some considerable atmosphere, especially at this time in the morning.

Sakellarakis prattled on as he walked slowly down the central isle, much of which had lost its roof. Soon they were at the other end of the building and Sakellarakis turned to face his congregation only to realise that he was being followed by just one of the students. The other was very carefully walking along the wall opposite. She turned at right angles at the top end of the building where she proceeded to carefully pick her way against the wall to join them.

***

Philomena was suddenly aware of a strong scent of wild herbs and then of something more … incense? The drone of prayers was at an end as on tiptoes she stretched to see over the crowds stood in front of her.

Then the great man spoke her name, he was calling her from the front; directing a way that she should take to reach him. She had been standing at the back with the women folk and the least important. Yet he was aware of her, he had recognised her and was now calling for her. This great man of faith, the bishop, had called her up to be in his presence. The congregation was packed, squeezed in and cross legged on the floor. There was only one way up to the front. She could not go through them; she would have to pick her way carefully around the edges. Eyes down, trying not to trip she made her way round. All the while she felt keenly, the eyes of the many hundreds boring into her very soul, and the question, unheard but perceived. 'Why her?' they exclaimed 'the non-believer,' unwanted and of no consequence. 'Why is it that she has been chosen?'

Then there was the feeling of the cold early morning once more and Philomena was back and awake in the present, lifting her eyes to meet the gaze of Dr Sakellarakis.

***

Oh God, Sakellarakis thought. *They've sent me a right pair here.* The girl joined them at last. She had been looking down at the floor, concentrating on where she was putting her feet. When she looked up, she flashed a big smile and said, 'Thank you.'

118

'You're most welcome Miss Philomena,' Sakellarakis smirked back.

* * *

To Philomena he looked like a real Greek academic. Grey hair to his shoulders, thick bushy grey eyebrows and moustache with a pointed grey beard. He wasn't carrying any extra weight for his age – a distinguished old Spartan. She noted how he was addressing them as Mr Giles and Miss Philomena. He either wasn't aware of their surnames or, more likely, he couldn't be bothered to remember them. She had a suspicion that he was just about being polite, that they weren't totally welcome and that he saw them as a bit of an extra burden.

* * *

'You've read about this site then?' Sakellarakis probed. He caught the male student rolling his eyes. The young man clearly had no confidence that the girl had read up on anything.

'Let's go through and up to the Odeon. This will be of greater interest for you Miss Philomena. We can take a look at the famous law code.'

Once out of the Basilica ruins, they joined the tourist pathway up to the Odeon. Well, at least two of them did. It took a good few seconds with Sakellarakis marching on ahead, before the men realised that Philomena was not with them once again. Turning, they both observed

Philomena climbing her way up through the scrub, caught in the beam of Sakellarakis' torch; she was heading toward the Odeon ruins.

'What is the matter with this girl?' Sakellarakis asked. To Philomena, he shouted, 'Miss Hutchinson! The pathway hasn't followed that route since late antiquity.' Philomena stopped and then made her way back down the slope and onto the modern path. She walked up to join them both.

'Sorry,' she said meekly on catching them up once again.

Irritated, Sakellarakis decided to respond to her in archaic Greek again.

'It's dangerous you know, to go wandering off. It's not yet fully light. You could trip up, break an ankle or worse, damage the archaeology.'

'I'm so sorry,' Philomena answered. 'I mustn't damage the archaeology.'

Sakellarakis looked at her, stupefied.

Bloody Hell, Sakellarakis thought. *The girl speaks Aramaic.*

9. War Band

Ruthin AD 525
Late December

The chatter had picked up in the hall, but the drama around Cynric, Cunewolfe and the captive woman were still the main event, the topic of whispers and discussion amongst the Angles and the local tribespeople in the hall this evening.

Cynric motioned for Cunewolfe to step closer and then, in a whisper, Cynric enquired, 'Cunewolfe, have you armed yourself?'

'No Cynric,' came the other's reply.

'Then do so,' Cynric responded. 'You will need eyes before, behind and on all sides this evening. Make haste and return, giving a clear show of your equipment. I'll make some announcements to keep the hall quiet, but I shall leave that which is of significance until your return.'

Cunewolfe nodded and left, leaving Cynric to address the hall, Gwen at his side.

'Friends, warriors, ladies, we find ourselves here across the mountains in Cambria. And we are here, largely unmolested as we pursue our hunt for Arth and the last warriors of Britannia.' Ale was brought into the hall for those who had recently arrived, and its distribution brought several minutes of distraction.

Through the corner of his eye, Cynric noticed the return of Cunewolfe, shield over his back, sword on his left side, battle axe in his right hand. Other eyes in the hall followed this warrior's entrance too as he assumed a position to one side of their leader.

'Followers of the hunt now is not the time for feasting and rejoicing for we are deep into lands which do not belong to us and we are unwelcome here as guests. This afternoon, Mordred, our Roman guide, was set upon and torn apart by a wild bear. His services are no longer. Our warriors have engaged the fighting men of Britannia, but we have no account of their dead, no captives save one.' Cynric pointed to Gwen. 'Here, I present to you Gwenllian of the Ordovices. You will know her as Wynefere.'

Immediately there came gasps and then discussion amongst the Angles.

'You see,' Cynric raised his voice, 'there is a clear peril in our position this evening and in the days to come whilst we are encamped within this place. The Britons, they will not let their queen be taken away so cheaply.'

* * *

LINDUM COLONIA (Lincoln) AD 525

'YOU, YOU ARE AN APPRENTICE TO A DISASTER, NO BETTER THAN A PUNTER AT THE BROTHEL. YOU ARE EVERYTHING THAT BRITANNIA SHOULD NOT HAVE BEEN. PROSTRATE YOURSELF BEFORE ME IF IT SUITS YOUR PURPOSE BUT YOU ARE OF LITTLE CONSEQUENCE TO ME NOW MODESTUS. I WILL COMMAND THAT THE GATES BE OPENED, AND YOU WILL BE THROWN OUT TO HAUNT THE FIELDS, THE FORESTS AND THE MOUNTAINS BEYOND. THERE IS NO VALUE ON YOUR HEAD, YOU WORTHLESS SON OF MEDUSA. I WILL AT LAST BE RID OF YOU AND THE ENGLISH WILL IGNORE YOU RATHER THAN BLUNT A GOOD BLADE TO GRANT YOU A SWIFT PASSAGE TO HADES. LEAVE THIS PLACE AND BE OUT OF MY MEMORIES FOR EVER MORE.'

Modestus lifted his scrawny aching frame from the floor before the lord who sat in judgement above him and considered hurling a tirade of bile and insult back. His mouth was open but rough hands held him firmly by both arms. He was being turned and marched swiftly out of the great hall. Still, Modestus twisted back to look over his shoulders only to be silenced at last for looking on the lord. His retinue were already engaged with the next item of business. He, Modestus, was quite forgotten.

Manhandled through the town streets he could see the great Newport Gates approaching ever closer. The town, LINDUM COLONIA, had been well chosen by AMBROSIUS for it had been easily refortified into a significant stronghold, one which was well beyond the current English resources to take.

Unceremoniously, Modestus was flung face first into the mire off the roadside on the outside of the town gates. These were then closed for the evening, denying him any further safety or comfort.

* * *

HMP Long Lartin AD 1987

After becoming what they liked to call 'volatile', Tom Evans had been returned to his cell. His cell mate was protesting that he was not prepared to re-join him for the shut down and insisted that he be re-accommodated.

'Tom Evans, you ready for visiting hour?' one of the two guards outside called through the hatch in the cell door.

'Sod off!'

'I'll take that as a no then Mr Evans.'

'No, I'll come, let me out of 'ere,' Evans responded.

'You'll need to be calm first Evans, I'm not sure you're balanced and in the right frame of mind for this visit, but we must let you know, offer you the opportunity.'

'I'm balanced, look I can stand on one leg. I'll come; I'll be quiet. No one been to see me before. Mustn't miss out now must I.'

There was a silent pause before the metallic click of the keys at the door sounded and two burly officers stood on the threshold to greet him.

With his hands up, Evans came through, 'I ain't doing nowt see,' and he allowed himself to be escorted off the level, down the stairs and over to visitors. This was indeed a new experience, a nice little walk, a bit of prison sight-seeing like.

The visitor's hall was a large room with a high ceiling. There was a row of long narrow windows high up at ceiling height on both sides and the late afternoon sun was streaming through on Tom's right. As he descended a short run of steps to the hall floor, officers on either side of him, clouds outside blocked the sun, throwing the room into shadow. From Tom's view point the shadow travelled from the far-right corner across the room's floor and walls to slowly welcome him. In that far corner, alone, sat a young woman, her head down and her long light brown hair falling forward. She did not look up; the greeting of shadows was enough; she knew that he had arrived.

10. Shout at the Wind

Gortyn AD 1986

The bus journey back to Matala soon became the best part of Philomena's day. The sight of the blue and white KTEL bus arriving to pick them both up soon after 6.00 p.m. lifted Philomena's spirits as she was no longer enjoying the experience of the on-site work at Gortyn.

Sakellarakis had been avoiding and ignoring her since that first day, giving her minor tasks which she felt were well below her experience and ability. However, in some ways, she accepted it, considering the events of her arrival with Giles. Sakellarakis must have thought he was dealing with a complete fruitcake. She was frequently asked to make the tea at break times; she guessed he probably didn't think she was of much use for anything else.

Sakellarakis had not been on site for many days now and there was some solace in that Philomena thought. This morning a letter had been left for her on arrival. She picked the envelope up, her name written formally in bold handwriting. His handwriting, she was sure of it, despite having never seen anything written by the man.

'Your marching orders; bus tickets for Heraklion and back home,' Giles announced from behind her shoulder. He too had come to the same conclusion on seeing the handwritten letter for her. 'I hope you haven't blown it for me too with your stupid behaviour,' came a further unwelcomed quip.

'Shut up Giles or I'll stamp hard on your toes!'

Giles just shrugged. 'Serves you right.'

During their walk on Matala's shingle beach that first evening, Giles had come close to being reasonable company. It was just about possible to sit with him for a meal in the taverna that night, but he wasn't really on the same wavelength as everyone else. Not very sociable, he was full of rigid thoughts and after their first meeting with Sakellarakis, Giles was very uncommunicative and dismissive full stop. She supposed that he didn't want to be connected with the 'mad' girl.

Her thoughts always came back to that – the 'mad' girl thing. These visions were getting far too frequent and too damn real. Philomena had considered that it might all be some kind of epilepsy or, as things were getting more out of hand, a giant bloody brain tumour, something that might explode inside her head any day now. She'd even done some reading on this subject but her symptoms, being able to see things from the past and speak languages from other times, didn't quite match up to those associated with epilepsy, brain tumours or strokes. Still, if it was something medical it was going to be pretty serious by now. She should really go and see a doctor or a specialist about these things. Yet, the answer at the end of many such internal conversations was always no. If she did have something nasty medically, she was just going to ignore it, keep going until whatever it was finished her off good and proper. Better that than sitting in some chair in a home, holding one of those double handled mugs with a drinking spout, dribbling and uncommunicative, or having to try to learn to walk and speak again after some twelve-hour operation. No way! It was better to die outright, to go out of this world with one great big bang.

Since arriving at Gortyn, her visions had become worse. Yet, when she was in Matala, she felt safe. The dreams, the smells and the sounds didn't follow her back from Gortyn. Whenever she was on site, she made a positive effort to be with someone else. She would shadow Giles in the beginning of the day and then pray that she'd be teamed up with someone from the Greek excavation party soon after. Philomena had developed a great fear of being in these ruins alone.

One of the main thoroughfares for the old city was, in particular, most problematic for her. Alone one day, the whole place had suddenly come alive, as it was once in ancient antiquity perhaps. This was surely in her imagination, but when the episodes took over, they were real and she was no observer, but a starring role.

She remembered this particular nightmare clearly, how she had come up on a crowd, jeering and threatening, and been spat at. She had launched herself back, arms flaying, then the vision had gone and when she'd looked around there was just the scrub, olive trees, dust and old stones. She had shouted at the wind. Maybe someone had seen her in this loss of self-control?

Still, being with others in this place was also a worry. What if she should have an episode in the company of others? Philomena convinced herself that being with someone gave her a focus, kept her in today so long as she held them in her sight. Somehow, the others had not seen a breach in her sanity since that first meeting with Sakellarakis, but it didn't mean that disaster hadn't come close.

Philomena was popular with the Greek team, particularly with some of the younger male students. She'd been asked to do a significant amount of levelling for the mapping work with Alexis, one of the Greek post grads from Athens. Of course, he worked the theodolite as only men could use such technical kit, whereas she had to hold the awkward bloody measuring stick, extending or collapsing the measure in response to Alexis' hand signals from the theodolite.

On one occasion they had stopped for a short break and were sitting on a low wall when she began to talk about the houses in front of them and how they dropped down in tiers following the slope. Suddenly she was aware that Alexis was scribbling pencil notes frantically in his little notebook.

'How do you know this, Philomena?' he asked. She had to tactfully avoid any further questioning – she couldn't tell him that she had actually seen them in front of her, could she? The slope was just scrub, thorn bushes and the odd olive tree, burnt out and waiting for the first of the season's rain.

So, the evenings in Matala were her escape. After a cold shower and clean up she'd wander over to Taverna Paradise from her digs. Giles had declined to join her after the events of the first day at Gortyn but to be honest she didn't mind, he was high maintenance anyway. She didn't feel alone in the taverna. In fact, she was made to feel very welcome.

After the first few nights of sitting outside, everything had been brought in as the restaurant returned to its out of season capacity, catering now for the locals only. The temperature, particularly at night, was dropping like a stone on this part of the island.

Behind the counter Philomena had noticed a photographic calendar which showed a black and white image of one of the offshore islands dusted in a light icing of snow for November. The image seemed totally whacky and out of place, yet winter could hit the islands of the Aegean quite hard.

By the end of the first week, the taverna owners had set her up with a table for two in one corner underneath an old heating device that was fixed high up on the wall behind her, its red-hot coiled bars pumping out heat and the smell of burning dust. She'd ordered a single glass of Logado, a dry white Cretan wine, with the intention of nursing it all night. Then a plate of home cooked Cretan food had arrived. 'I… I haven't ordered anything,' she had said in Greek.

'This is on the house. When you come from now on this will be on the house and you are welcome every evening,' Dimitra, the old matriarch, had said, coming over. 'Look, see—' she'd gestured with her arm to the other tables in the room '—when you are here Philomena, others will follow. You are very good for business. Besides, you are too thin. You need some more meat on you if you are to attract a nice Greek boy.' Dimitra had smiled. 'That English boy, too tall, too pale. He is not the boy for you.'

They had been remembered from the first night. This was a real family taverna, it did not shut at the end of the tourist season. It was here to serve the Cretans of Matala, and they had very much taken a liking to Philomena.

On one evening, Great Uncle Stavros came in to dine. Great Uncle Stavros, a local celebrity by all accounts, had spent a tough life as a shepherd in the hills and mountains of Lefká Óri – a harsh, remote world. They made much fuss about his presence at the taverna and of course they were very keen to introduce their guest, the Greek speaking English girl.

Great Uncle Stavros observed her closely and engaged her in general chit chat, who she was and where she was from. He listened very closely, not much slipped past Great Uncle Stavros.

'Which university are you from in England?' he asked.

She politely replied, 'Oxford sir,' taking care of her manners in this gracious interrogation.

'Oxford, yes now that explains it,' he said. 'You speak Oxford Greek. The Greek of Herodotus and Homer, for you do not know all our words of today do you, young lady? I have seen this before. I have experienced your Oxford Greek. I helped a British spy during the occupation. Hidden him in the mountains, safe from the Nazis. He spoke Oxford Greek too.' And Great Uncle Stavros nodded and beamed at her.

'Dimitra!' he called out. 'We must make a toast to our English friends, past and present.'

Two small shot glasses of twelve-star Metaxa Brandy were brought over. The old man held up his glass in salute and sank the lot in one go, bringing the thick bottomed glass back down with a bang on the table.

Philomena held her glass up to follow and knocked the shot back before being consumed by a fit of dry coughing. The stuff nearly blew her head clean off!

* * *

Throughout the evening, she had been absent-mindedly tapping the unopened envelope on her table.

'A letter. You must open it Philomena,' Dimitra said, coming over to clear up as the taverna was closing.

'Letters can bring very bad news,' Philomena replied. 'I think they're going to ask me to leave.'

'Who are? No, we will not let them Philomena,' Dimitra said with indignation.

Philomena sighed and ripped the envelope open, pulling out the letter inside.

'I suppose I've got to know one way or another,' she said, and she unfolded the handwritten note. Philomena was aware of Dimitra watching her, a concerned look on the old lady's face.

On opening the letter, Philomena frowned.

* * *

LINDUM COLONIA (Lincoln) AD 525
April

MODESTUS lay face down, eyes closed, arms outstretched. Could he, will his life to an end? Was it possible to terminate his own breathing and wish himself to fall into a never-ending sleep? Though the winter winds had turned, and green shoots had once again broken through the crust of earth, as the light faded so did whatever warmth the sunlight hours had brought. Still, unmoving, MODESTUS began to feel the damp chill rise up and into his body from the ground as his own body warmth dissipated away into the cooling air.

However hard he tried to prevent his own breathing; his body overruled his mind. A coward, yes, but he could not even manage a coward's death. What lay before him in the following hours of darkness, alone, hungry and with nothing?

His body shouted to him, 'Get up!' and slowly, aching with discomfort he brought himself up onto all fours and there a minute he delayed.

The Angles of Bernicia had decided to bide their time. LINDUM COLONIA stood in the great wilderness as an island of Roman dominance and civilisation, but it was largely surrounded by the fens and marshes, the low flatlands into which the Angles had penetrated. Dominant now, the Angles knew that this bastion of the past would decline over the years to come, political insecurity and the encroachment of lands would weasel away the influence of this great city and her people. Still, the Angles kept watch; they monitored the comings and the goings of trade and of people.

So it was, early one spring evening that an expulsion was observed. An older man, an individual with a Roman countenance, was unceremoniously pushed out of the gates as day turned to night and the Angles questioned, 'Who is this man?' A criminal perhaps or possibly a political rival? Expectation would suggest that such an individual would have been dispatched with the sudden violence that was seen as the Roman way.

MODESTUS, finally on his feet, began to ramble this way and that, looking back at the gates or forward along Fosse Way. Round he rambled, directionless and confused, all the while the light of day faded, and the dark shadows crowded in as night assumed its place in the great cycle of things.

Thoughts raced across his mind. Where next? What now? Could he walk all night, walk on forever? Who would rescue him; take him in? British farmsteads seemed so few and so far apart in this lonely desolate landscape. Would he freeze tonight, die after all? No, he could not, would not face the thought, for MODESTUS was too afraid to die out here like some stricken animal.

Circling ever further away from the city, the plumes of smoke, fires and lamps diminished as the fugitive distanced himself step by step until the great walls were just as one in the landscape. A dark silhouette of indistinguishable shapes, random and ill-defined.

There came a loud bark and MODESTUS froze, terrified, having been brought back to his senses, reality slipping back into sharp focus. Heart beating, eyes peering into the blank nothing that was the night, he prepared for the ambush, the sudden pounce from whatever lay beyond, for it knew more of him than he of this silent predator.

Seconds felt as minutes, the silence overwhelming in the grey stillness of night. At last, with all the ferocity and venom he could muster, MODESTUS roared out his challenge to the void. 'GER AWAY!'

A large rough hand grabbed him by the scruff of his neck. Raw, guttural excited voices from all around further shattered the silence and MODESTUS experienced the emotion of relief – these were people, not the wild wolves of his imagination. He was being held, shaken as three, no, five animated shapes conversed around him. Listening hard now in an increasing state of alarm, MODESTUS tried to decipher, but only the briefest understanding did he glean. The harsh sounds were those of the English tongue and he wished now that he had taken a

135

stronger interest and devoted greater time to learning more in the past. As was so often the case however, he had chosen not to put in the effort when chance he had, dismissing these people as barbarians with no future. Far too often he had backed the losing side and would learn to regret his own stupidity.

'Arth!' MODESTUS called out. 'Know I the Briton Arth. Find him I shall for you.'

There was a silence from his captors as they considered his shouts of nonsense. Then there was more talking from the shadows followed finally by a sharp whack on the top of his head. One of the great lumps grunted and gesticulated the direction to which he wanted MODESTUS to go. It was followed by a kick up the backside, a further encouragement to get MODESTUS to walk on.

The walk was not of any great distance, but MODESTUS stumbled and tripped in the darkness, his eyes not well adjusted to this new situation. Pushed and kicked, he certainly felt humiliated, but the physical prompting never hurt as it could. They had clearly decided to keep him in one piece. The encampment, when at last they arrived, was well hidden as perhaps it needed to be, so close to the great walled city. These men were now silent, gesticulating only for communication.

He was unceremoniously pushed down and forced to lie face first on the ground. Old noxious hides were placed on top. Maggot riddled with the strong pungent smell of defecation, these skins at least provided some warmth and a wind break for the evening and night. The greasy pelts made MODESTUS gag; he felt like a pig in a sty.

Whilst voices whispered around a campfire, MODESTUS was denied both civility and nourishment. This first night's captivity was perhaps to be one of many.

MODESTUS was poked with a stick at first light; the group were moving. Standing in the early morning murkiness, MODESTUS' calculation of the night before was confirmed – five unkempt, rough living Angles had apprehended him. Now they were off, and he was once again kicked and poked to move him along in the direction that his captors chose.

Within minutes it was clear that only two of the Angles would be escorting him, leaving the other three behind. The stinking pelts had been tied and parcelled up as a backpack which he MODESTUS had the indignity of carrying. It proved heavy, particularly in his weak state, and the package had been knotted around him in such a way that taking it off would take several minutes and, with it on, there was no way that he'd be running off; his captors had planned it so. MODESTUS was stuck with his lot, at least for now. He would have to play the beast of burden, behave and do just as he was told.

They followed a path that to MODESTUS seemed unmarked in anyway, but the Angles clearly knew their direction of travel. The clouds had gathered since daybreak and the air temperature had dropped in the gloom. Predictably, the first rain shower caught the travellers some two hours or so into the journey and the three were forced to take shelter under a large tree that was fortunately in leaf early for the season. Nevertheless, they all got wet, and as they sat trying to avoid the worst of the weather, their teeth began to chatter and their bodies shake with the cold and damp. MODESTUS was particularly affected. One of the Angles offered him some hard, dry meat to chew on. Salty and tough it was nevertheless welcome and MODESTUS savoured the chewing for as long as the morsel lasted. He was then presented with some water from one of the leather flasks his captors carried. It was fresh but already tasted and smelt of the leather container from which it came. The rain showed no real signs of abating, so a decision was taken to press on. At least this way the walking produced body heat.

MODESTUS' silver white hair was matted against his skull and dribbles of water from the rain dripped off the top of his distinguished Roman nose. One of the Angles observed him, a smile broadening on his face.

The Angle then said something, but MODESTUS caught little by way of understanding and was confused when the Angle stopped him and began to untie his backpack. There followed an altercation between the two and MODESTUS was not able to follow what they were saying. One however, seemed to be more concerned for his welfare than the other.

When they finally stopped for the day, MODESTUS was very much at the end of what he could endure. By this time both captors were concerned for his wellbeing and come evening they ensured that he ate, drank and spent time before the campfire. They had begun to talk to him, engage as if he was part of their conversation but MODESTUS could only just manage to understand the odd word. Perhaps his captors felt that he could understand because he was an educated Roman and they were meant to know everything.

The second night in the open air was traumatic. He had never experienced cold and damp such as this. The morning, when it came after a relentlessly uncomfortable night, was a pale washed out canvas. The new day brought with it clear open skies. The damp and the drizzle had gone.

MODESTUS suffered three more days and nights before the party arrived at journeys end. Now he was truly in a barbarian world. These people built nothing that would last. Instead, they had returned to an altogether more organic existence. Wooden huts and shallow dugouts encroached around some stone buildings now disused and roofless. The settlement was on a slight elevation, more MODESTUS judged to avoid flooding from a chocked stream that pooled its way round the rise, than of any necessity for defence. There was some evidence of industry, the sounds of sawing and of tapping mingled with the gentle scolding of some hens that wandered free.

One of his captors placed his hands on MODESTUS' shoulders, indicating that he should now sit. When he did so his captor joined him on the floor, legs crossed, rubbing his eyes and yawning. The other had walked off in the direction of a larger wooden building. Now that MODESTUS considered this, he was aware that it was an altogether much more massive structure. A great hall whose timbers had been expertly fashioned and fitted together. The entrance pillars and a lintel were fantastically carved.

The two of them sat there waiting, dozing as time went by in the relative warmth of the afternoon sun. The peace and tranquillity were, however, at last broken as their colleague called them over from the entrance to this great hall. MODESTUS allowed himself to be led; he had mixed feelings now about his future as it was currently well out of his control.

The hall was gloomy, with overpowering odours of woodsmoke and alcohol and MODESTUS blinked in an effort to adjust to the darkness. A fire smoked in the centre, just embers smouldering but fresh piles of timber were being prepared for the evening and night-time to come.

Beyond the fire stood several members of the warrior class, deep in animated conversation. Then they became aware of the visitors and one, a tall, powerful, blond individual, turned to observe what had been brought in through the door. This warrior then addressed the others.

MODESTUS fell to his knees. There were two reasons for this action. Firstly, he considered the deference to this upstart leader might help in the minutes to come and secondly, he was frankly too exhausted to stand up straight. MODESTUS kept his head bowed whilst the other man considered him intently.

This warrior spoke again and MODESTUS could pick up a sneering derision from the man's tone. MODESTUS decided that he'd better continue in the manner of the humble captive where he waited patiently, catching no man's eye whilst the conversation, no doubt about him, erupted.

'HOW NICE TO SEE A ROMAN IN HUMILITY. THEY DID NOT WANT YOU DID THEY NOT, AT LINDUM COLONIA?'

The hairs on MODESTUS' body stood up on end. The savage spoke good Latin. Suddenly, there was a sharp point under MODESTUS' jaw. The blade was raised and brought MODESTUS up from the floor and on to his feet. The eyes of the two men at last met.

'INTERESTING, A MAN OF SOME REFINEMENT I CONSIDER. YOU HAVEN'T DONE A HARD DAY'S WORK IN YOUR LIFE BY THE LOOKS OF YOU.' Bringing his face right up close, he continued, 'I'M INTRIGUED. WHO ARE YOU?'

The man continued to stare into MODESTUS' face. MODESTUS remained silent.

'OLD AMBROSIUS IN HIS BRICK CITY DOESN'T WANT YOU. HE HAS CAST YOU OUT, A PUNISHMENT WHICH HE SAW FIT FOR YOU.'

There was silence in the hall; the others watched and waited, without understanding.

'YOU WERE THERE WEREN'T YOU? THERE AT BADON FIELD. I CAN SMELL IT ON YOU. COME ON, GIVE US YOUR NAME.'

'I AM JUST A MERCHANT, FALLEN ON HARD TIMES,' MODESTUS began, but was quickly interrupted.

'NO, NO, YOUR NAME. WASTE NO MORE OF MY TIME OR I'LL HAVE YOU CHOPPED UP AND FED TO THE DOGS.'

'MODESTUS,' the Roman half mumbled back, and the name brought great excitement to his muscular interrogator.

'MODESTUS CORNELIUS ANTONINUS! YOU KID ME NOT. FOR THIS IS TRUTH FOR SURE. I CAN SMELL YOUR FEAR.'

The Roman's eyes flitted this way and that. Great Jupiter, who was this savage? Who would know of his name? Then the reality came flooding into the Roman's mind. He had been thrown out of the cooking pot at LINDUM COLONIA only to fall straight into the molten embers of the fire.

The Angle leader addressed the others of his rabble. MODESTUS heard the name Mordred, his name in the English tongue and the warrior was pointing. MODESTUS felt a threatened, bedraggled, scrawny wreck before this man who looked down upon him. The sound of his name inspired an excited discussion amongst the English.

'Croeso Mawr MODESTUS,' the Angle bellowed at him. 'IS THIS NOT HOW THE GREAT VOTADINI WOULD GREET YOU?'

MODESTUS now knew the name of his tormentor and wished that he had found the path to Hades on the night he had been turfed out of LINDUM COLONIA.

Cynric approached him again, sneering. 'YOU KNOW WHERE URSUS ~ARTH ~ HIDES. BOASTED THIS TO MY MEN WHEN THEY FOUND YOU. WE BOTH KNOW YOU LIE BUT FIND HIM FOR US YOU WILL.'

* * *

Chania Crete AD 1986

Another bus. Philomena's life was all about buses she concluded. A bus here and a bus there and to be honest she had got to quite liking them. You could sit on a seat and watch the world go by through the window. You didn't have to do anything, just show your ticket, get on and enjoy the ride. It was an opportunity to let your mind wander or people watch. This was a later bus than the one out to Gortyn and Iraklion and she wondered how Giles had got on earlier that morning. Philomena had been around to his studio digs at the end of the evening to borrow one of his guidebooks to Crete.

'I won't be in with you tomorrow,' she had said, 'but I'll get your guidebook back to you.' Philomena had made no further comment; as far as he was concerned, she'd be making ready to go back home.

This bus was headed for Chania, Crete's second city in the west and by all accounts the guidebook saw this as an altogether much more agreeable place than Iraklion, the capital. She believed this to be the place where Sakellarakis lived. The letter had given a series of instructions for her arrival; she was being invited out to lunch by Sakellarakis who had written in his letter how he was keen for her to meet a colleague of his. Perhaps she had got the wrong end of the stick in her opinion of the doctor; his letter was quite engaging, excitable.

'On leaving the central bus station head for the harbour,' the letter had said, *'follow the harbour round to the old mosque and join us at Taverna Oasis.'*

Chania was indeed a different beast to Iraklion. After some initial confusion outside the bustling bus station, she followed in the direction of travel taken by most pedestrians and was soon walking past the great indoor market before entering a street with grand old merchant houses on either side. In one there was the Chania Archaeological Museum and Philomena dithered at the entrance but pushed on as time was not on her side for exploring. Finally, she was at the grand venetian harbour with its wide promenades and walls stretching out to the old Turkish

144

lighthouse. There was the strong scent of the sea and the chill of a stiff onshore breeze.

Oasis was a street or two back from the harbour front and being less exposed had attracted a number of locals sitting, braving the outside. Sakellarakis had clocked her approach and was standing to welcome her. His colleague had also taken to his feet. Philomena smiled as she walked up to join them. Sakellarakis greeted her warmly and pulled out a seat for her between him and the other gentleman.

'Philomena, welcome, this is my colleague Yosef... Dr Yosef Ben-Zvi.'

She shook hands with them both before taking her seat.

Philomena observed the two men; she wasn't sure about the relationship here. Ben-Zvi, complete with kipper, was clearly Jewish.

'Yosef is a visiting researcher from Tel Aviv University with an interest in ancient Middle Eastern languages,' Sakellarakis, the old Spartan, nodded towards the other man. 'We're both very intrigued.'

Philomena looked from one to the other. 'With me?'

Ben-Zvi nodded. 'You and your languages Miss Hutchinson.'

Sakellarakis began an engagement with the waiter; they clearly knew each other.

'Err... a coffee Philomena? Greek or cappuccino or...?'

'A cappuccino would be really nice.'

'I'll order some baklavas for us all too. It's made here and it's very good,' Sakellarakis continued.

Throughout this exchange, Ben-Zvi had observed her, seemingly in anticipation.

'Miss Hutchinson, I can't wait. I'm just so intrigued. Would you... would you take a quick look at something for me?' He brought out a small A4 bundle of photocopied photographs stapled together on the top right-hand corner. There were some handwritten notes alongside the photographs – English and... Hebrew? Many of the notes had been blotted out in black ink. The top sheet photograph was of a stone or clay tablet, a bit like the Rosetta Stone in that there were a range of texts, different texts one under another. Unlike the Rosetta Stone there was no Greek, no Egyptian Hieroglyphs either for that matter. It looked like cuneiform stuff; Philomena had seen that in books from her general reading. From the front photograph the image was too small to make anything out, but the following pages had captured each of the scripts, enlarged one at a time. Philomena turned over the pages before returning to the front sheet once again.

'I'm sorry, I've put you on the spot. Do you recognise anything?' Ben-Zvi was pushing her for an answer.

Philomena shrugged her shoulders and began to take a closer look. She guessed that the texts were perhaps saying the same thing, like the Rosetta Stone. On her first glance she'd recognised some of the scripts in that they were markings she had seen before in books or from things she'd seen in museums. Quite which language was which however – she wasn't sure. And what any of these scripts actually said, well that was something again.

Ben-Zvi was watching, waiting.

'I can read Latin and Greek,' Philomena offered, the weight of expectation suddenly concerning her. 'I'm not proficient in any other ancient languages.'

'Cymraeg.' Sakellarakis had joined back into the conversation; she'd been unaware of him for a little while but despite his animated conversation with the waiter he was clearly tuned in.

'Take another look Philomena,' Sakellarakis encouraged.

Philomena felt a little ambushed and under pressure. She'd never looked at stuff like this with the aim of actually reading it. Now that she was focused, there was a vague familiarity with most of the texts as she turned the pages once again. There were different languages for sure, translations and each text was conveying the same message more or less.

She came to rest on one of the middle pages – the odd one out. This one had been shuffled; it should have been the last page in the bundle for it was at the base of the tablet and the other copies had been arranged top to bottom from the tablet. Strangely, it was the one with which she was most familiar. The two gents were testing her perhaps. The handwritten notes would have identified the different languages, but they'd been blacked out. She was none the wiser regarding which language was which but guessed one was some form of Hebrew.

The two men continued to watch her.

Philomena shrugged her shoulders. 'I thought you were going to dismiss me Dr Sakellarakis. I haven't been much of a success at Gortyn have I?'

'You've had your moments Philomena,' Sakellarakis responded.

Ben-Zvi tapped the table with his right index finger. 'What do you know?' he asked. 'That one in particular, you've stopped on that text. Why?'

'The author...' Philomena stopped herself.

'She knows. Sakellarakis where have you found this wonderful girl?' Ben-Zvi exclaimed, almost joyously.

'You know this language, Philomena?' Sakellarakis nodded encouragingly 'I had this feeling...'

Philomena shook her head. 'I don't know, I really don't know what this is.'

The refreshments arrived and the waiter made a great play about placing down all the bits and bobs on the table. Ben-Zvi was tapping his teeth with the fingers of his right hand. The interruption was a distraction. He was clearly desperate to get back to the conversation.

'This is the text we are unsure of. It's a form of Aramaic but...'

'It's the odd one out.' Once again, Philomena checked herself – what did she know anyway?

The waiter had finished with the nonsense of setting all the refreshments out and Sakellarakis was once again taking some charge of the discussions.

'You speak Aramaic or something like it, Philomena, and I was wondering if this was something you picked up as an extra study at Oxford?'

Philomena shook her head. 'I don't think I do. Speak Aramaic I mean. I've only studied Greek and Latin at Oxford.'

Sakellarakis was observing her closely now. 'You've done quite well by all accounts since you'd received no formal instruction on either before entering your undergraduate course, had you? Interesting.'

Philomena noted that Sakellarakis spoke very good English. There was none of the 'Miss Philomena' nonsense. She'd been right, they had not been entirely welcome when they'd arrived.

'Why don't you just tell us what you think? What was it that came to you when you first looked at this particular text?' Ben-Zvi tapped the photocopied page in front of her.

'Don't forget your cappuccino, Philomena. I'm so sorry, we don't mean to interrogate you. I hope we're not making you feel uncomfortable. Try the baclava.' Sakellarakis held out a dish with pastries for her to choose from.

Philomena twitched her nose. 'Hmm, OK, I'll just try a small one.'

Ben-Zvi helped himself to a couple.

'Always a real treat when in Crete,' he said. Both he and Sakellarakis had opted for the Greek coffee – black and in a small cup. Philomena tried not to make a mess. Her chosen pastry looked like shredded wheat and disintegrated as she bit into it. There was a little silence and Philomena knew that she was expected to speak. She bit the bullet and blurted out her ideas.

'I think all the texts relate to the same subject and I guess the content would be important for a biblical scholar. Some of them mean nothing to me. One is different. This one, because it's informal. The author made it so. It relates to the same subject but...' Philomena stared at the image and the markings again before continuing. 'I don't know how I can recognise any of this, but this text is not a standard err... it's saying more about this subject than the other texts. There is within it an additional message, a play on words that shares a point of view or an opinion perhaps?'

Ben-Zvi leaned back in his chair, nodding in agreement. 'It could be interpreted, translated in different ways. Some words are lost in translation or are used as you say, differently to their intended meaning. I would really like to hear your take on what you think the author is trying to say here. Somehow you have a feeling for all of this.'

'Philomena, you have visited Crete before, yes?' Sakellarakis enquired.

'No, this is my first time on the island and my first time in Greece actually. Mum and Dad have a time share in Madeira, so all of our family holidays abroad have been there. I haven't been about much otherwise.'

'And how are you enjoying the work at Gortyn?'

Philomena looked Sakellarakis is the eye. 'To be honest, I find the place a bit oppressive. I'd expected you to ask me to leave and perhaps I'm resigned to leaving. It's the atmosphere there, it doesn't feel like here or Matala.'

'Yet you know Gortyn so well. My student Alexis, he contacted me after you'd described the city. Your following of ancient paths, lost and blocked today and that little, how would you say, episode in the Basilica that first morning. My team have observed you err...'

Philomena could feel her cheeks going red. *Oh my God*, she thought. *Have they seen me?* She felt sure she would die of embarrassment if Sakellarakis went into details.

'Your languages are very interesting. I sent for a copy of your thesis on ancient graffiti,' Sakellarakis sensed her discomfort and changed the direction of the conversation.

'An excellent piece of work,' Ben-Zvi interjected. 'Worthy of a first.'

Philomena looked from one to the other; it really felt like an ambush now.

'I very much want you to stay with us in Crete, at least for this season Philomena. There are two reasons for this. Firstly, your knowledge of ancient languages without having previously studied

151

them and secondly, your in-depth knowledge of somewhere that you have not visited before, well, not in this lifetime.'

There was a short silence as Sakellarakis considered his words. 'Perhaps you have lived before. You have experienced life in ancient antiquity, and you remember.'

Philomena blinked. What had he just said?

* * *

11. Cold Trail

Rhyl AD 1988

For the first time in thirty years, John Morris, former Detective
Inspector John Morris, had some time on his hands. Recently retired,
John had not elected to engage in any part-time consultancy work with
the police force though offers had been made and it was the expected
gradual slow down into retirement for an officer of his rank.

His children were growing up, with the oldest away in university.
Angharad, the ever-faithful Angharad, who had put up with his career,
the unsociable hours, the nights and weeks away from home. She had
made it abundantly clear that now it was her time. As a result, John had
become the stay-at-home husband in a full reversal of roles. He was the
cook, the housekeeper and the whatever else that had been left to his
wife in times past. At first, he had wholeheartedly embraced his new
routine. Blimey, he actually found ironing almost satisfying! As the
weeks and months began to slip by however, the stay-at-home husband
stuff, well, it just wasn't enough. The urge, the yearning for some
greater purpose began to bubble up and John Morris was soon mindful,
watching out even, for some new opportunity in life.

Once or twice a month he'd meet up with some of the old gang,
the wrinklies – retired police on a get together, low profile over a
lunchtime drink and a pub lasagne. So it was, that an opportunity had
come at one of these lunch time gatherings. It had been a chance

observation that had rattled some memories with his old drinking partner. John had been absently staring at the comings and goings at the bar and his eye kept falling on one of the younger women in particular.

Bob 'Charlie' Charles had followed the DI's gaze.

'Ah, Kelly Evans, now that's a young lady I wouldn't much want to meet down some dark alley.'

'Why so?' John Morris questioned, turning to face his companion. 'Do you know her?'

'Dark core to that one,' Charlie resumed. 'First got involved with her when she was perhaps fourteen or fifteen. Teenage prostitution. She'd come from a pretty poor background. They say her old man was some kind of clairvoyant – a lot of pretty unsavoury behaviour to boot I'm afraid. I'm sure there would have been a child sexual abuse investigation today; Kelly would be seen as the victim and I'm sure it starts with that but, well, there's a core of nastiness in that girl. A beautiful but sinister black darkness, you watch for those eyes, something special. Speckled and flecked she can look deep into your soul.' Bob 'Charlie' Charles paused for a moment, before continuing. 'I picked her up once with a social worker after being called over to the house and she proper gave me the creeps somehow. It's all in the eyes with her. She's been with a lot of partners, unsuspecting losers sucked in by the outward beauty, the sexy looks. She's had some maladjusted sprogs too, all different dads and odd as hell the lot of 'em. They'll be keeping the social busy for years to come I shouldn't wonder.'

154

John Morris let Charlie talk on, it was a way of collecting a story, a quick account of the facts known by the other professional and Charlie well knew the importance of this sharing.

'Go on then,' Charlie continued, 'What's your interest in Kelly Jade Evans then?'

'I hadn't any interest Charlie, at least not until you shared that nice little story with me. You did quite a bit with the family by the sounds of it. Now that you shared your little bit mind, perhaps I should be more interested in young Kelly over there. That nice little tale from you just reminded me about one of the things I'd been planning to spend time on during my retirement. Something about a case involving, well, unless I'm very much mistaken, that family and, in particular a master Tom Evans, the older brother of Kelly perhaps? The clairvoyant, he'd be Mod Evans?'

'Yeh, he would, and the brother, proper bad 'un,' Charlie chipped in. 'I had some dealings with him too. Liked to break into peoples' houses did Tom. At first it was just breaking and entering but pretty soon he started to stay and lie in wait until the owners got back. Then he would jump out and surprise them hitting out at folk with a cricket bat. Would leave little calling cards too. A turd in someone's bed or in the fridge that sort of dirty nonsense. Not bright like his sister, just plain nasty was our Tom. So, you've got a bit more of a story of this young man have you John?'

The DI smiled. 'You might remember he ended up with a promotion into the murder league. There was a slight link with the clairvoyant bit. Perhaps you'll remember Tom's father had died, the result of an enormous stroke which young Tom blamed on a group of teenagers from Ruthin. They'd been in the house, visited Mod Evans for a reading but had nothing to do with the old git's stroke and had left unawares. Mod's wife had witnessed the old man fitting but she was so frightened of him she'd left him in his chair dead and rotting for days. Tom turns up having been released from prison and less than happy that nobody had turned out to meet him on getting out. Loses his temper see, smashes his stepmother up and charges off to Ruthin after the teenagers to avenge his father's death. Somehow, he manages to find one of the youngsters and pow, one sharp punch with a knife and there's some poor kid who loses his life.'

'Nice.' Charlie nodded. 'Hare mad bugger never had anything going for him. You know he topped himself whilst inside. Won't be missed, no loss to society that one.'

The DI continued, 'Open and shut case really, it was several days before we caught up with him mind. Tom had been living rough and was in a real sorry state when we found him. Opened up to us after the offer of a cup of tea and somewhere warm to sit. Took us to where he'd hidden the knife, spilt the beans tidy he did with very little prompting. There was something more to the case though. Something I didn't follow at the time. He'd done it alright and there was no one else involved in the murder that night. There was just this odd interview, some months later.' John left the story hanging, knowing Charlie would now be intrigued and up for more.

'I'm waiting, 'cos old DI Morris doesn't go over a story like this one without a good reason. What you doin' then with your retirement John? I'd keep away from Kelly over there, the girl's like Medusa. Don't you go looking into those eyes. Master of the black arts that one. The force could never pin anything serious on her but believe me, she's up to her neck in evil that one.'

'You believe in clairvoyance, talking to the spirits and all that Charlie?' the DI chipped in. 'That's my interest for my retirement you see. The odd things in some of the cases I've worked that didn't quite get explained away rationally.'

'You're writing a ghost book then are you John? Super!' Charlie picked up his glass and tipped the last swig of beer into his mouth. 'Got to be going,' Charlie continued, pushing himself up from the table and pulling his coat on. 'You pay and we'll touch base next time, yes?'

The DI nodded.

'Oh, and if you go talking to Kelly over there – you watch those eyes, you hear' and Charlie was gone.

* * *

Denbigh AD 1988
November

'I know who you are.' The voice came from an older gentleman who had stepped into the charity shop. Thickly set with dark but greying hair. Anya paid him no attention– she was sure he wasn't talking to her. She continued going through the second-hand clothes for sale on the rail, pretending not to notice the man. She'd spent some time avoiding his type – tall, smart, straight, ex-military perhaps or police.

'It's been a few years since that trial,' he continued. 'It is Miss Richards isn't it? Anya Richards?' He held out a hand in greeting.

'Err... do we know each other?' she replied on turning to face him, and only then did it begin to dawn on her who this might be. It was a face from the past, but she wasn't quite connecting the face to its owner.

'John Morris,' he responded. 'Detective Inspector John Morris.'

'Oh, right, hello.' Anya's mind was now in a whirl.

'We only met briefly, and in unhappy circumstances. I've been retired a year now,' he continued.

'Oh, OK.' Anya wondered whether this was just the DI being nice or if he wanted something. She had developed a suspicion of police officers, her own habits and lifestyle recently meant that she was far from what one might consider to be a model citizen.

Anya peered at him. 'So, what do you want?'

Morris smiled. 'You've had a very tough time haven't you, Anya?'

158

'Maybe, not that you lot were all that bothered.'

Morris nodded. 'I'm truly sorry for what you went through. We could have done better, provided some real support for you. And things haven't improved much for you have they – since the murder I mean?'

'So, you've looked me up?'

'Maybe,' Morris replied and because it was a natural reaction, a throw back to when she was a girl, Anya suddenly felt anxious and guilty.

'You think you made a mistake, that I murdered Tim all along?'

'No, Miss Richards. It is still Miss Richards isn't it?' the DI enquired.

Anya regarded him with suspicion. She had the feeling he knew the answers to his questions; he was prepared.

'It's still Miss Richards,' she replied warily.

Morris nodded again. 'I've been looking out for you. It's not police business now mind and officially your case is all done.' He looked around for a moment. 'This isn't the best place for a chat. Could we set up a meeting?'

Anya stared at him. 'I don't know. I don't know why I should if it's not official police business. You people haven't exactly done much to help me, and I can't offer any more today than I did back then when Tim was murdered.' She edged away from the DI.

'OK,' he responded. 'I just wanted to clear something in my mind. Sometimes, very occasionally, you come across something that doesn't quite make sense. I quite like exploring things like that.'

'Oh, really?' Anya said without enthusiasm. She was wondering how she could end this conversation, how she could get off and out through the shop door.

'There was another witness you see, or at least it would now seem that there was another witness to the events of that night. A young lady like yourself – Philomena Hutchinson.'

Anya hesitated. She had made no progress with tracking Philomena down. Anya was certain that Philomena could offer much more information on this story. She met the DI's eyes properly for the first time since he'd entered the shop. 'Are you going to buy me a coffee or something then, as part of this meeting?'

* * *

Later that evening, Anya rummaged through her mangey bedroom. Somewhere, she knew not where, she had put what she was looking for; she had kept it safe all these years. It was something her mother had given her ages back when she was a little girl. At the time, it had seemed an odd gift. Anya had been too young to receive such an expensive item, an item better suited to an adult. Perhaps that's why her mother had presented it to her, knowing full well that it was something that her daughter would use as she matured and grew older. It would then be something to treasure for the rest of her life.

The item, an expensive Kaweko fountain pen, had been brought back as a gift. Her mother and father had gone on a business trip to Germany. It was in school term time and so they hadn't taken Anya with them. Strange, up until this trip Anya had only fond memories of an idealistic childhood. But on her parents return, Anya distinctly remembered that something had changed. Soon after, her mother had become very ill and she had died suddenly. This pen seemed to be the last connection between mother and daughter. Beautifully finished in a smoky blue steel shell the pen was a balanced precision instrument, relaxing and indulgent to use.

'Got you! You bugger!' Anya exclaimed with some delight on apprehending the hiding pen. Unscrewing the barrel, she was able to access the plunger, charging the pen with a luxurious turquoise ink – the only bottle of ink she had.

Anya's handwriting was a true work of art, a crisp style of ascenders and descenders looped and joined in a broad confident flow. Today, for the first time, some progress had been made. The quest had truly begun at last. Her meeting with the DI was one that she now considered to be of great success.

Ms A Richards
15 Love Lane
Denbigh
10th November 1988

Miss Philomena Hutchinson
The Archaeological Department
University of York
Kings Manor and Principals House
Exhibition Square
York
YO1 7EP

Dear Philomena,

I wish to make contact with you about Timothy James who you met in Ruthin in August 1985 and who I think we both very much liked.

It was kind of you to return soon after Tim's death and I'm so sorry that you were unable to meet any of us, his friends, when you visited. This was a very sad time, and it has been truly difficult for many of us to come to terms with the tragic events of that August. It is only recently that I have noticed your signature in the book of condolences. I've visited that church from time to time. It's a calm, quiet place and I like being there.

I've had some personal difficulties; I won't go into details, but it is only recently that I have started to come to terms with what happened to Tim and the experience of being with him that night.

Philomena, you will remember Tim's garden dig, I thank you for the rather silly photograph you took of him in his excavation. When I look at it, it makes me smile and I can remember just what he was like.

I had been visiting our reference library here in Ruthin, and I was, on this occasion, exploring the ancient history section when I noticed a book that clearly did not belong on the shelf with the others. It was a little scrap book full of newspaper cuttings, drawings and notes made by a teenager. It was Tim's. Here I found your photograph of Tim together with notes on some of the events of his last few days. He writes in some detail and from what I read I can see that he liked spending time and sharing things with you. I'm sorry to bring the past back up Philomena, but this little book has thrown up all sorts of questions which I think might relate to what happened to Tim that summer. There are things that puzzle and frighten me a bit and I think there is truly a mystery here to be solved.

Philomena, I am so sorry to bother you about all this, but I feel that I really must. I would be grateful if you could spare me some time. Perhaps we could just meet for a coffee and a chat? I promise I'll not keep you for too long, but I so desperately would like to meet you and share memories.

I look forward to hearing back from you soon.

Yours faithfully,

Anya

12. Artefacts

Carmarthen AD 1989
June

Philomena retraced the paper folds and then replaced the letter into its envelope. This correspondence had been sent to her months ago and yet Philomena had only just received it. Initially she had been perplexed, but the envelope was not the original and had been redirected on to her here in Carmarthen by the good folk at the York Archaeological Trust. After careful inspection of the letter Philomena had been able to confirm that it had not been sent directly to the Trust. Indeed, had this been the case then she would have received it whilst she was working for them. The writer had taken the trouble to put the intended address down, as The Archaeological Department at the University of York. The two however, were not the same and there was clearly some sort of back story as to where the letter had been up until now.

Philomena had been fortunate, having spent just over a year in Crete and managing to get an MA out of it with recognition from both Oxford and Athens, which gave an exotic edge to the qualification. Although she had conducted some further work at Gortyn, Sakellarakis had placed her principally between the two museums at Heraklion and Chania. Unfortunately, funding inevitably came to an end, and she was back in the UK. After a week or two back home she was all prepared to take up a job in a Wrexham supermarket when the York Archaeological

Trust picked up her CV and she was asked to join them for three months of digging.

In a very short space of time, archaeology had suddenly become professional. Volunteers were a thing of the past, discouraged even. Archaeology had become a more popular discipline offered by most universities who churned out armies of graduates who had little hope of ever really making it in their chosen field. However, changes in the law around planning regulations meant that developers were now obliged to wait for a survey and/or excavation before works could begin and overnight there was a demand for very low paid professional staff. Philomena's three months were extended once, twice, and so on. Mind, there was no real future in it and so when an opportunity arose, she jumped ship once again, leaving the Trust at York for this place.

Trinity, a university college in Carmarthen, was essentially set up for training would-be teachers. For some odd reason it was now developing a faculty in archaeology. Philomena had seen the advert for a research fellow and had applied. For some time, there had been nothing, not a touch of the life she believed she had once lived in distant antiquity. York, where she had been living and working for the last year, clearly held no memories. She had begun to think that she'd made it all up, that it was some daft teenage notion.

In Carmarthen, however, she knew there was something strange going on for her. If there had been a past life, because of her teenage experiences in the town, she knew that at least some of that life may have once been spent when the town was called MORIDUNUM.

This was a chance to re-engage with her pasts if they indeed existed. However, it wasn't going to be all plain sailing. There were the lectures and tutorials to manage alongside her research work. The college had offered her either Batchelor of Arts or Batchelor of Education students for her tutorial groups. Knowing absolutely nothing about teaching either in secondary or primary school settings Philomena had wisely opted for the BA students. The college assigned ten BEd students to her tutorial group. She was actively putting the thought of managing that little problem to one side for the time being.

In the first few weeks of work her rational beliefs were being seriously tested. Well, if you invite the Devil to tea, you couldn't then complain if the bugger turned up. The Devil, on this occasion, couldn't have played a stronger set of cards. The letter was unexpected. Its author had clearly done her research. The addressee marked Miss Philomena Hutchinson; the author had really set out to track her down. At no stage back in August 1985 at the end of that long balmy summer had she ever disclosed her surname whilst spending time in Ruthin. As for the author, she knew of her all too well, but they had never met. And now, here was a letter, polite and without detail, but Philomena felt a little threatened, nevertheless.

Of all the players in this strange drama, Anya was the one that had made Philomena the most uneasy. They were perhaps rivals, but

Philomena knew far more about the other girl than was shared in kind. There was a darkness about Anya, a feeling of relentless tragedy. Quite why and how were just beyond Philomena's reach of understanding. There was however, always that unsettling feeling, a precursor for some great loss – death?

Philomena searched her memories, could she reach back? Could she still read the thoughts of the others as she had once done for those brief few days? There were the three boys. Cooper, as obvious and straight forward as they could be. Dan, always with an eye for the pretty girls, looking out for the next Mrs Jones. Then there was Tim, the one she'd seen years before, the one, well, now that she was thinking about it, the one for her. She had felt so comfortable with Tim, that she could share anything and everything and he would still accept her, respect her. Talking to Tim was so natural and safe. Like the other two boys, he liked girls, but he was very shy. He hadn't any idea when a girl fancied him – he was too scared to look for the signs. Tim didn't believe anyone could have a crush on him, least of all her and certainly not the beautiful Anya. For Tim, Anya was just the impossible, but Philomena knew different.

There lay the difficulty, you see, whilst Philomena and Tim were getting along quite well, Tim was still holding a torch for Anya. Anya was the girl in the way and Philomena didn't like competing with someone else – she wanted Tim for herself. Now, a few years on, that someone else was writing to her. Time and life had moved on surely, and yet this other girl was writing to her, now and in this place. The past had once again caught up with her.

As soon as Philomena had walked into the Middleton Arms on her first night out in Ruthin, she'd been aware of Anya, minutes after walking into the bar. Philomena could listen in to her thoughts. Had this extra sense happened today, then Philomena was quite sure she would have been frightened silly by the experience, but back then it was like an adventure.

Thinking about it now, how on Earth could she have just accepted those strange powers? There was nothing normal about being able to read and listen in to the thoughts of others, yet she'd somehow accepted, even welcomed, this strange gift. At least at first.

Philomena tapped the envelope on her chin gently as she considered the situation before reaching up for the A4 file box on the top shelf of books and boxes that graced her office. She pushed a plastic knob on the side, releasing the lid. Within was the rolled-up self-portrait that Tim had presented to her almost four years ago, held together as a tight roll by the original elastic band. Not once since had she pulled the elastic band off and looked at the portrait. Now, roll in hand, she felt a little fearful. She felt that she still had a strong mental image of Tim; her memory was sure and true. Philomena considered the roll of paper in her hand. What if?

In a wave of curiosity too strong to suppress, she pulled at the elastic band with her fingers. The scroll unwound, paper slipping outward as the roll diameter increased in size.

Would Tim be as she had remembered, or had she been nursing a make-believe, almost too good to be true, image all these years? Philomena gently unrolled the scroll further, pulling it out straight. For a second or two, her heart beat faster. The pencil marks were lighter, less defined than perhaps they once were, but the image held nothing to disappoint her memory. A handsome youth with near shoulder length wavy hair gazed out at her as he had when she had first held Tim's sketchbook, when she had looked up to compare the images. Tim had dismissed the work as something less than competent but to her eyes he had caught the likeness, it was a near flawless self-portrait. Then as now, however, there was something more.

Philomena swallowed hard to hold back the emotions. He was still here; the lines on the page breathed a credibility into her recollections. A modern piano tune on the radio, melancholic but warm, gave a background setting to the moment and suddenly her mind was racing through the memories of their meetings, days in the sunshine, her teasing conversation, and his painful shyness. All these things came back to her as if the events were but days before. There were tears in her eyes as she whispered, 'You're still with me. You'll always be with me.'

Philomena considered the image for a little while longer before rolling the paper up once more. Retrieving the elastic band, she returned the scroll back to its box.

'I shan't leave it so long next time,' she said, clipping the lid closed. There it could wait with the letter, artefacts from her own past story. There they both could stay until the time came for these things to come into the light once again.

* * *

DEVA (Chester) AD 525

The girl had come to the table through the chatter and wood smoke in the room. Pulling a chair, she sat directly opposite him, her head bowed, strands of hair that had escaped her plaits falling forward.

MODESTUS considered her for some minutes. A waif of a creature but not unattractive. Perhaps she, having followed him, was offering services because she considered that he may have some coinage to offer in return. Times past he would have paid a girl such as this and left her naked on the floor when he'd had enough. People like this, they were of no value, just commodities to be used. MODESTUS cared little for the circumstance of others, how they would live, eat, survive.

Still, with this girl there was something of a recognition, something that made him hold back and look more carefully. The girl raised her head and gazed directly into his eyes. With this movement, the memory of his wife, FLAVIA, came to the forefront of his

171

contemplation. Married for the power and the prestige that such a union would bring, FLAVIA was intelligent, but he considered her dull, unyielding and sickly. MODESTUS found the serving girls more attractive and had used them at will. There was, however, one physical feature that made his wife unique – her eyes. Flecked and speckled the colours were different between left and right. He considered it the consequence of years of restricted breeding. Families of the rich and powerful, there were but few here in Britannia, and they liked to keep the arranged marriages very much amongst themselves.

No, the eyes, there was something alluring, even perhaps attractive about them. The girl silently gazed on, her face perfectly proportioned and her eyes, was this just a simple coincidence?

'WHERE ARE YOU FROM GIRL?' he asked, and a sneer broke the calm serene beauty of her face.

'I AM FROM SOUTH BRITANNIA,' she responded. 'THEY SAY MY PARENTS WERE OF THE RULING CLASS AND THAT MY MOTHER DIED HORRIBLY WHEN BRINGING ME INTO THIS WORLD. OUR HOME, OUR ESTATES, I'M TOLD THAT THEY LAY NEARBY TO THE TOWN OF GLEVUM. THESE HAVE ALL GONE NOW, TAKEN FROM US BY THE ANGLES AND THE SAXONS.'

She had in these words confirmed his suspicions. MODESTUS reached over and took her hands in his. She had recognised him long before he had her. Perhaps another who knew him had pointed him out. Here was the reason she had trailed him throughout the morning.

A heavy hand fell on his shoulder. It's owner, one of the two Angle warriors who always had him in sight like a dog on a chain. The girl glared up at the man.

The warrior's tone when he next spoke was at least respectful. Perhaps her glare had made the oaf considerate. 'Mordred sir, it is time that we move on.'

MODESTUS maintained his grasp of the girl's hands and looking back into her eyes he said, 'DAUGHTER, WE WILL MEET AGAIN IN ELYSIUM.' He let her go and pushed his stool back in readiness to stand and leave.

Months had been spent passing away time with the Angles, a people Rome had considered as barbarians. People who were on the edge of and should have remained outside civilisation. It was a different existence. Austere plaster walls, intricate mosaic floors and the grand vaulted halls had been replaced by smoke-filled wooden halls and roaring central hearths. The polite and political power games of elite conversation, swapped for the epic stories of gods, heroes and monsters. There was a warmth and a comradery in the hall of the Angle king. It seemed clear now to MODESTUS that it would be these people who would inherit Britannia. These were a people akin with the common folk, a structure in their society was developing, and it offered something more to those who had nothing.

The Angles had put up with MODESTUS, he was fed and his lodging, although little better than the absolute basic, was at least adequate. He was still alive. There were not the creature comforts that he was used to, and he commanded little if anything it terms of respect but, he had the confidence to face each day because he was required, at least in the short term. However, his keepers had set him to work on tasks both menial and demeaning from dawn until dusk. There had been no time to be idle and this was certainly well out of custom from MODESTUS.

The spring had gently warmed, and the days of summer were ablaze. Crops, for the first time in years, grew strong and proud in the fields. Harvests would be good, and people would be fed.

In this time of summer MODESTUS was called once again before the warlord Cynric who at last seemed set upon a course of action in relation to his dealings with what was left of Britannia. MODESTUS had been dispatched with a group of armed warriors across land and over the Cheshire plain. Cynric considered that news of Arth and British resistance would best be collected at DEVA. MODESTUS found himself in agreement, for Arth had come from the lands of the Votadini, from a kingdom now termed as Gwynedd. DEVA, the old legionary base in the north, stood on the edge of the lands of Cambria from where the hills rose to become the mountains of Gwynedd beyond.

They had not found DEVA in the same state of organisation or preservation has had been the case at LINDUM COLONIA. The place was a chaotic ramble. Some districts maintained pockets of more permanent habitation but much more was now long lost to decay.

The good weather had brought people in from the countryside hoping to exchange a surplus for high value goods and the forum centre was a maze of makeshift stalls, carts, sacks, animals and people. Around this were the old shops and kiosks offering the daily needs and requirements – food, drink, medicines, manicures and surgery. Lean-tos of pole and leather sheets, dens of smoke, of bartered deals and hectic, sometimes desperate, conversation.

MODESTUS walked through this hubbub of humanity, alert and attuned to the comings and goings, shadowed by his armed guard. As a group they attracted little attention from most. Armed bands were clearly a regular phenomenon in this tangled run-down place.

MODESTUS had enquired as to news of armed warriors, collections of fighting men and the allegiances in this frontier town. He was met for the most part with ignorance or silence, but his life depended on what intelligence he could discover, and he was thus persistent, speaking and asking his questions in all the tongues he could muster. There had been the odd nod towards the smoke-filled dark corners, places where alcohol was freely available, where those of the under-class lurked in the shadows.

As the morning wore on, both MODESTUS and his guards were aware that they were being observed, followed even, as they made their way around the stalls and then the side streets, choked now with rubbish and excrement. There was graffiti, markings and signs on walls and street corners. Some of it old and deliberately carved, it had been present for a great many years, whilst some was new, and it was these new markings that were of greater interest to MODESTUS. As he stopped, so stopped his observers. He noted one in particular, a girl.

MODESTUS brought his Angle guards into the dark drinking dens. MODESTUS considered it early in the day but many of the degenerate earwigs were already drunk and apt for begging. It was here he found himself facing this girl, his daughter. As he was being ushered away from the table and his meeting with her, so she had also stood and there was command in her eye. She no longer looked the stray waif, there was a strength and dignity in her demeanour.

His parting memory was that of her shawl, or perhaps more accurately, the pin that fastened it in place. This was nothing of Roman or German invention. There was a flowing style, an imagination of wild things in a swirl captured in the deep red of crushed cut garnet. This was a pin of ancient Briton; a symbol of Albion before the Romans had disembarked on her pebble washed shores.

'ARTH, HE LEFT SOME SHORT WEEKS PREVIOUSLY. FOLLOW HIM ACROSS MERE AND MARSH, TO WHERE THE HILLS RISE, AND THE LANDS OF CAMBRIA BEGIN,' she called out.

He praised her under his breath. To the Angles he shared but a simple instruction. 'We need to leave this place and an audience with Cynric we must seek.'

13. Huw Gog and the Old Antique Shop

Denbigh AD 1989

Huw Guto Roberts, HGR to some, and Huw Gog to many more, had been running his house clearance and antique business on Vale Street in Denbigh for a good few years. It had been purely focused on house clearance when his father had been in charge. A bit of a rough diamond, his father had relied on selling stuff on cheaply in bulk. When it came to Huw's personality, he had more in common with his mother.

Having attended college and then university, much to his father's disapproval, Huw had picked up a degree in fine arts and was trying to guide the business more into antiques since his father's death. He was keen to use some of the knowledge he'd gained from his studies and to prove the point that he could be successful in his own right.

Huw Gog was the butt of jokes around town; overweight and slightly bohemian in his choice of dress and language, he fitted one's idea of an antique dealer to the tee. Big, fat chubby hands managed to handle the most intricate jewellery and time pieces. However, while he handled merchandise well, he was more than clumsy about his own person. His gaudy ties most usually bore the stains from that morning's breakfast boiled eggs.

HGR had a magic touch when it came to finding antiques, but his skills weren't so well balanced when it came to be selling them on. Sure, he was very knowledgeable about his subject, but he was absent-minded and caved in all too soon when it came to haggling on price. Huw had none of his father's sharp sales edge and nose for profit.

Huw Gog didn't fit in socially. Brought up public school, he had become a classic English gent but was stuck in a town that was world renowned for its support of the Welsh language and the Welsh nationalist movement as a whole. HGR had an eye for the ladies; problem was, they had no eyes for him. Generally, he was teased and ridiculed, but this didn't stop him from propping up the bars on Friday nights, a chance to admire the fast women on a night out, dressed to kill in their tight-fitting jeans and skirts.

Quite how he'd got around to accepting Miss Richards to join him as his shop assistant he wasn't too sure. He longed to be accepted by someone nice, someone at all would have been good, but he guessed his looks and reputation put women right off. He still lived at home, a carer for an ageing and increasingly helpless but demanding mother.

Huw was perhaps a good ten or fifteen years older than Miss Richards, but he'd noticed her when she was a teenager on the occasional night out in Denbigh. Someone like that was way out of his league but he'd watched her with her friends in the pub and he'd wondered who the lucky bloke would be. Some years later he'd observed her slide into drug abuse, petty crime and, it gutted him to think it, prostitution. What the Hell had gone so wrong? She had everything: good looks, talent, friends, and a real position in society, but she had thrown it all away. He had seen her almost reduced to living

179

on the streets, literally. A changed person, she had become an animal living hand to mouth and very much on the edge.

This winter, Huw had caught sight of Miss Richards in Denbigh town on several occasions. Each time he found himself looking back after her. There was a change, both in her looks and demeanour. Had a phoenix begun to rise from the ashes?

It had been a late morning encounter and he hadn't expected anyone to call in, least of all Miss Richards. It had been quiet in the shop since opening and with lunch hour rapidly approaching business would soon be in that lull period when the few shoppers who were out in Denbigh would be heading for a bite to eat.

Huw liked working on his own. No, that was perhaps an understatement, more he feared having someone else to work with him, but he now had to admit that he was not good at all the jobs that the business required. If things carried on the way they were, his father's profits would all be spent and his little commercial enterprise was liable to become extinct due to a distinct lack of sales. HGR had procrastinated a great deal about getting help to a point that if he didn't do something about it really soon, he wouldn't have the spare cash to pay anyone and that would be the end of the show. Finally, he had half-heartedly placed a scribbled note in the shop window – *situation vacant, one shop assistant required*. There was little else by way of information as he was still undecided and had opted for chance or the hand of God to provide a solution to his dilemma rather than being directly proactive himself.

He had been fiddling with an Edwardian pocket watch, concentrating, sat behind an excessively cluttered back desk for the shop that was both a work top and sales base. Perched on a high stool, a small eyepiece magnifier over his right eye he'd struggled to perform a near surgical operation on the cogs and wheels that were the innards of the time piece. For several minutes HGR had been oblivious to the young woman stood at the counter in front of him. Eventually Anya had made a little cough to clear her throat before addressing him.

'Excuse me, I'm sorry to be bothering you Mr Roberts, but I'd like to know how I might apply for the vacant situation?'

Somewhat startled, HGR had responded, 'What situation?'

'The one advertised in your front window Mr Roberts,' Anya had replied.

'Ah... right that, erm...'

'Are you still looking for someone?' Anya had fixed him with her brown eyes.

'Yes, I suppose I am, and you'd be interested because err... well it doesn't pay too well. What experience have you got?'

'Working in a shop, none, but I've got maths and economics A levels and I can speak Welsh quite well.'

'Yes, but the trade, antiques, what do you know about that?' HGR had asked.

'I'm a quick learner and I'll have the best of teachers won't I Mr Roberts?'

Huw Gog had blinked a lot. Flattery, that's what it was, and he didn't get much of that ever. He hadn't the wit or the wherewithal to seriously go out and employ someone properly so perhaps he could take the easy route as he wasn't exactly fighting off the applicants. He was about to say 'Yes, OK' but then he'd remembered her drug addiction.

'Err … it's Miss Richards isn't it? You've got a bit of a reputation, can I trust you?'

She'd looked sad and he'd been afraid that he'd really hurt her feelings.

'I've got a reputation, done lots of bad things and made too many mistakes, you're right. But I want to try and improve myself. I want to get away from the drugs and … I want to get my life back. Will you help me?'

Once again, he'd been caught with a pleading gaze from those brown eyes.

'OK, perhaps we could try you out. You could start the beginning of next month.'

'I could start straight away, right now, if you'd like?' Anya had responded.

'Err…'

She was still looking at him. He wasn't used to women looking at him for so long and against his better judgement and with God whispering as his inner voice, he ended up saying, 'Yes, err... OK.'

And so it was that Anya Richards had come to take up a job in Huw Gog's cluttered ramble of an antique shop. He had been more than nervous for the first week or so, lest she wasn't to be trusted and robbed his till or flogged off all his precious stuff to pay for her drug habits. You could never judge a book from its cover mind, and by the end of the first week several items had indeed been sold. By the end of the first month the shop takings were up, and for the first time ever, Huw found himself raiding his lock up to replace the stock that had been sold. Many locals had found HGR a bit odd and women would avoid the shop because he was there. Now there was a helpful young woman serving, more people were inclined to call in.

Quickly, Huw had very much got to like the idea of Miss Richards being around. From his experience, most women would whisper sly comments about his appearance and giggle at him when his back was turned or they'd ignore him and take no notice at all. Miss Richards was different; she tended to listen and was quietly spoken. Her interest in his business was clear. She had borrowed and devoured all the information in his well-thumbed antique guides. Miss Richards made well considered responses when he brought in any new finds for the shop to sell and she listened without judging him when he rambled on about all the problems he was having looking after his ageing, disabled mother.

So, he liked being in her presence. She made him feel a little important, a little special. Above all perhaps, for Huw, were her looks. Miss Richards was definitely attractive, had done something nice with her hair and that slightly turned up nose! She was natural, wore very little make up if any – he wasn't sure, but those deep brown intelligent eyes made his heart melt. Huw could have happily stared all day, but he didn't; he was determined that she should never feel uncomfortable in his company.

* * *

Anya was considering her change in fortune too one morning. She'd done some rearranging in Huw's shop, whilst he was out at an auction. Anya had discovered that what a great many callers to the shop wanted most of all was to talk about themselves and their obsessions. She'd picked up on this early on and was a good listener – always made the customer think that she was interested in what they had to say. She also noticed that most shoppers, having taken up so much of her time, then found themselves duty bound to make a purchase, to buy something they didn't really want or need out of politeness. Through this approach, Anya was getting to know the shop's clientele. She was tuning into what the punters were looking for and would put out things of interest for them, guiding them to the right place. Visitor numbers increased – the customers liked her.

Of course, there was always the 'What's the best price you can do on this?' line, but since most of the stock had come in from house clearances that Huw had picked up for next to nothing, there was a sure profit to be made on just about everything that sold. Mind, old Huw Gog had an eye for the interesting and this, matched to her sales and presentation skills made for a very sound business partnership. Huw was not slow to notice; the antique sales were really picking up and after some months he announced that he was happy to make her a permanent member of the team and that he had great faith in her.

Life was looking up for Anya. There wasn't a fortune in this business, but what money there was made a difference. She was busy during the day in the shop and she was out one night a week at an adult learning course with the aim of progressing on to a further qualification. She'd opened up a bank account and for the first time since leaving home she was building up a small amount in savings – the means for a return to further education perhaps.

The weeks had gone by and with some encouragement from everyone at the night class, Anya had made an application to study a BA in archaeology. The institution wasn't in the same league as her first choice of university after leaving school, but it was a start. A letter of acceptance from Trinity College in Carmarthen followed a month later which did wonders for her self-esteem. The letter of acceptance, however, didn't please everyone.

'If it all goes wrong, you know, with the education thing Miss Richards, there'll always be a place here for you in the business,' Huw would repeat. Clearly, he was struggling with the thought of losing his business prodigy.

'I've got lots of contacts down there in *Caerfyrddin* you know' Huw announced one day, emphasising his knowledge by his use of the Welsh name for Carmarthen. 'I'll give you a lift down with all your stuff in the van when the time comes.'

'What stuff?' she replied.

Ignoring her, he continued, 'Perhaps I could relocate the business? There are lots of good clearance opportunities down there you know. The place is full of ageing farming families stashing interesting valuables away in isolated farms. They pop off you know, with no real close relatives and then it's just a race to get the places sold. No one really cares about the contents or considers that there might be real treasures hiding away in these places.'

Anya didn't doubt Huw's analysis. That battered white van of his cast a very wide net in search of old junk.

Anya had quickly realised that Huw was not averse to engaging in some shady deals, particularly if they meant obtaining the unusual, the historical or the mysterious – things he liked. He had been intrigued too, by her interest in archaeology. He suggested that such an interest would, one of these days, be of great value for the business.

After coming back earlier than expected from a buying excursion, he had pushed open the door, bell dinging to announce his arrival, and called out, '*Paned* Miss Richards?'

Anya noted that in all this time he had always been very formal. Not once had he ever used her first name Anya.

'Got some things here to show you my dear. I'd like you to take a look; give me your specialist opinion?'

He unrolled his canvas bag and exposed several curious items. Anya came over. Huw picked up some flint arrow heads to pass to her. They were smooth to the touch but razor sharp on the edges and at the point. Exceptional quality but on handling one she noted that the colour was all wrong.

'Nice pieces Huw and if they were real, I reckon you'd need to be taking them down to the museum,' she said.

'Real, what do you mean by that Miss Richards?'

'Well, you see, the colour's all wrong,' Anya continued. 'Look, this one has a distinct green shade so it's no real piece of flint. I'd say its glass. The North American Indians worked on glass as if it were flint. Interesting and beautiful quality – just not what you were hoping for Huw.' It's at this point that Anya froze because she'd seen something else in the cache of stuff Huw had brought in.

187

After following her gaze, Huw said, 'I'm not sure what that is. I picked it up with a box of fossils. Quite nice examples actually but not ones you could sell on. I gave the fossils to the lad next door, mad keen on dinosaurs he is, but that item I kept. Mind, I think, judging from your reaction, that you know something about it?'

Huw picked up the item and held it out towards her. Anya paused; she had seen this stone before, or at least the pattern engraved upon it. Tim had made a careful drawing of these markings for his notebook. This stone was most definitely the subject of his drawing.

'Some sort of writing or symbols I reckon,' Huw added. 'Does it match anything you've seen or read about before Miss Richards?'

He gestured for her to take hold of the artefact. Anya was hesitant, she wasn't sure what she would feel if she held the stone; here was a direct connection to Tim, an object he would have held in his final few days. It was something he had studied carefully before the events of that final night with her.

When she did finally take it from Huw there was nothing, just the touch of cold stone. Anya held it in her right hand; it was smooth and easy to handle.

She looked up, daft really but her emotions were suddenly taking over, big tears welling up in her eyes.

'My boyfriend found this,' she said before she was overcome with emotions and memories. Anya began to sob uncontrollably, great big sobs that racked through her body. She felt Huw's hands on her shoulders, gently guiding her to sit on an old mangey chaise longue. He sat next to her. Anya brought her hands up to her face and was gritting her teeth, breathing in slow deep inhalations of air, determined now to regain her composure and self-control. A few uncomfortable minutes of silence passed between the two before Huw once again opened up the conversation with a question.

'Miss Richards?'

'Anya, its Anya, Huw. You are one of the few friends I have so please, just call me Anya.'

'So, Miss Richards' – she gave him a look – 'Anya,' he corrected, 'what happened to this boyfriend?'

'He was stabbed by some nutter. I tried, I really tried so hard to keep him with me, but it was too dark, and he bled away in my arms.'

There was another period of silence between the two before Huw once again raised a question. 'So, this is why you turned to the drugs?'

'No,' Anya returned, shaking her head. 'No, my soul had gone to the Devil long before then. My mother, she died early and when I started in secondary school my father did things to me, things a man should never do to his daughter. My stepmother knew, she knew all along, but she did nothing to protect me.'

Glancing now at Huw she caught a look of horror and disgust on his face. She fell silent, head down, looking at the stone which was now in her left hand.

'My God,' Huw began, 'You, you are braver and stronger than I can imagine.'

Anya placed her right index finger on the stone's markings and began to trace the carved circles. As she did so, a powerful, deep throb of electric pain built to a crescendo, a nauseating wave through her arm which terminated painfully in her armpit. Violently she pulled her finger away.

'Ouch!' she exclaimed, breathing quickly, gasping for air. Her heart was pounding against her rib cage.

'What's wrong?' Huw demanded. He had caught the stone before it hit the floor. Huw looked down at the stone and followed her example, tracing the circles with his chubby right index finger. Nothing happened.

Ding, ding – the shop's front door opened and like naughty school children, the two jumped up from the chaise longue. Huw headed off out back whilst Anya, pulling her jumper straight and taking another deep breath to compose herself, made her way to welcome the caller.

'*Bore da*, good morning. If you need any assistance, please let me know. Otherwise, I hope you enjoy looking around.'

The visitor simply nodded.

Anya didn't recognise the woman and guessed she hadn't been in before. *The silent non-communicative type*, she thought. Sometimes this type would know exactly what they were looking for and if they found it there would be a sale.

The visitor went in the opposite direction to avoid passing her. Anya made no more effort to engage in conversation. Looking back toward the counter she noticed that Huw had scooped up his collection of unusual antiquities and had gone down the narrow corridor at the back of the shop towards the back store like some badger down a tunnel. Her stone however, he had placed where she could see it, next to the till.

The customer, their first that morning, had gone round the shop once, perhaps twice, and was heading back out through the front door. Perhaps she'd just come in to get out of a shower of rain. There were no thanks or goodbye, just a ding as she opened the door and a clunk as the door then shut behind her.

'Don't tell me—' Huw had returned '—she's spent a thousand pounds and wants all the purchases delivered first thing tomorrow morning.' Huw was carrying two mugs of piping hot tea, one in each hand, steam evaporating from the surface of each one. Anya gave him a weak smile when he passed one of the mugs to her and wondered just how he'd managed to achieve all he had in such a short period of time.

Huw nodded in the direction of the till. 'I think that stone there rightly belongs to you Miss Richards.'

'I'm not sure I'll feel all that safe with it.'

'So long as you don't go tracing those circles with your fingers, you shouldn't get hurt again,' the big man replied, settling himself down onto the chaise longue once again.

Huw's statement was good advice as she had indeed held the stone in her palm without any ill effect and deep down, she knew that there was something more, that this stone was very significant and important to her. It was for her to look after this artefact now, whatever it was.

14. Lazarus

Denbigh AD 1989
June

Back in her little mid link house that evening, Anya set about getting ready to go out. It was her one and only social night in the week. The adult learning group were going to meet for a drink at the Boar's Head in Ruthin. She was considering walking over from Denbigh and catching the last bus back. To do so she would have to get going because the walk in would take some time. Chances were that one of their group would offer her a lift back, especially if they wanted her to stay a bit longer.

She needed to freshen up. Business had really improved in the shop that afternoon and they'd been busy. Perhaps the improvement in the weather had brought more customers into the antique shop with it. Strange, Huw's joke about the morning's big spender had kind of come true that afternoon. Out of the blue they'd taken a good thousand pounds worth in sales.

'It's that magic stone, it's a lucky charm you know,' Huw had said at the end of the day. 'I think I should be keeping that in the shop to bring us more good fortune.' But he'd still made sure he'd passed it on to Anya before she left for the day.

Anya stood before the sink in her vest top to wash. The joy of cupping warm water between two hands and bringing it up to her face and arms was a real pleasure and she repeated the act several times.

There was such a contrast between her circumstances now and the previous autumn. She had money to put in the electric meter, she had warmth and warm water at the flick of a switch.

Finally, she pulled the stopper chain for the plug and the water gurgled away and out of the sink. She watched the whirlpool of water empty before reaching out for a towel. She buried her face in the rich warm cotton and then dabbed each arm dry. She took extra care with her inner arms, as they bore many scars.

It was at this point that she stopped and held both arms out to the mirror so as to compare them. Her heart beat faster. The left underarm was disfigured and ugly, but on her right the skin was pure, unblemished. A prickling sensation crept up from the base of her spine and hairs across the whole of her body rose up as one. The feeling was not one of this world.

Anya closed her eyes, fearful, a great pounding in her chest. With her eyes shut, standing there shaking in front of the mirror she whispered a prayer. A prayer to God.

'Oh God, forgive me, forgive me my sins. Please do not harm me but look after me and see me safe as I stand here before you.'

Anya kept her eyes closed for some more minutes. When at last she peeked through her eyelids, she expected the illusion to have gone. There was, however, no illusion. So was this a miracle?

Turning, she gazed at the stone that lay where she had placed it. There was a strong temptation now to test this strange magic once again by tracing the circles on the stone for a second time. Would doing so with her left index finger mean that she would be clean on both arms, that she would be whole once again? She remembered the pain from the morning's encounter with this strange power and suddenly she felt unworthy of this gift, undeserving in the shadow of God.

* * *

When she had finally joined the other adult learners on their evening out it had proved to be a very pleasant experience and a nice diversion, a chance to escape back to the real world. When at last she had returned to number 15 later that night, grateful for a lift, she had deliberately ignored the stone and had gone straight to bed. Her dreams however, had been haunted, wild and disturbed.

The arrival of the post early in the morning broke the cycle of nightmares, leaving her with a feeling of relief. Post was not a regular occurrence, especially packages as large as this one. The postman had clearly struggled to push it through the hatch. Anya imagined that he would not have wanted to knock on the door to get her up.

She bent down to collect the fat A5 manila envelope and guessed immediately what it was. She had sent off for a new college prospectus, the one she had being a little out of date. She brought the envelope in from the doorway, ripping it open before sitting down to explore its contents. The new prospectus for Trinity College was a real step up from the old one, fatter and more professional in its presentation.

The courses were arranged in alphabetical order and archaeology was right up there in the front. Anya scanned through the course description and the departmental team list that brought up the rear in the text. There were several new names for the department, names that meant nothing to her, that is with the exception of one.

Philomena Hutchinson, reader in Roman Archaeology. Specialising in Roman Frontiers, Latin as a living language and the end of Roman Britannia.

There was more but Anya wasn't taking it all in.

'Bingo! So, this is where you are,' she whispered. Any doubts about returning to further education evaporated from her mind. There had been no reply to her letter which she'd sent to the University of York Archaeological Department and here clearly was the reason why. Philomena was no longer in York, and no one had forwarded the letter on. This little quest had stalled, but now, well perhaps at last, some new doors had opened, and her quest could continue.

The excitement quickly faded, for Anya caught sight of her right arm. Last night, whilst out with the others she'd pushed the miracle out of her mind. Surely this sort of nonsense was only taken seriously by the Catholic Church. She didn't believe in God, well not usually at any rate. She considered religious people with suspicion. There was always something wrong, something missing in their lives, and they needed the religion to prop themselves up because they couldn't cope with the real world. Drugs and alcohol had replaced religion in recent years and then

Anya began to consider her own weaknesses and how she had used drugs to escape the pain of life.

She looked at the stone through the corner of her eye. It was still there, silent and just where she had left it last night. What the bloody Hell did Tim kick up whilst walking over that old burial mound four years ago? What forces had he unleashed? The excitement of the quest – this adventure she had conjured up in her mind was again fading fast. This was no longer some fancy, some *Famous Five* adventure trip. She was scared, and every hair stood up on end as a wave of ice cold rushed across her body. Last night she had prayed to God but what if this was something from the dark side? Anya had initiated all of this, opened up Pandora's box and taken the first few steps out on her own free will. Now she was taking more steps, but she no longer felt in control. A pathway was already there, but someone or something had taken her by the hand and was leading her along.

Anya fastened a watch onto her left wrist. It was nothing special, something she'd picked up from work. A small simple dial with Roman numerals painted onto a fine white disc with a gold surround. The stamp on the reverse indicated nine carat gold. Anya had replaced the cheap metal strap with one that had been made up for her in the leather shop. There were no digital bits or bobs, just the necessity to wind the timepiece up once or twice a week. Huw was all for her having the watch as a gift. 'Take it,' he had said, but she had insisted on paying.

Anya paid her way now. She needed to be careful, but she was no longer a charity case or a benefit scrounger.

As she turned the watch round on her wrist, she noticed the time. She had half an hour before opening time and today she knew that she'd be alone in the shop, at least for the morning. She sighed regretfully. She wanted Huw to be there; a hug would have been nice and a chat over a cup of tea. Huw was always one for his *paned*. He was warm and easy going. Clueless when it came to women and a clumsy, bungling clot when with her most of the time. Nevertheless, she felt safe when Huw was about.

Anya pulled an old shoe box from under her bed and lifting the lid off she retrieved her prize Kaweco fountain pen and some sheets of lined paper that she had tucked in the box with the pen, some envelopes and a bottle of Waterman turquoise ink. You see, she wasn't alone, there was perhaps someone else on this quest with her and suddenly she was writing at pace. She was calling for help, reaching out to share her news.

* * *

Ruthin AD 526
January
Gwenllian caught the village headman's eye. A native, he was someone whom she could trust. She beckoned him to come closer.

'Sir,' she enquired, 'can you keep this safe? Can you fashion a container whereby we can hide this item through all manner of weather and time for a day when Arth will come to collect it?'

She looked apprehensively in all directions. The woman's captors, it seemed, were more preoccupied with preparations to evacuate and begin the journey back out of Cambria, than they were on her. Gwenllian held out her hand, offering a small leather pouch to the headman.

'My lady.' He took the package with a nod.

Gwenllian edged back into the shadows and was gone.

The local people here had warmed to Gwenllian from the day of her arrival. Calm and beautiful, she treated others with respect. Gwenllian was one who would notice the day to day events, knew everyone by name and spoke only in friendship and encouragement. She would enquire after folk expressing an interest or sharing a concern. So, the locals took her to their hearts. She was the human side of the Brythonic entourage, and the locals were keen for her to stay. They observed where she went, with whom and when. In this way they had been aware of the oak tree, her trips to the waters and her meetings there with Arth.

The headman gauged the situation. A meeting with others to discuss anything other than routine or the work set for them by their English task masters was discouraged for their own safety. Now a different breed of warrior was in town. These English would not stay long. They would not invest in the community as the warriors of Britannia had done earlier in the season. Theirs was a smash and grab visit.

Outstretched and far away from the security of their homelands the English were both nervous and suspicious. They expected an imminent attack and considered the locals as little more than the enemy within the gates. They were aggressive and bad tempered as a fear had spread through their ranks like a voracious disease. There were frequent scuffles with the village men who endured much bad language and threat.

Under these conditions the headman decided that he alone would secure this package. With an ear to gossip and chat, he decided on the young oak as a best location to bury and hide this leather pouch in readiness for Arth's return. When he opened the pouch to inspect the contents, he was most puzzled. For within, nestled in moss and dried grass he found a fragile, incomplete wooden goblet. To him it looked old, quite an antique, and he pondered the item's significance for a few minutes. He also put his mind to consider just how this goblet might be preserved. On the latter he concluded that he would wrap it in a parcel of lead piping. Such a material, to his knowledge, did not rust or degrade when buried in the earth. Lead used on rooves was also waterproof. He had no hypothesis, however, in regard to the former – the item's significance.

Denbigh AD 1989

The rain started to come down heavily, so she pushed open the door to the nearest shop. She would not usually choose to visit a place like this – full of old junk and dead people's stuff. And yet, once she'd committed, clinking a bell on the door as it opened and stepping down from the street through the doorway, straight away she became aware of something, a charged atmosphere, a connection from the beyond.

'*Bore da*, good morning. If you need any assistance, please let me know. Otherwise, I hope you enjoy looking around.'

An attractive young woman with troubled brown eyes had greeted her. Despite the polite warm welcome however, the shop assistant was distracted.

Nodding back, she walked around, pretending to show an interest, picking up the odd item, bringing it up close for further examination but really looking beyond to observe the young shop keeper each time. The shop keeper – who was she? There was an aura, the atmosphere was chilled and heavy in this dive of a shop. The eye of this intangible storm – the woman at the till. A past life called but the distance in time was so great. In her mind's eye an image flickered, crimson on white.

She took her time and went around once, twice in a figure eight before leaving, pulling the door to with a cling, the bell announcing her departure. While the shop keeper looked up briefly from her distractions, she did not notice that she was being observed still through the street side window. The observer, a dark shadow of a silhouette against the bright sun that shone now through the shower clouds.

15. A Communion of the Covenant

Ruthin AD 1989
June
Dan screwed his eyes up, right hand massaging his temples as he looked out over the field at the back of his mother's house. It was perhaps a little less damp than it was in his days of childhood but otherwise, not much had changed. The mound where he had observed Tim four years ago no longer showed the scars from the JCB attack. It was just a low unassuming rise in the field.

'Jesus,' he exclaimed, holding his forehead between thumb and fingers as a shot of pain rose behind his eyeballs. *I should go and see the GP about this*, he thought. Doctors, however, were one breed that Dan could not abide. He'd always been squeamish; blood and bodily functions, especially when unusual, made him feel physically sick. He made a point of keeping well away from the medical profession. Perhaps an optician would be better placed to help, considering the pain was behind the eyes.

He continued to massage his temples with both thumb and fingers, hoping the movements of distraction would somehow sooth the pain away. Perhaps there was an underlying tension. Anya. Since their meeting in Siop Nain in October, he hadn't heard from her. Now and then, round lunch time, he'd stuck his head into Siop Nain just to see if she was there, but there had been no sign. A postal address was all he'd had, and the echo of her voice saying, *'I don't want you coming around to my place, I couldn't bear it. I couldn't bear for you to see what I have become.'*

Then out of the blue, Anya had written to Dan.

Dan, we must meet. I have things to share, exciting things that you must know about, things that shine some light on our mystery.

He had repeated the words again and again in his mind. Perhaps today, being the day of their meeting, the expectation, that nibbling emotion of concern, was what had driven this bloody damn migraine, if that was what it was. Dan had other worries about all of this business mind. At the end of this story there had been a murder. Scum like Tom Evans might not think twice about exacting vengeance again – might it be Cooper or him the next time around?

Nowadays, life imprisonment seemed to mean a few years and you were out on good behaviour. Were Anya's enquiries just going to end up bringing trouble back to his doorstep? Dan had serious nagging doubts about all of this. He had been intrigued about how she was doing, whether there was anything more to all of this but now that she had reopened the contact, suddenly the implications of the whole affair made his blood turn cold.

* * *

'Hi Daniel, we must stop meeting like this,' Anya greeted him as he stepped down into the café through the door on the street. 'These meetings make me feel like a spy – adds to the excitement of our adventure don't you think?'

'Not sure about excitement or adventure,' Dan responded as he pulled up a chair to sit opposite her on the little table for two. Anya shot him a puzzled look.

'Yeah,' he continued, 'before we get going, I've something really on my mind about all of this. Something, no someone, is really worrying me. If you're doing your little investigation, unearthing things so to speak, well, this family from Prestatyn, they might find out and we know they can do some proper harm.'

'Wow,' Anya looked slightly taken aback. 'How are we in any danger?'

'You seem to forget there's an unbalanced murderer in all of this,' Dan blurted out.

The waitress had arrived to take their orders. Anya was quickest to respond.

'Mr Jones here will have a tea and it's a black filter coffee for me please.'

'Anything else?'

'No, that will be all for now,' Anya countered, and the girl was off with her order. Anya turned her gaze back towards Dan. 'Well Daniel Jones, I'm pleased to inform you that our Tom Evans is out of gaol. He left, I believe, in a box.'

'What?'

'He's dead. So, you have nothing to get so worked up about on his account. That clairvoyant guy you lot upset, he had a daughter too you know, but again if you've had no bother from her up until now then I should think you're not going to in the future, wouldn't you agree?'

'Yeah, that does make me feel a whole lot better. So how do you know all of this then Miss Richards?' Dan returned her earnest gaze, still massaging his forehead and temples.

'You got a nasty headache or something? You seem to be screwing up your eyes and rubbing at your forehead a lot. I'm sure there are some crystals for that – you know, to drive out all the nasty toxic energy, the stress and pressures in the lives you jet set sales people like to lead.'

Still massaging his temples, he said, 'Don't get me going about all that yoga meditation nonsense. Go on then, spill the beans. What do you know Miss Richards and perhaps more importantly, how do you know?'

'OK,' she began. 'Well, where to start? A chance meeting with DI John Morris I think.'

'Who?' Jones interrupted her.

'The lead detective on Tim's murder case that's who. Except it wasn't any chance meeting at all because he had specifically set out to find me. He's retired now and is writing a book about the odd unexplained events in his detecting career. Yes, I think I've explained that right.'

'So why did he bother to find you – seemed a pretty open and shut case to me,' Dan interjected, listening to her every word despite the tempest that was raging behind his eyes.

'Yeah, that was my response too,' Anya returned, 'but, identifying the murderer wasn't the unexplained bit in the case. Apparently, a certain Miss Philomena Hutchinson had called in to the station and had given a statement sometime after the event. Some of the details she gave could only have been known to the murderer – Tom Evans.'

'Oh,' Dan replied, still massaging his temples. 'You're not serious. How could that be? Was she there Anya, at the Woodlands?'

'No, she was hundreds of miles away and that's the bit the DI was struggling with. The information about the demise of Tom by the way, that came from the DI as well. There's something else too.'

'You've been planning this little story for me haven't you Anya,' said Dan.

'Oh yes, I've been looking forward to this for a little while.'

Anya began to roll up her sleeves.

'Take a look at my arms Dan,' she encouraged.

Dan looked on, puzzled. 'What? What am I looking at your arms for?'

Anya had rolled up her sleeves on both arms to beyond the elbows and presented the undersides for him to inspect. The skin on her right arm was clean and unblemished. That on her left bore the tell-tale

207

signs of self-harm – the view quite put the squeamish Jones off, and he guarded his eyes with his left hand.

'OK… I still don't know what I'm supposed to be looking at,' he stated.

'I showed you my right arm last time we met; do you remember?'

'Showed yes, but I didn't look. Can't stand stuff like that.'

'You're far too squeamish Daniel Jones but look, my right arm is clear, and it wasn't when we last met.'

Dan looked again but didn't respond.

Late, but better late than never, their drinks arrived. 'Sorry about the wait,' the waitress said as she put the drinks down heavily on the table, tea in front of Anya and coffee in front of Jones.

'Thanks,' Dan responded somewhat sarcastically, and the pair swapped the cups round.

'After meeting you last time, I got a job.'

Jones stirred his tea, listening.

'Huw Guto Roberts of Denbigh Antiques and House Clearances, you might know him.'

'Yeah, I've heard of him, bit of an odd job bloke,' he said.

'Yes, perhaps, but he's been good to me, and the business is doing really well. He wants to make me a partner to try and stop me from leaving I think.'

Dan raised his eyebrows.

'Yeah, I've been doing an adult learning course, perhaps I said. Well, I've had an offer of a place at this tin pot university college in Carmarthen. I wasn't sure about going because I was enjoying working for Huw, but I've changed my mind. Anyway, Huw brought this into the antique shop one morning.'

She retrieved an object from her backpack which was by her feet on the floor. Wrapped in an old tea towel the object was solid. Anya unwrapped the tea towel to give Dan a view of the object within. There before him was what looked like that marked stone from Tim's notebook. Dan reached out to pick the stone up, but Anya quickly intercepted him, gently pushing his hand to one side.

'Careful, you need to know how to touch this stone.' She presented the undersides of her arms once again to Jones. 'The stone generates some sort of deep electric power.'

'Bullshit!' Jones responded and he reached out to touch the markings on the stone. He began to run his index finger around the markings cut into the stone. For a few seconds nothing was happening and then, suddenly, Jones hissed, 'Jesus!' and yanked his hand away.

'What the…!' he exclaimed, knocking his teacup to blazes and causing something of a commotion in the café.

An anxious waitress came over to investigate.

'He'll be OK,' Dan heard Anya responding to her. 'I'm sorry for the disturbance, can I pay the bill?'

Dan had doubled up; he was sweating profusely, and his breathing had become very fast. He could hear muffled voices.

'Looks like he's 'avin an 'eart attack to me,' the daft sounding waitress was saying. He could catch snippets of conversation but the pain and nausea he was experiencing made much of it a blur.

'No, he'll be fine trust me,' came Anya's voice again. Dan's world was swirling around him. Anya had taken a note out from her purse.

'Take this for the drinks and keep the change. It can pay for the breakages.' Dan felt her take hold of his good arm.

'Come on Daniel, let's get some air.' Anya led him out of the café.

Dazzling lights seemed to be obscuring his view of events, but once out he felt his breathing stabilise but he still felt very rough. There was a painful throb in his right arm and this together with the sweating brought some considerable panic to his mind. Perhaps the daft girl of a waitress was right, and he really was having a heart attack.

'Told you not to touch didn't I,' Anya piped up as she propped him against the outside wall of the café.

'Jesus I'm going to look proper daft out here like this,' Jones responded. 'Good God let's get out of view or people will think I'm bloody ill or something.'

'They think that already dear the big scene you made in there. You men never do what you're told do you?'

Dan's senses were slowly coming back as they made their way up Well Street past the Nat West Bank to sit on a bench outside the Wine Vaults. Anya must have picked up the stone in all that commotion in the café and she now set about wrapping it carefully once again in its tea towel before placing it back in her backpack. This gave him a little more time to recover.

'Strange,' Anya began, 'the stone affected you and I but had no effect on Huw when he touched it.'

Dan shook his head but made no effort to reply.

'I wonder if it only has that effect on people who knew Tim?' Anya asked.

'So, you're suggesting the stone miraculously healed your right arm, is that the point you were trying to get over in the café?'

'Yes, later when I was washing, I noticed the difference between my arms, and I'd traced the markings with my right index finger.' Anya flashed Dan a sideways look. 'How's your head now?' she asked.

Dan considered; for just a minute he'd seen the fresh-faced cute girl from comprehensive school again. For the first time there was a spark in her eyes.

Rubbing his temples, Dan replied at last, 'Bloody headache's gone.'

Anya was observing him closely now, 'After you touched the stone; it's a miracle then,' she said and there was a quiet pause between them both.

211

'You know, there seem to be pieces to a puzzle in all this, and I think I'm starting to find some of the pieces.'

'Are you?' Dan responded.

'Yeah, I think so. You see, there's one more thing that I forgot to add. Philomena, I know where she is Dan.'

'Oh yeah, where is she then?'

'Carmarthen,' Anya replied, 'She's a lecturer there.'

'And you're going to Carmarthen to study? That's a bit of a coincidence. Does she know you're going?'

'No,' Anya answered, 'I don't think she does, unless the lecturers actually look at all the applications they get.'

'Then I shouldn't tell her in case she disappears again,' Dan replied.

* * *

Ruthin AD 526
January

Gwenllian had been pushed out of the great round house by a large sais warrior, wrapped in his sheep skins, breath shunting out from his mouth like a steam engine. It was cold outside with a ground covering of wave-like drifts of very fine snow that had built up overnight on the hard floor. The locals had a saying *'Eira mân, eira mawr'* or 'fine snow, deep snow'.

There was an urgency about the English encampment today, a need to get out and off on the journey across the mountains towards home. The sais pushed her in the back again, prodding her like some cow, toward a tall powerful looking warrior who stood up ahead on the path waiting for them.

'AH GWENLIAN,' he addressed her in Latin. 'WALK WITH ME.' He held his hand out in expectation that she would take it in her own. She came up to him but did not take his hand of friendship, rather she pulled her heavy woollen cloak around her more tightly to fend off the chill wind; flakes of snow lifted and settling in her long, matted hair. She felt dirty, cold and tired.

'STILL NOT SPEAKING?' He nodded, indicating the direction of their journey. When she did not respond, he continued. 'WE HAVE NOT FOUND HIM.' Turning to look at her once again, he added, 'SO I SUPPOSE YOU STILL HAVE HOPE.'

They continued to walk on slowly before he continued once again in an attempt at conversation with her.

'YOUR ESCORT, WHY DID HE BRING YOU BACK HERE? ARTH, WHY WOULD HE LET YOU COME BACK HERE? IS IT PERHAPS THAT HE DOES NOT KNOW THAT I, CYNRIC HAVE COME ACROSS THE MOUNTAIN PASS, THAT WE ARE HERE?'

Gwenllian shrugged her shoulders in mute response.

'PERHAPS ARTH IS NO MORE,' Cynric pursued, 'AND YOU MY LADY, YOU ARE NOW ALL ALONE.'

GWENLLIAN LOOKED THE ENGLISH LORD IN THE EYE BEFORE FINALLY making a response. 'I CANNOT TELL, I DO NOT KNOW, AND NOW, NOW THAT YOU HAVE ME WHAT IS IT YOU INTEND TO DO WITH ME MY LORD?'

'SO, GWENLLIAN, YOU ARE NOT MUTE BUT SPEAK IN CALM INTELLIGENCE,' Cynric responded. 'I HAVE MANY OPTIONS. WE CAN WAIT HERE BUT I SUGGEST SUCH AN ACTION WOULD BE DANGEROUS. ARTH IS ONE PROBLEM, BUT THE KINGDOM OF GWYNEDD LIES YONDER AND THE VOTADINI MASS IN STRENGTH THESE DAYS. THEY HOLD THE GROUND HERE AND FURTHER BEYOND TO THE VERY LIMITS OF BERNICEA.

'THEN, WE CAN LEAVE, AS WE ARE, AND IF ARTH STILL LIVES HE MAY FOLLOW, HE MAY ATTEMPT A RESCUE?' Cynric observed Gwenllian.

'WHAT WOULD YOU HAVE ME DO GWENLLIAN? I WILL TAKE YOU WITH ME BUT HOWEVER MUCH I MAY WISH TO KEEP YOU THE ANGLES WILL BE MUCH AGAINST SUCH ACTION. THEY ARE SUSPICIOUS OF MY MOTIVES HERE WITH YOU. THEY HAVE TRAVELLED FAR AND INTO DANGER, TO ACHIEVE IN THEIR VIEW, NOTHING OF GREAT CONSEQUENCE.'

Gwenllian considered the man by her side.

'WHO ARE YOU CYNRIC?' she enquired. 'AN ANGLE WHO CAN SPEAK LATIN, PERHAPS

CYMRAEG TOO. YOU ARE AN ANGLE, BUT YOU HAVE THE FEEL OF THIS COUNTRY ABOUT YOU.'

'I WAS BORN HERE MY LADY,' came Cynric's reply. 'MY FATHER CAME AT THE REQUEST OF THE GREAT KING. I AM BORN TO BRITANNIA. I AM ONE OF MIXED SPIRITS, RECOGNISED BY ALL BUT ACCEPTED BY NONE.'

The path had brought them to a young oak tree, a brown scar at its base where two of Cynric's warriors had dug into the hardening earth. One of them approached and handed Cynric a heavy parcel of lead.

'This is what we find here sir,' the warrior reported.

Taking the object, Cynric turned to eye Gwenllian. 'AND THIS MY LADY, WHAT IS THIS THAT YOU HIDE FROM OUR EYES?'

Gwenllian responded with an expression of puzzlement and observed as Cynric peeled open the lead parcel before her to reveal its contents.

'WHAT IS THIS?' he enquired again.

She shrugged her shoulders.

'IT IS OF IMPORTANCE. YOUR HEADMAN, HE HAS LOST HIS LIFE AFTER ALL, FOR FOLLOWING YOUR ORDERS. SO, LADY, THIS, WHATEVER IT IS, BROKEN AND IN PIECES, IT HAS SIGNIFICANCE DOES IT NOT?'

The shocking act of cruelty shared as some common place deed left Gwenllian numb. A tear in her eye, but with command in her voice she demanded, 'WHY DID YOU MURDER THE HEADMAN?'

Cynric met her gaze before responding, 'WE DON'T TRUST THESE NATIVE PEOPLE. THEY'LL BE IN LEAGUE WITH THE HOUSE OF GWYNEDD, AND THIS' – he held out the parcel of lead – 'IT IS SOME SIGN, SOME MESSAGE?' He looked into the lead parcel containing moss and some broken pieces of curved wood.

Gwenllian, holding her right hand across her face, her hair falling in front, struggled to suppress her anger and frustration.

'YOU'VE KILLED A MAN FOR NOTHING!' she spat out. 'YOU'VE COME HERE FOR NOTHING. THERE IS NO BRITANNIA. THE GAME IS OVER, IT HAS BEEN OVER THESE LAST FEW YEARS. THE BRITONS WILL NOT RISE AS ONE AGAIN.'

Cynric, clearly giving her words no regard questioned once again, 'THIS MESSAGE, WHAT IS IT YOU LEAVE BEHIND HERE AND IN THIS PLACE. A SPECIAL PLACE, YES? KNOWN TO OTHERS WHO MIGHT COME LOOKING?'

'IT IS NOTHING. IT HAS NO MESSAGE FOR BATTLE. IT IS A RELIGIOUS ARTEFACT WITH MEANING ONLY FOR THOSE WHO MIGHT BELIEVE.'

'Wynfere,' he spoke with the English version for her name. 'INDULGE ME, WHAT RELIGIOUS MEANING HAS THIS?'

So, Gwenllian indulged the Angle's curiosity. She retold the story of this object, a wooden cup that had been brought from the east and made as a gift to Arth. The cup from the last supper when Christ broke the bread and shared out the wine.

Cynric shrugged his shoulders in distain. 'CHRISTIAN FAIRY TALES THAT PROPAGATED WEAKNESS LIKE A DISEASE ACROSS THE EMPIRE.' She could see him looking into the parcel, taking out pieces of curved wood that were once a goblet. He counted the shards in front of her: one, two, three, four and five.

'THE OAK?' he enquired. 'WHY BURY THIS HERE?'

'SO THAT IT MIGHT BE FOUND AND TAKEN TO HOLY SANCTUARY,' Gwenllian replied.

'BAH, YOU BELIEVE IN RUBBISH LADY!' Despite his words, Cynric observed her closely. He pushed the lead package back into shape and motioned to one of his men. Taking the package from Cynric the men dumped it back into its hole and kicked the clods of earth and turf back as infill.

Cynric had turned back towards her but she looked down so as not to catch his eye. The cold was bitter and she crossed her arms tightly over her chest as her body shivered violently against the icy wind. Cynric unclipped his heavy sheepskin throw from his shoulders and, walking up to her, he wrapped it over her shoulders. The two men at the burial had stopped; they had noticed this small but significant display of affection.

16   The Roman Girl

September

Philomena had spent the entire summer setting up for her first semester at Trinity. She had initially fostered a now misguided notion that most of her work time would be dedicated to research with just the odd tutorial or lecture. In reality the teaching schedule was pretty full on and there seemed to be a high commitment to the students here.

A big surprise had been meeting up with Giles once again. *How on Earth had he managed to secure a position here?* She'd wondered. A nod and a curt 'Miss Hutchinson' had been the welcome on her first day before the long summer break. He'd probably been appointed at about the same time but hadn't been able to start and all she'd known was that another research fellow was joining her in the department. From the initial introductions in July, Philomena reckoned the surprise was as much for him as it was for her with his wide-eyed look of astonishment. Their paths hadn't crossed all that often over that summer.

They shared an office and today he was moaning.

'We're working with bloody students!' he exclaimed.

'You have prepared for your courses I hope Giles,' Philomena responded, a quip designed to irritate, as she knew full well that he'd spent the summer on his own research work believing that he was above any involvement with the students. The departmental head had put him

219

straight this morning and he was now sliding into a meltdown having received his confirmed timetable for the autumn semester.

'You were a student once,' Philomena continued, getting a bit of her own back, but she couldn't be too mean. He was going to go down like the Titanic with students and she was more than a little fearful on his behalf, so much so that she was considering trying to help him out. Mind, who was going to be there to help her out?

The semester had begun, and she was already finding after a first week with the students, that there was just too much to do and that you couldn't fit it all in a day. The students were going through what counted for freshers in Trinity. During the day they were turning up for introductory sessions for modules and deciding on the structure of their courses. There were going to be changes throughout the week as modules filled up or because students had to change as their first-choice options wouldn't fit in the timetable.

Today looked to be a busy one, with a group in for an introduction to one of Philomena's learning modules this morning. First year students fresh in. At lunch time she had a meeting with a Ken someone from the Clwyd Powys Archaeological Trust and Philomena needed to check his surname along with some notes for the meeting straight after her lecture; she knew the surname sounded French. He was working for the Clwyd Powys Archaeological Trust, now that was a job she quite fancied. Charging around Wales, checking in on known ancient monuments and sorting out rescue projects for those that were in imminent danger of being lost to erosion or land management.

Instead, she was here getting increasingly nervous about the teaching commitments which seemed to be growing daily thanks to her head of department. Being conscientious, Philomena tended to over prepare – better having done too much than too little and the sessions she had taken so far this term hadn't been a total disaster; moreover, her lectures were very well attended.

This morning's lot were going to be a mix. There could be straight archaeology students here, but the module could also be taken by those on a BEd course. The module explored life in Roman Britain and Wales. She was using her own slides to illustrate the introduction and the darkened room made talking to the students easier – they were a quiet lot once she'd got started and seemed happy to sit through the talk. Perhaps there had been a big night in the Student's Union the previous evening as the students seemed quiet with none of the usual questions. The room was also dark so the faces in front of her weren't so distinct.

Suddenly the time was up, and she brought the lecture to an end with reminders for the students about the time and place for the next lecture. Philomena then busied herself with the lights, opening the blinds and packing up the projector. There hadn't been any questions, just the buzz of students packing up and leaving for the next session.

She checked her watch. Her timing was spot on and she was pleased – she could award herself one smiley sticker for today at least. Looking up, she noticed that one student had remained, standing towards the back of the room. Philomena experienced a sudden feeling of dread and her heart beat faster. A little voice in her head said, *Oh not today, please not today.*

This student had a small purple and black backpack slung over her left shoulder. She was wearing a light, patterned, long-sleeved blouse, faded baggy jeans frayed at the pockets and knees, and a pair of worn leather sandals. Philomena took all this visual information in very quickly. The student made her way up to the front, giving Philomena a clear view of her facial features. The student had dark shoulder length hair, deep brown eyes and freckles that ran across the bridge of a dainty, slightly turned up nose – Philomena had seen this girl before.

'A fantastic introduction Miss Hutchinson. You've got a real passion for your subject, and I can see I'm going to very much enjoy your lectures.' Holding out her hand, she continued, 'We never officially met; it's Anya, Miss Anya Richards.'

Philomena pushed her hands deep into her front pockets. She hadn't prepared for this meeting, despite the fact that there was every chance that one day such a meeting was bound to take place and inside, she was cross with herself about her unreadiness.

'I got your letter Anya. Thank you. I'm sorry I haven't yet replied,' Philomena said.

Anya smiled weakly, placing her hand back by her side. 'Never mind, I'm here now. Perhaps we could chat?'

'Yes, sure,' Philomena responded. 'I don't want to seem unpleasant but, I'm not sure I want to shake your hand just yet.'

Anya's eyes widened.

'It might be me just being silly but strange things have happened to me when I've touched people from…'

Anya was now observing her closely.

'Would you like a coffee or something?' Philomena asked trying to make the meeting less awkward and Anya nodded in agreement.

'We'll go over to the office I share. Could you take some of my files over for me and I'll carry the projector?'

Anya dutifully scooped up the files and followed Philomena out through the door, along a corridor and down a short flight of stairs that led out to a somewhat beautiful garden where Magnolia trees had recently been in flower, their rich pink petals littering the pathways.

'It's just over this way at the other end of the garden,' Philomena said, turning back to Anya. 'We're underneath where the old coal fired boilers once were. Something of a joke I think with the college authorities. Put us in the dark at the bottom they have. They know we archaeologists like digging in deep dark holes.'

They arrived at the building which had an entrance at ground level and a set of steps going down to a basement on the right-hand side. Philomena led the way down, pushing open the door and entering a corridor beyond.

On entering her office, Philomena considered how it must look to Anya. Something like Indiana Jones' storeroom she imagined. The floor to ceiling shelving was crammed with books and file boxes, stacks of maps, another slide projector and boxes of slides. There was a double table which divided the room in two, one cluttered with trays of pottery, the other side somewhat more organised with what looked like an Apple Mac II computer all wired up and ready for action. Philomena plonked her pile of stuff on the first table.

'Now, what the Hell has he done with the chairs in here?' Philomena stated, somewhat exasperated – Giles had clearly taken them all out, leaving just one for himself. Philomena left the room in search for one, giving Anya the opportunity to nose around. Luckily, she didn't have to look too far and Philomena lifted the additional chair into the room, catching the door frame with the chair legs as she did so.

Taking a seat, Anya pointed to a photograph on the other desk. 'Oh my God,' she whispered, 'it's Paul Pot. You share an office with Paul Pot?'

Philomena responded with a broad smile. 'So, you've met my colleague then?'

'Christ, the most painfully boring person on Earth,' Anya stated. 'I have him as a lecturer *and* as my personal tutor.'

It was just as Philomena had thought and she couldn't help laughing. 'It didn't take you lot long to come up with that nickname.'

Anya rested her arms on the table. The sleeve on her left arm rose up, displaying the many scars on the underside of her wrist. Philomena's eyes narrowed observing this and Anya quickly pulled the sleeve down.

Philomena hadn't observed things like this first-hand before; she was a little shocked, this was something outside her own experience of life.

While Anya was attractive, particularly from a distance, up close Philomena could see the fragility. Anya wasn't quite what she remembered; didn't match her expectations somehow. Philomena was picking up a feeling about her too – Anya was quite shy perhaps, quietly spoken. That would explain why Tim had such a crush on her. Yet, when Philomena had last seen her... Anya had looked stylish, obviously coming from money.

Had something happened there? There was an aura about her, one of deep sadness.

'Can I show you something?' Philomena offered, to break the ice. Without waiting for Anya's response, she reached up to a box file on the top shelf in the office. She put the box on the desk between them and depressed the release button so that the lid flicked up. Opening the lid fully, Philomena brought out the roll of paper.

'He gave this to me before I left Ruthin. I found it again recently, took another look. Don't know, hadn't wanted to look until now because, well, I didn't want to spoil my memory of him. I'd kind of developed an overly flattering image of him you see, in my imagination. Didn't want to spoil that image, shatter the memory. Take a look,' she said and in so doing she rolled off the elastic bands and pulled the paper out flat so that Anya could see the image.

'What's this?' Anya pointed out the sword that ran through the middle of the portrait.

'Excalibur. Tim had an imagination, but I guess you'd know because you were in school with him.'

'He tells me a lot about you,' Anya responded.

Philomena raised her eyebrows, noting Anya's use of the present tense.

Anya smiled and released the paper which rolled back up on its own. 'His notes – Tim talks about you and I'd like to know, I'd like to understand better some of the things he says about you.'

'Notes?' Philomena questioned. She held an image in her head of Tim writing until late in the night. It was part of her being able to read him, read his mind. Her last night in Ruthin when she had left him early and in bed she had turned over on the pillow and closed her eyes. The writing was for him – she didn't need to know everything. Not then, not at that time.

'Are you going to tell me what he wrote?' Philomena asked.

'Did you know about Tim's notebook?'

'He never talked about a notebook to me Anya. When did he give you this notebook?'

'He didn't. I found it in the library – I think he'd left it there for me to find.'

'So, you've got it with you? May I see it?'

'Later perhaps,' came Anya's reply. 'Some things he said, they're a little fantastical.' Anya had fixed her with a serious look. 'I think I could ask you a lot of questions about your visit to that clairvoyant or the warning you gave Tim,' Anya stated.

'Warning?' Philomena asked, somewhat puzzled.

'You told Tim to be careful, that there were a lot of ghosts and that some of them weren't dead.'

Philomena narrowed her eyes. 'Not sure I put it quite like that – what did he actually write in his notebook?' She was slightly irritated. Anya clearly seemed to have lots of more detailed information about the time she and Tim had spent together – Philomena wasn't sure she wanted that known. As Anya had put it – the details were more than a little fantastical, weren't they?

'These languages you can speak, that's clever isn't it? And the mind reading, that's rubbish, yes? You were just trying to impress Tim?' Anya continued, ignoring her question and putting her on the spot.

Philomena rested back in her chair, twitching her nose.

'You've made your mind up about me then Anya. I'd made it all up just for fun because I liked leading Tim on. I liked the Famous Five adventure of it all.'

'Why did you all go and see that clairvoyant? If you are for real, wouldn't you have known?'

'Known what?' Philomena responded.

'That it was a dangerous thing to do. That family, you'd have known,' Anya persisted, and Philomena was now shaking her head.

'I'd like to see Tim's notes. I'd no idea what was going to happen in that house. The photograph, Andrew Cooper wanted to know something about that ghost he'd photographed, and he'd heard about this Mod Evans. We went with Andrew, more for moral support really. It seemed like an exciting, if slightly scary, thing to do at the time, but I didn't believe in all that nonsense. I kind of thought there was going to be someone with a crystal ball, and it would be all theatrical and a bit silly. I wanted to go and join in – it was a chance to be with Tim. I got to sit next to him in the back of the car.'

Now Philomena returned a serious look back.

'You didn't know that did you? You didn't know that I liked Tim, that I wanted to be with him.'

Anya didn't respond straight away, and Philomena could see that the other girl was considering, thinking about what she was going to say next.

'Then why just leave him?' came Anya's response finally.

'I didn't know it was all going to end the way it did. That Mod Evans guy was proper bonkers and nasty, but he was alive when we left him. He scared us all but...' Philomena paused. 'I don't think Tim liked me in the same way – there was someone else you see.'

'And you'd know because you can read other people's minds, right? Could you read my mind too Philomena?'

'Miss Hutchinson!' There was a call from the corridor outside and a knock at the office door. 'Your appointment, a gentleman from the Clwyd Powys Archaeological Trust.'

Philomena pushed her chair back to stand. 'I'm sorry, we're going to have to finish here for now.' She held the door for Anya to leave. 'I'd love to see those notes though. I don't know what Tim wrote but I'm very sure he didn't say that I could see into the future Anya. Perhaps we could look at them together?'

Anya nodded and left.

* * *

Llandudno AD 1989
October

The book had moved on very little these last five months. There had been this very flattering, nice request from North Wales Police for him to do some interesting consultancy work and he'd been dragged back in. Angharad wasn't too impressed at first but hadn't kicked off too much – the work got him out of the house, out from under her feet.

This afternoon's meeting of the wrinklies was at the Royal Imperial in Llandudno for lunch. Superb service, excellent food and stunning surroundings. He hadn't been inclined to pass on the invite, but the luncheon meeting was a squeeze on his time today. The usual crowd were present and as was customary, conversation started with fishing, grandchildren, house improvements and pretty pointless small talk but it drifted back to the old job soon enough. Once a copper, always a copper John Morris supposed.

John left his seat to make a trip to the gents. The rest room was actually a work of art in this place, better than the bogs back home with posh hand towels, a spray of flowers, liquid soap and hand cream on tap. It was all a far cry from the seedy 'spit and sawdust' dumps most often frequented by their clientele.

Leaving, he entered the corridor, but his way out was blocked. A younger, attractive woman smouldered against the narrow wall, an insincere smile on her face. The DI wondered if she was the wife or partner of some villain he'd locked up in the past, he was struggling to place her. Strange, he had a good memory for names and faces.

'Not talking about me this afternoon then Detective Inspector.' She spoke with a deep silky-smooth voice and then she leaned in and the door for the ladies opened, allowing her to slip away and out of view.

His eyes met hers for just a fraction of a second and a name came to him – Kelly, Kelly Jade Evans.

Trinity College Carmarthen AD 1989
September

Now, time to take stock. Why was she here in Trinity? Why had she chosen to study archaeology – it was hardly a good career choice. Had she picked this to do because of Tim? Was she now in Trinity because of a desire to meet and find out what had happened to him from Philomena?

She'd picked archaeology as something to do in a night course – to keep her social worker happy. It would be an easy subject she'd thought, but there was also the connection to Tim. She had come to Carmarthen – why?

Be honest with yourself Anya, she thought. *You're here because of Philomena, no other reason. You'd have changed your mind had you not seen her name in the prospectus. So, what if there is nothing behind all of this in the end?*

Just what did she believe? Anya was summing up. She believed that there was something more to Tim's death – there was something supernatural. She had physical proof – her right arm. That being the case, then how much of a leap of faith did she need to accept Tim's notes about Philomena. The girl could either speak the languages or she couldn't. With a first from Oxford she probably could; she was almost certainly quite gifted with languages. Then there was the reading of minds? Could she believe that?

231

What now did she, Anya, want from all of this? She wanted things explained. Did she suspect Philomena was somehow implicated in Tim's death? That didn't seem likely now, but Anya didn't think Philomena was being all that open with her either. Could she blame Philomena for that? A serious professional would be careful about discussing their own supernatural powers or a belief in… reincarnation, as Tim had suggested in his notes.

What about her future now – this course would be interesting and she had a chance at being a student again, but she should select her modules with care. The longer she was away from the antique business the more she missed it. Perhaps she should do some of the design or history of art modules.

Anya came to stand at the window overlooking the street below. She'd opted to live outside the college accommodation in a shared student house on College Road. Some of the students had already given up and she pretty much had the house to herself at the moment.

Anya's thought returned to Philomena. She would be about the same age. Perhaps she could invite her out for a drink one night – that would be less confrontational. Maybe they could talk this through together.

* * *

'I'm not stalking you, honestly,' Anya greeted Philomena as the other woman came out of the Halliwell Lecture Theatre.

'Oh, Anya hi.' Philomena looked up an expression of wariness on her face.

'Tough lecture – busy day?' Anya continued. 'I thought perhaps we could meet up for a drink some time? I'd bring the notebook with me.'

Philomena was obviously in a rush to get away at the end of the lecture. Anya was having to walk quickly to keep up with Philomena. The woman walked quickly.

Philomena shrugged her shoulders. 'I'm not sure you'd believe a word I say.'

Overtaking Philomena and turning to stop her, Anya said, 'Try me, I just might.'

Philomena frowned.

'I'm stuck on my own here at the moment,' Anya went on. 'I'm in one of the student houses off campus. It was full last week but a load of them have already quit, given up. So, there's just me and Lottie. She's got some long-term boyfriend. Seems to be at home with him more than in college.'

'Right.'

'I could do with some good company and well… if it doesn't work out, I won't bother you again – I promise.'

'I drink Bacardi and Coke. Can you stretch to that Anya?'

'If you can stretch to Vodka?'

'That's hard stuff.'

'Oh, you can add some blackcurrant to it if you like. So?'

'OK, you've talked me into it. We could meet later this evening. Do you know the Ceffyl Du pub?'

'I've heard some of the students talk about it. Sounds a dive – they all go there to get drunk,' Anya responded.

'Yeah, that would be right.' Philomena gave a smile which Anya reciprocated and then Anya noticed an observing, questioning look from Philomena. Anya guessed that she would have questions. Questions about her own story these last few years. Philomena would have noticed her teeth and there was a pang of sudden distress in Anya's heart. She was not the same now; she was damaged and that had all been self-inflicted.

* * *

Y Ceffyl Du AD 1989
September

As Philomena approached the bar, she wondered whether she had made a wise choice in the venue for her meeting with Anya. It had been an almost instinctive suggestion earlier that afternoon but now, on entering this place she felt the risk all too keenly. The name had meant very little to Anya.

Philomena had arrived early to check the place out – just in case she felt something here. The Ceffyl Du was full of farmers after the mart – these would be the lost and the lonely, hanging around to stretch out their one and only day in the city before heading back to their

234

isolated farms or small holdings. Married farmers would have been dragged off by their wives by now – those who were happily married that is. In these parts farming was a tough existence for most, tending to vast tracts of rural agricultural land, much of it only just viable especially as you headed inland.

There was a wall of noisy, wellington boot, Macintosh clad men at the bar and Philomena waited for one to head off to the loo in order to get in through the gap. She neatly side-stepped up and made her order – her Bacardi and a vodka and black for Anya.

There was suddenly a thick arm around her waist as a short fat drunken farmer pulled her in close to him.

'*O Duw, Cymro neu Sais?*' He'd truly hit the jack pot with Philomena.

Untangling his fingers and pushing him away she spat out, '*Cer! Shiw!*'

There followed a great deal of expletive grumbling in Welsh from the love lost man, but Philomena ignored him and paid, grabbing her drinks and heading off.

'Anya!' Philomena called over from a corner, as the other girl entered through the main door. Philomena pointed to an empty seat. 'Do you want to sit where I am, facing the bar or…?'

'I'm OK here,' Anya responded and thanked Philomena for the drink.

'I'm keeping an eye on the bar,' Philomena continued, 'on who comes in. If you see a distinguished old gent, silver hair pulled into a ponytail, cowboy hat, posh wellies, dungarees complete with ferrets, let me know.'

Anya gave a slightly bemused look. 'A boyfriend of yours? And what happens if we spot him?'

'Don't know,' Philomena returned 'but you can expect drama if he's here that's for sure.' Before Anya could ask any more questions, Philomena continued, 'Did you bring those notes Anya?'

'Sure.' Anya took the notebook from her bag and passed it on to Philomena.

It brought a smile to Philomena's face as she turned the pages one at a time. 'Good at spelling, wasn't he?' she commented before stopping at one of the press cuttings.

'It gets much more interesting towards the end,' Anya added.

'No, for me it starts here.' The cutting was an article from the *Daily Post* with a *'WE DIG THE ROMANS!''* headline. Philomena could almost remember the people in the photograph, familiar faces all lined up for the picture preparing to dig with their spades down. There was a lively quote from Professor Bari Jones, spicing up his excavation at Rhyn Park for the reader. Tim had made a comment in biro next to the cutting saying that he had spent two days helping out in August 1980. He hadn't mentioned seeing a girl there and although it confirmed for her that he had been at the excavation she was disappointed in the fact that there was no mention of anything more.

'That was my first dig. I joined it as a very enthusiastic innocent schoolgirl. When I left things were different, I was different, haunted even. Ever since, piece by piece some strange jigsaw has been coming together.'

'What do you mean?'

'From the very first night camping out at the dig I had vivid consecutive dreams. Then I saw Tim. I wanted to meet him. I wanted to talk to him so much because somehow, he was part of it all. I was living in Coventry then you know. What are the chances of me having a grandmother living in Ruthin, in my meeting up with Tim again?'

'Slim,' Anya responded. 'Are you sure the boy on the dig and Tim were one and the same?'

'Absolutely, and this little press cutting, this confirms for me that he was there.'

'OK, I'm going to accept that there is definitely something odd going on Philomena. If you could do what Tim said in his notes and you believe it then OK. I know from personal physical experience how strange things can happen and I don't believe Tim's murder was just a random incident. I think there was more which I guess is one of the reasons I'm here in Carmarthen. The haunted feeling Philomena, what do you mean by that?'

'The dreams at Rhyn Park were too real, like I was being reminded about a life before. There were ancient languages in my dreams and after I'd woken, I still knew them, could read Latin and understand it for the first time' Philomena responded. 'There's a ghost in Ruthin too – I saw the photographs. It's like there was some presence with us and I remember feeling uncomfortable about that. But I didn't really feel threatened, not like Tim. I think he was frightened, especially on his own on that path.'

'The path?' Anya questioned, 'he's got some notes about that. Where is it?'

'It's a short cut up from town to where he lived. It's where we met for the second time and that ghost is part of all this. A photograph of it in the church and then on that path – coming closer. Gives me the shivers when I think about it now.'

'A presence?' Anya took a sip of her vodka. 'I feel Tim is still with me sometimes Philomena, but he's stronger, wiser. He knows, and he's waiting. He's been waiting for me'

Anya pulled up her left sleeve. 'I caught you looking. These cuts across my wrist – they should have been much deeper. Things hadn't exactly been going well for me before and after Tim's death. I wasted three years of my life on drugs.'

Anya fell silent for a short while. Philomena said nothing, sensing that Anya had more to say. A thought came into her mind. Anya had been someone else, someone important from the past.

'At the end,' Anya continued, 'Tim pulled me closer. He said he'd be there for me when… when darkness comes and that he would be waiting for me.'

'I hadn't realised he'd spoken to you at the very end.'

Anya gave a puzzled look. 'You hadn't realised Philomena? What do you mean?'

Philomena looked seriously into her drink. 'That night, I was here in this pub. I had some kind of vision and saw it all happen… I watched Tim walk into the packed disco, looking for you. He was pushing through the crowd towards you. Tom Evans was already there waiting. Tom calmly walked through the crowd towards Tim and as he did, he dropped a blade he was hiding. It slipped down his arm and into his left hand and then, without warning he punched out towards Tim. I called out, willed you to do something and you shouted and then the connection was gone. I could see no more, and I was no longer with all of you. I heard nothing more until I was back in Oxford and Gran wrote to me, sending a newspaper cutting about the murder.'

There was a silence between the two girls before Anya spoke.

'The DI said you'd called in to make a statement to the police, that you'd given an accurate description of Tom Evans and that your account of the events matched the statement Tom made to the police. That baffled him a bit I think.'

'I didn't think Tim had been murdered,' Philomena responded. 'In my vision your shout distracted Tim's attacker and the thrust was off target. I thought because of that vision I had helped to save Tim.'

'I didn't shout out,' Anya whispered. 'I had no warning.'

Philomena shook her head. 'I don't get it. Why then did I have that vision here?'

17 Tumulus

Ruthin AD 526

Late Spring

Meugan had positioned himself at the very front of the canoe, eyes watchful as his father, Llyr, at the rear, provided the power that enabled the vessel to glide through the shallow marsh waters.

Meugan had spotted something out in the lake, glinting in the mean pale light of a winter's afternoon. It had however, taken many weeks to persuade Llyr to take him out onto the waters in the log cut canoe. You see, Meugan was dreamy and prone to fanciful notions. Heaven knew, the autumn and winter months had brought so much this year to fire up the young lad's imagination.

Arth and the last warriors of Britannia had arrived in their village at summer's end, just as the nights were starting to draw in. They were followed by Gwenllian, the first-born daughter of the Ordovices, a princess, betrothed to Arth and Britannia. Then the Britons had left and soon after, the Angles had arrived. Crossing the high pass at Bwlch Pen Barras they had descended into the Vale and Cambria for the first time; arriving as unwelcome visitors and hunters in the pursuit of Arth. It had been a brief but uncomfortable visit. Armed and aggressive, these Angles cared little for their hosts.

All this coming and going was more excitement than young Meugan could manage. Then there had been Gwenllian's return and her capture. There followed the awful news that a body had been discovered up on the high pass. The details, shocking as they were, had not been shared with Meugan who was far too young and sensitive to know of such horrors.

So here he was on some fool's errand urged on by his excitable son. The child's insistence, rather than fading away, had persisted day after day, week after week. Not wanting to give in to this stupidity, Llyr had relented with an excuse that it was now high time that the eel traps be checked for repairs.

'Dad, dad!' The young lad was gesticulating and pointing from the bow of the vessel.

'Well I never,' Llyr uttered, dropping the paddle to bring the canoe through a sideways glide to a resting position.

'Reach out lad!' Llyr called to his son 'Reach out and hold on hard as she'll have a good weight I reckon.'

The boy reached out with eyes on the prize and no thought to his own balance. Two keen hands clasped pummel and grip and the great blade slipped from its anchorage. The boy leaned back to set the length free and clear of the mire.

So, the boy had been right all this time; more, this was not a common piece for use in combat today. This was a long sword, the grip fashioned in the style of an ancestor god, balanced and true. A weapon for heroic combat, one on one, in the time of the ancients.

As the two gazed on at this great prize, the canoe, stirred on by the boy's movements had continued to slip gently through the waters

242

before being brought to a rest against a rise of land that just cleared the mere, deeper today following the winter rains. The canoe snagged now in vegetation, but the father could see beyond and what lay on the rise. Metal and leather fittings, although disarticulated and in some cases chewed, were still enough to identify a scatter of bones that lay there. Llyr pushed the paddle deep and with one smooth powerful motion reversed the canoe, taking it back out once more into open waters and away from this island.

'Well boy,' Llyr addressed his son. 'Hold on tight and we'll land our catch on firm ground.' With this, the father turned the canoe so that it faced away from the island and he propelled it back to the bank, Meugan jumping out with the rope to pull the vessel in.

'Father, what was it?' the child enquired. 'You know, on the island back there in the middle of the marsh?'

'Best keep away son,' came the reply. 'It's an ancient place. A place where the wolves gather.'

Returning to the village with his son, Llyr observed new banners flapping atop the tall poles in the forum square. His heart sank with the thought of yet more new arrivals, more unwelcome guests. The banners, long pointed triangles, depicted some sort of animal in red on a white background. Llyr could make no identification of this animal; neither could he identify the visitors from their banners. Another English war party perhaps? He did not know.

Llyr and his son came up and into the village through a side entrance. The boy had also seen the banners and excitedly fired questions at his father. The boy did not know the seriousness of such events. To him this was just another adventure.

'Shall we show these visitors the great sword Dad?' the boy suggested.

'No lad let's keep our discovery to ourselves for now,' Llyr responded. The reply took the wind out of the boy's sails.

'Are these visitors, will they not be so friendly like the Angles Dad?' came the boy's returning question. Llyr nodded and put his index finger to his lips to silence any further discussion from the boy.

Llyr carried the great sword but had taken the time to wrap it well in some sacking. This had taken a few minutes on landing the dugout canoe but the decision to do so now seemed to have been a good precaution. Llyr guided his son away from the village centre and the main thoroughfares. He had decided to make for the house via the side alleys where he hoped they would not be noticed. They had clearly been on the marsh for longer than he had planned, and they had visited not one single eel trap.

'Llyr!' A call from behind stopped both man and son in their tracks.

'We've been looking for you. There's someone here that wants to speak to you. We have visitors. Come, you're needed at the old forum, the officers' building.'

Llyr considered passing the sword onto his son to take on home but thought better of it. He was the adult, and it was his duty to take the responsibility for this find. Llyr sent the lad home, encouraging him to keep his tongue and make haste. Llyr then turned and nodded to the villager who had hailed him and together they went back around to the officers' building at the village forum.

The larger, more imposing structure within the village had been so remembered as one connected with control from when this place acted as an auxiliary station. The building had several steps up to the main set of entrances and in its prime it would have been an impressive structure. It had, however, fallen into a state of disrepair, no longer having quite the wow effect that it must once have surely commanded.

Tall banners had been planted in front of this building, their brightly coloured cloths flapping in the breeze. On the steps, several visitors stood in discussion with some of the locals. On the other side of the square were men at arms. They were stood down, but Llyr considered that they could rapidly redeploy with a bark from the right man.

'Ah here he is!' one of those on the steps called out by way of a greeting.

'Llyr, our new headman, yes?' came an encouraging voice and one of the men scampered down the steps and made his way towards them, flanked by several others who were armed. The visitor held out a hand of welcome.

'Your reputation and good name travel far beyond this place,' he stated. They shook hands as the visitor continued, 'I'm a good judge of character and it will be on your shoulders to be the new headman for this place and govern in my name Llyr. I need someone with a sound sense of justice and purpose; someone strong here on the edge of my kingdom.'

Through this statement the visitor had identified himself and Llyr bowed quickly with reverence and respect.

The visitor eyed the wrapped package Llyr was holding.

'Not very well disguised,' the visitor stated, and he reached out to touch the wrappings.

'Sir, I have bad news.' Llyr gave an explanation of what he and his son had discovered earlier that morning.

The visitor listened; he was silent and thoughtful.

'Your son, Meugan, I should like to meet the lad one day. I'm sure he does you proud Llyr.' He then nodded towards the sword. 'It's too late now, you and your son, you must go back out in the canoe and return this to the mere.'

'I will see to it sir.'

The Lord of Gwynedd nodded, placing his hand over Llyr's shoulder, guiding him towards the forum building. 'And of Gwenllian, what news?'

Llyr shook his head and looked down at his feet.

'She is also lost then.'

The two men began to mount the steps up to the doorway. On the third step, the lord stopped and addressed one of his armed men who stood rigid and on guard. For Llyr there was a sudden recognition of the man's face, he had been one of Arth's men, Huail. He had been picked out to escort Gwenllian. The silence was crushing as the lord gently tapped on Huail's shoulder.

'My brother entrusted you with an important task.' He left the statement hanging. Huail's eyes blinked; he was sweating. Then calmly the lord brought his hand down, washing his hands of the man that he had addressed. This man, Huail, he was nothing, as if he was no longer there.

The lord nodded at Llyr and the two continued their ascent. At the top, the lord clicked his fingers and Llyr could hear a scuffle as other armed men held Huail who was taken away and out of sight. The screams, the pleading, the wailing, was unsettling, traumatic. Llyr closed his eyes and wished that time would move on.

The condemned man was brought to a rough chunk of rock that sat in the centre of the square. It was something that did not belong, as if it had been dropped by some giant, discarded and yet strangely revered. It was on this rock that Huail was crudely decapitated in a horrid, squalid scene.

* * *

Carmarthen/ Trinity AD 1990
January

Philomena and Anya had met perhaps two or three times since their first encounter. For Anya, the story had developed little further. Today she'd agreed to meet Philomena after one of her lectures. The room had emptied but only slowly and Anya observed the last students in her group amble past and out through the door. Philomena had quietly come up to sit before her at the high worktop. This was a science lab which the archaeology department used for a number of their lectures.

'So, what have you got for me?' Philomena questioned.

Anya took something out of her backpack, it was wrapped in a in a tea cloth. She placed the object reverently on the table-top in front of Philomena and said nothing.

Philomena reached over and opened the package up. Anya watched, but said nothing, allowing the other woman to explore without guidance.

'Ah,' Philomena announced 'I've seen this before. Tim's cool little stone. He showed it to me the day before I left. He said he'd found it on the old burial mound in a field just out of town.'

Philomena picked the stone up; it sat quite comfortably in the palm of her hand. 'How did you come by this then?'

Anya said nothing, just observed, waiting in anticipation for what might happen next. Philomena was studying the markings closely.

'You know,' she began, 'back in Tim's place these markings just looked like scratches, no meaning. No language that you could make out but now… now I can see something in this. The markings in the outer circle, look.' Philomena held out the stone to Anya so she could have a clear view.

'These markings, I'm seeing little pictures, no, figures. Looking for a second time, I think these are people,' Philomena stated. 'What do you reckon Anya?'

Anya was somewhat perplexed. She had expected Philomena to trace round the circles with her finger but in all of this Philomena hadn't touched the surface markings once. Why not?

'Yeah, the more I look, the more I see.' Philomena was now in full archaeologist mode. 'Five figures in all, two girls or women, look, there's a slight suggestion, head, chest.' Philomena was pointing out with her finger, but not touching.

Anya found herself nodding – they were there if you looked hard enough, if you squinted your eyes.

'Cup shapes, female – kind of an agreed representation. And these, well use your imagination, I'm guessing they represent male figures. Yes, three male figures and two females. I didn't see it at the time and Tim was thinking about some sort of compass, like some sort of directional device.'

'Tim, Jones, Cooper, you and I,' Anya announced.

Philomena observed her, narrowing her eyes. There was a short silence.

'Why are you linking this stone, these figures, to us?' Philomena asked. 'How can this possibly have any connection to us?'

'Put your finger on the surface markings Philomena, and you'll see what I mean. You'll, experience the connection.'

'What are you saying?'

Anya shrugged her shoulders 'Do you want to see?'

'See what?'

Anya pushed up the sleeves of her top exposing the skin of her arms which she turned so that her palms faced outwards. Philomena looked and shrugged her shoulders.

'What are you showing me?' she asked. On one arm the skin was quite undamaged, whereas on the other, there were scars, the tell-tale signs of someone who self-harmed. Anya lowered her arms and pulled down her sleeves.

'Go on, feel the power, experience the glory,' Anya egged Philomena on.

'What? Touch it, how do you mean? I'm touching it now, aren't I?' Philomena responded.

'You've done everything but touch the damn thing. Run your finger across the markings, or do you already know, have you already found out?'

Philomena moved to run her finger along the markings. 'I don't know what you think is going to happen. I touched these when I was with Tim, sure I did, and nothing happened then.'

As Philomena's fingers were just about to make contact, Anya deflected her hand, pulling it away from the stone surface.

'Changed my mind. Perhaps you shouldn't touch it after all. I believe there's some sort of spell, a power in those engravings but I don't know if that's a good or bad thing. If you felt nothing before then perhaps you shouldn't touch it now. You won't be tainted if there's something dark, something sinister in those engravings.'

Anya pushed her sleeves up to show her forearms. The left arm was scared – the remains of self-harm and abuse. 'They were both scarred before I touched that stone with my right finger,' Anya stated.

'So, how did things get so bad that you were self-harming and taking drugs?' Philomena asked. 'Where was your family in all of this?'

'Don't you know. I thought you could read minds?' Anya replied.

Philomena returned the stone to the bench and looked Anya in the eye.

'I felt a great sadness in you; that you were somehow lost.' Philomena paused. 'I guess this is the bit you can never believe. Like Tim, you can't accept that I had the ability to read other people's minds, know their thoughts and share their experiences. I knew just what you looked like from Tim's dreams, swimming naked in that dark lake. I saw you at the clock tower on Ruthin Square one afternoon and I knew then that we are all linked. You, me, Tim and the two boys.'

'Dark lake, what lake?' Anya asked.

'That lake in North Wales with the mountains. Llyn Tegid?'

251

'Mum and Dad would take a boat out there to sail when I was in primary school. But I've never swam in Llyn Tegid, not naked and certainly not with Tim. You've got some imagination Philomena.'

'You do swim though don't you, or at least you did. Always bloody thinking about you he was. No, somehow, at some time, you swam in that lake together. The day I drove down to Carmarthen with Gran I knew you were going to meet Tim. I knew you'd talked with Dan Jones before, and he'd helped you to meet Tim.'

Anya pushed her hair back behind her ear with her right hand. She gave Philomena a seriously long hard stare.

'You liked him too and you could see all of this?' she questioned.

'I remember feeling pushed out at the end, that you'd come along and I'd be just a spare part. Perhaps that's why I was warning him. I was being jealous because I'd met him before and...'

'Go on, don't stop there Philomena,' Anya pushed.

'There's a memory in that picture he drew of himself, but Excalibur, it didn't look like that. Not the real Excalibur. The picture, it's Tim and yet it's not. When I looked at that picture, I suddenly had this visual image that he was holding my hands and I remember looking directly into his eyes. I was in another world, in another time for a minute, and then it was all gone.'

Anya was shaking her head; this last bit was just nonsense.

'Are you telling me that you've lived before Philomena? You're an archaeologist, one with a growing reputation at that. You can't believe in reincarnation, surely you can't?'

'No, no I can't, can I?' She lifted her head to look Anya in the eye. 'But it's here Anya, doesn't matter where I go, what I do, my past life it's here and it's with me.'

Anya shook her head again. 'There are some mad things in all this, but Philomena, people write silly books about things like reincarnation. It's all made up, it's not real. People don't die and come back again as someone else, and no way did you ever meet King Arthur because he never existed anyway. You've got a good imagination and perhaps you're good at reading people – guessing what they might be thinking.'

'I know what I know Anya,' Philomena replied with some force.

'Well, this isn't really helping me to understand why Tim died.' Anya started to pull her things together from the lecture.

'I'm sorry, I don't know why he died. We didn't get anything special from the clairvoyant – only the dogs. Perhaps just a good guess – I think Tim was frightened of dogs.'

'Dogs?' Anya questioned.

'Yeah, Mod Evans said something about how the dogs would crush his bleached bones.'

'They sound a nice lot – kind of glad I wasn't there with you when you met up with Mod Evans. I've got to go. We'll catch up again?' Having pushed everything into her backpack, Anya swung it onto her shoulder and started making for the door.

'Yes, OK Anya.' Philomena nodded. 'We'll meet up again.'

18. The Old Dog

Prestatyn AD 1990
June

An ageing woman sat in her comfortable armchair looking out impassively through the living room window. Her right arm rested on the shoulders of her large dog who sat on the floor beside her chair, eyes forward like hers. Together they were enjoying the deep red colours of a sunset on an early summer's evening.

Much had changed in this house over the last few years. Much indeed, Candy Gail considered, after the sudden but welcome passing of Mod, her husband – a vile, embittered, bully of a man.

Life had not dealt a fair hand of cards to Candy. Her own childhood had been chaotic, unbalanced. There had been little real warmth or encouragement. One of six siblings she had not been blessed with intellect and had never developed much in terms of skill. The only possession Candy had once brought to the table had been her physical good looks, but years of emotional strain and oppression had wiped the beauty clean away.

When as a young teenager, she'd fall for any boy who showed her attention; she chose unwisely time and time again. Two tacky unstable marriages and then there was Mod. She'd fallen for him because he too had shown her attention and had admired her. She could not foresee how this man would let her down. Mod, for his part, had taken his time. He had feigned respect and concern for her wellbeing, had spoilt her with affection and gifts and had so lured her quietly into his web of hatred and abuse.

There were both monsters and ghosts in this old woman's world. When with Mod, life had been a nightmare, an endless storm, but, out of the holocaust ash a promise of better times had risen.

Candy ran her tongue along the gaps of her front jaw, confirming the memories of her contemplation. Here, the teeth had been knocked clean out in an explosion of violence that had put her in hospital for days after. She massaged the great dog's neck seeking comfort from her own memories. Tom's attack and her subsequent survival had over time enabled her to build up an inner strength.

Tom, Mod's offspring from a previous relationship with another woman, had lived with them at Mod's insistence. Candy saw him as a troubled child from the start and had never liked him. After the attack, she had learnt how the police had caught up with him. Candy closed her eyes, shutting out the fearful memories. In her mind she could still feel Tom's shouts, him punching her and the bang of the door when he had finally stormed out. These events remained as vivid and real today in her recollection despite years since the passing of that dreadful day.

When Tom had been charged with murder, Candy had made no attempt to support her stepson, the freak. The police had wanted her to press charges too for assault, but his murder conviction had been assured. Besides, at the time she was in no fit state, physically or emotionally, so, she washed her hands of Tom Evans.

With Mod gone and Tom in jail, Candy had time to explore this slum of a house. A house loaded with secrets. There was the downstairs room, locked and bolted; this had been Mod's lair. Now there was an opportunity to investigate. Months had passed before she had felt brave enough to open up the door and explore the room beyond. Even then she had, with every move, expected that harsh growl of a voice, the vice-like grasp hurting her arm. Mod storming back from the dead.

The room contained Mod's bed, two old, battered wardrobes, and piles of magazines that frightened her. There were heaps of bulging A4 envelopes too, of cheap brown manila, shoved under the bed or stacked and crammed in the wardrobes. Mod, the nasty tyrant, had stashed money away, money that could have seen them all fed well, money for the children, all kept for himself. Where had this money come from? She did not know and cared not to find out.

After she'd investigated the room, she'd sat in the front room, an episode of *Emmerdale Farm* on the TV. She'd placed herself in front of the little battered coffee table, with a glass of Mod's best rum, a pack of elastic bands from the newsagents and stacks of these brown manila envelopes. She'd began counting and bundling up the ten-pound notes. On she went through the evening as light turned to darkness outside and still, she was counting. In the end she'd bundled up thousands of pounds worth of notes. It wasn't small money. Now she could afford to live like a queen.

Soon after she'd arranged for a clearance – all Mod's junk and trashy furniture went to the tip. Candy would spend a bit of money now on the house, lift it up, make it habitable. A disinfection to wipe those dreadful memories away. Good days, there hadn't been many, and Candy could remember them all.

A police officer at the door, and Candy was revisiting her memories once again. She could remember the fresh innocence on the young officer's face. The visit, months after Tom's trial had been a surprise.

'Mrs Evans,' the officer had begun, 'I'm really sorry to be the bearer of such bad news. May I come in? Candy had stepped aside and led the officer through to the front room.

'What news officer?' she had questioned nervously.

'It's regarding your stepson Tom. I'm so sorry but he was found dead in his prison cell.'

Candy had nodded, urging the officer to divulge more and motioning for the policewoman to take a seat.

'A suspected suicide,' PC Janes continued. 'Once again, I'm so, so sorry for your loss Mrs Evans.'

Candy remembered smiling broadly at the nervous officer. She had looked so young, too young, and too nice to be in the police.

'A cup of tea, a chocolate biscuit, would you sit with me and chat a little while?' The officer had nodded gratefully.

The young PC had stayed perhaps half an hour before Candy saw the young woman out to the door. Candy had washed her hands of Tom and when the letters came regarding Tom's arrangements, she'd ignored them all, thrown the lot in the bin. And so, Tom Evans had left this world pretty much as he had come into it, unwanted and unloved.

The time when she had truly cried for a loved one was the day that her old dog passed away. Poor old mangey bugger had struggled to even stand up in the end. One morning on coming downstairs Candy had found him curled, stiff, cold and still in his dog basket. At least, in the end she'd been able to bring him in, he had been warm day and night and free from Mod's swearing, his pinching and his thumping. The pitiful yelps of pain still burned into Candy's memory to this day. The loss of her only friend in life had left her truly shattered.

This was not a house you'd want to be alone in and Candy was very quick to find herself another companion. She had bought the Rottweiler as a small pup. Candy had checked the breeding and paid good money for her new companion. She had set about a comprehensive training regime so that he would be, at all times, true to her, his mistress. There were times when he would bark, especially up on the landing at the top of the stairs and she'd make her way up, but there was never anything to see. Once, the dog had got into Mod's old room where he had become hysterical and she had dragged him back out barking, wild, with slobber on his muzzle, and she had slammed the door shut. The house was haunted, and the place would have been an uncomfortable proposition for most people – they'd have moved out.

There was the time when she had called on Dick Abbott the local handyman to fix a lock back to the door for Mod's old room. Dick would never have come by when Mod was alive. Decent, respectful people stayed well clear.

'What you locking this old room up for then Candy?' he'd enquired innocently.

'Mod's old room see,' she'd replied. 'Haunted proper. No one'd want to be wanderin' there by mistake day or night.'

Dick had opened the door and looked inside at the bare, freshly painted room, a window at the far end with a radiator beneath, plain 'Marley' tiles on the floor. He'd quietly pulled the door to, engaged the padlock into its clasp and dropped the keys onto Candy's expecting hand.

So, the house had its ghosts and Candy could just about put up with that. Ghosts weren't solid, couldn't cause you physical harm, could they? Sure, they'd leave the odd dank smell, a touch of cold, but they were no more than air, just ether drifting. Monsters mind, well they were something again.

Some of these monsters had the inconvenient tendency to turn up on the doorstep late at night, hammering at the door of Number 43. Usually, they were creatures from Mod's past. Often drunk, they'd have been on the receiving end of Mod's malice in some bygone time. Years after, brave from the drink, and sound in the knowledge that Mod was not there to face, they'd turn up to have their say. Candy was prepared for such eventualities. The ghosts made sure she was on edge, ready for action, and such unwelcome visitors would face the full rampaging fury from her great Rottweiler dog.

There was one other monster, one that terrified Candy the most. She had expected a visit, had felt now that one was well overdue. Candy knew that she would need to show a great resolve when this visitor finally showed up. There must be no holding back with what she felt she must do should this monster ever call and if needed, the great dog she must command. The creature must do her pitiless bidding; he must launch at the throat and rip all that was life, clean away.

19. Eira Mân, Eira Mawr /
Fine Snow, Deep Snow

The High Pass AD 526

January

The following days after her encounter with Cynric beneath the oak remained bitterly cold. In this time the Angles readied further their departure under pale washed out skies. There had been no thaw but neither had there been fresh snow. What snow that there was lay as small ripples or was wedged up against edges, posts and filled up the gullies in drifts. When the wind blew, a fine swirl of iced powder came with it. Winter now held the world in its vice-like grip.

Some of the Angles had already broken camp to be out and away from this place. These, the first off on the journey, were those of a lower caste. It was for them to test the dangers of the high pass, but with luck they would clear Cambria before the next fall of snow.

Many of the villagers had now absconded, slipping silently away into the countryside, leaving the Angles to make their own preparations. Such moves, considered as treachery, conspired to make the visitors more irritable, apt to lash out, to kick and to swear.

Gwenllian, fed the mean scrapings and pushed to the edge of the hearth's warm glow, became consumed by the winter's deep chill. Her body, frail now, shivered and her teeth chattered continuously. The glowing ember of life deep inside was turning from amber to ash. Pinched, beaten and abused she had been put to menial tasks when it suited, tethered like an animal when it did not.

An argument erupted around her as daylight slipped into darkness, but Gwenllian was near oblivious in her glazed numb state. The English tongue, a mass of jumbled sounds, meant very little to Gwenllian but amongst the voices was that of Cynric. Harsh and commanding, he would not yield. Of this warrior there had been no sign this last day or so and with his absence her treatment by these English had been poor. On his return he wasted no time in broadcasting his displeasure. Counter arguments he beat down but the mutterings of displeasure, these he could not silence. The English, they wanted her stamped out and kicked into the earth, like the last embers of a fire, to put an end to what was once Britannia. They need not stamp so hard, for the fire in her soul had already died.

A cold bitter morning followed and the English broke camp. In the half-light, they moved on so as to catch as much daylight as the season afforded. The arguments continued around Gwenllian; she was aware that she had become the subject of much discussion, was aware that she was not approved of by those who were the more senior of the English. All that was but for Cynric; he remained a lone voice in her support. Not that she heard with much understanding. Her mind was now a numb fuzz as one of the sais tied her wrists together, the rough twine biting sharply into her skin.

A lack of food and her own low spirits had brought on a physical sickness, a dazed weakness. Gwenllian, promised to Arth, last mistress of Britannia, allowed herself to be kicked and dragged into line, the back of the line, with the sick and worthless. The scouts had left long before light, checking the way forward as the vanguard. Cynric had support for the early start. Chances were that they'd make the high pass long before anyone even noticed they'd gone and, in these conditions, they were unlikely to be met by anyone intent on ambush.

The convoy moved on under grey heavy skies along well routed paths which made pleasant easy walking up to the base of the hills. Here the Clwydian mountain range made a sudden sharp rise and the level tracks gave way to prolonged climbs. A cart had lost a wheel at the point where the old Roman road made a steep switch back. Chaos and panic were the result of this unfortunate calamity as the drivers frantically set about rescuing their belongings. Snow had begun to fall as small fluttering particles of ice, silently drifting in little flurries. Then, as the party climbed further, the view of the valley floor below was lost; a breeze had picked up and the air had become a swarming mass of grey and white flakes. The heavy clouds had released their load and now the front of their party was lost from sight to those at the rear.

In all this Gwenllian plodded onwards, white iced powder billowing up at her every footstep. There were ominous shouts and those who would do her harm had seized the advantage. Oblivious, she was dragged away from the line, off the road and down the steep incline, her cape pulled roughly from her head and her long dark hair pulled pitilessly away from her bare neck. There was then a silence as she was pinned, head pushed down towards her knees. Perhaps those who had planned to do her harm were considering their options, the consequences for the actions they were about to take. And in all this, just briefly, there was a break in the blizzard and the skies opened, affording Gwenllian one last longing look at the valley below and Cambria spread out before her.

The window closed as suddenly as it had opened, and the grey swirl of the blizzard returned. Vision was her remaining sense now for the rest was just a bleak, empty, silent stillness and her body had not the time to assimilate the sharp slam down of blade. The crisp white snow before suddenly coloured in deep jets of crimson. Her body was kicked downhill into the deepening drifts. And there she was left, wasted as her assassins climbed back up through the tufts of heather and gorse, dusted in icy white snow, to join the convoy and the journey home to Bernicia.

* * *

Ruthin AD 528

Llyr's heart sank, visitors again. This meant he was in charge and should anything go wrong, on his head be it. It was a fair comment to make that the place felt safer, more secure than it had done in many years. A return of the Angles from across the mountains seemed less likely now that the Kingdom of Gwynedd grew in strength. The old king had regimented his tribe into a military unit, tight and safe in the mountains. The old man didn't live to see the kingdom grow for that was a task he left to his sons.

After a period of consolidation, the eldest son of the House of Gwynedd was ready. Not that he was especially keen and confident to take up such a calling. That, however, made him more suitable than he liked to recognise within himself. From the day of his succession, he had taken no undue risks and like a skilful chess master he had planned his moves in detail with full regard to the consequences of his actions.

So it was that the Britons began to nibble back the lands they once held, lands taken away from them by the Angles. Surely, steadily, the Cymru had moved across the fields and rivers beyond DEVA and up into the Pennines where once the great hillforts of the Brigantes had towered in the mists. These a forgotten people now washed clean away from the face of Roman Britannia. Now, Cymru edged to the very heartlands of Bernicia and for once the Angles were considering their position on this island.

Llyr had set the villagers to opening the great hall, once the officers' block it had become the administrative centre of this place – the red fort, a name the Llys had been given by the lords of Gwynedd.

Llyr was managing well with the general organisation of this place, felt he had actually been correctly chosen for the headman role, but he handled formal occasions with less ease. He would become nervous and worried far too much over minor details. These visitors had not arrived in great numbers, just a handful of riders on this occasion. Perhaps the town could get away without staging such a great welcome event. Llyr considered how he had liked both royal brothers on meeting them. Arth the younger, whose bones had lain bleached on the mound that rose just slightly from the marsh waters, and the man who paid visit to their settlement today. The elder brother who had acceded to the throne.

'We are only passing through this evening.' The elder brother could read his mind now. He well knew his key subjects, understood that his headman here was uncomfortable with formal hospitality events.

'It will be nice to be served just a good meal Llyr, whatever makes good eating for this time of the year.' So, the preparations were made and many of the women folk were far more excited about the coming evening than he. This was a chance to enjoy preparations, see new people and catch up on news from afar.

Later that evening their guest addressed the village headman.

'Llyr, I'm told that your son is a bright young man. One of a caring nature but not too suited for the hard work of town or field. A proposition I would make to you.'

Llyr nodded. 'You have my ears Lord.'

'We need some learned folk Llyr. Do you think he would take to reading and writing? Meugan, your son's name is he not? What are your thoughts to this as his father?'

'It would be a great honour for me Lord and a matter of great wonderment for the lad.'

'I'll send him on then. He'll not be alone. You'll remember I executed Huail on one of my visits here. Perhaps I was too hasty in my decision, but the man had failed to complete the orders he'd been given, and great tragedy was the result. The thought of young Gwenllian's corpse yonder as a result of a man's failing, somewhat upset me. I always liked Gwenllian. Far too young for me of course but she was fair, and we enjoyed giving her a warm welcome at court when as children.' Shaking his head, the visitor continued, 'Such a waste Llyr, such a waste.'

There was silence between the two men, as each considered their memories of such events before the visitor spoke again.

'Huail has a younger brother and I consider that I owe the young man a better chance. Besides, he's a mouthy pain in the arse and sending him away for some learning might be the politic thing to do. I know of a learned teacher down south, an old gent going by the name of Illtud. It is in my mind that both boys, your son and this Gildas, why they can travel south together and be schooled. Illtud, our wise old boy is perched out on some cliff edge down there they say; he has a reputation for good teaching. Christian faith and that, no use for you or I Llyr, but my memory prompts that this faith was important to Gwenllian and so the education, it will be something for which I will pay by way of remembering her.'

20. Dark Angel

Carmarthen AD 1990

May

Anya had kept in touch with Huw through her first year at Trinity, despite not having returned 'home' for either Christmas or Easter. What was there to go back to? She'd let the little house on Love Lane go when she'd become a student in Carmarthen, for it held lots of painful memories. A place where she had been at the lowest point that could be imagined. She was ashamed of the life she had lived there. Anya did not want to return to Denbigh and Huw had not travelled down South to see her.

As the year went by, she had begun to think of him more often. A true friend, nothing physical, no desire, but a friend whose company she missed the longer she was away. She would sit down on a Friday and write to him, and what had started as a once a month event had become once a fortnight over a coffee with the old radio playing away in the background. She well knew how he treasured each letter.

Pouring out her news, her innermost thoughts, sharing the sad days, the good days, it was a release, a kind of therapy. She never got much back in return – Huw was crap at writing letters and non-existent when it came to phone calls, but this was him. No doubt he believed that by replying, by being too enthusiastic and opening out his own heart it would make him seem forward. A stiff old bugger was Huw. So, the traffic was largely one way, not that she minded in the least.

At Trinity you had to go to the porter's office at the main gate in front of Dewi – one of the old halls of residence – to get your mail. Anya was living in one of the college houses so the post should have gone there but for some daft reason it didn't, and she had to collect her post from the porter as if she was on campus. She made a habit of calling in once a week and most of the time there was nothing there. On this occasion, however, there was a letter for her, a handwritten envelope in a clumsy awkward style. Anya recognised the handwriting straight away.

'Oh Huw,' she said out loud, 'it's not like you to write.' She ripped open the envelope to access the letter within. It was clearly one of Huw's longer efforts as there were several pages in blue Basildon Bond. In the letter Huw shared the unhappy news that his mother had recently passed away. He was writing to ask if Anya would attend the funeral. Anya felt a strong sense of sadness for him. The guy didn't have many true friends and his request for her to attend, despite being somewhat economic in written form, was really a desperate plea. In truth Huw was a bit of a sad lost cause, so that made the two of them. His father, from what she could gather, had been a bully and Huw never matched up to the man's expectations. He was very much his mother's boy, but these last few years her physical health had deteriorated, and this, married to a well-established and deepening Alzheimer's condition, had very much taken over his home life – the business being his only escape.

Anya made straight for the payphones on reading Huw's call for help. Of course she would attend. He would have done anything for her, of that she was quite certain, so at the very least she would be right at his side to help him though this ordeal.

* * *

The funeral saw the Church of Wales at its most solemn. To Anya it seemed a dry, emotionless service and she felt Huw had been talked into the hymns and prayers which, although appropriate, weren't exactly a celebration of the life of the recently deceased. Huw had made a stab at a eulogy but struggled greatly with his emotions whilst a handful of somewhat odd-looking relatives and attendees looked on. At the end of the service, she stood by Huw because he had asked her to do so whilst he shook hands and passed pleasantries with the mourners before thanking the gormless vicar. Anya was the focus of many disapproving looks as they all wondered who she was.

The wake was a short affair in the Bull. Sausage rolls and a glass of beer and within the space of an hour they'd all gone home.

'Oh, Huw.' Anya put her arm around his waist as she came to stand beside him at the end. 'I'm so sorry about your mum.'

There were tears in the big man's eyes.

'If you'll have me,' she continued, 'I'd like to come back and help you over the summer?'

For the first time, he put his arm around her.

'I would like that very much,' he replied.

* * *

Prestatyn AD 1989

May

There are some subjects that should never be discussed – secrets to be well hidden from view. In Candy's experience, there were many such taboos, shameful secrets that she had endured and kept. A shared life with Mod Evans would have been more than enough for any sane person but for Candy, unfortunately, life's dark passages did not all end with Mod. There was also the boy, her stepson Tom, a vicious thug who had been long out of control. In Candy's mind however, both Tom and Mod together were in some ways insignificant when she considered what had become of her daughter. Kelly. There was a burning shame that somehow Candy was to blame, that she could and should have done so much more to put things right.

A very bright, pretty girl from an early age, but beyond the attractive sugar-coated looks, Kelly brought before her a banner of dark shadows. Behind the sparkling eyes lay a vile evil steak of malevolence. Even as a little girl Kelly could throw out violent tantrums that brought a great fear to anyone close by; these tantrums were disturbing to witness. There was something sinister and unbalanced about the child. As the girl grew older, the tantrums faded away. They were instead to be replaced by the girl's highly developed powers of manipulation and control. These were honed into a sophisticated art form. There was the precocious illegal interaction with men significantly older than herself. There was the unnerving second sense, a knowledge of things that could not be known and a delight in using such facts to humiliate and destroy others.

The girl was Mod's prodigy and the blame for such a monster lay firmly with the girl's father. Candy was terrified of Mod, but she had shown great strength in the protection of her daughter. A mother knew, understood, that the two must be separated. From the first signs Candy had called on the social services for help, but the veins of poison ran deeply between Mod and Kelly. Far too often father and daughter would act in parallel, rubbishing Candy's witness, taking full advantage of a long line of inept social workers, workers who favoured taking the easy options rather than squaring up to the vile, intimidating Mod Evans. Then Candy would be left alone to face the music.

Eventually Kelly had been removed from the family home. The authorities had acted and there was to be no contact between father and daughter but somehow there was always a connection. Candy had often considered her husband's 'gift' of clairvoyance, how everyone was frightened because they feared for what he had seen in their pasts or what he could predict for their futures. Candy was doubtful; she saw her husband as a clever fraud. But he had access beyond the normal senses. That access came through Kelly, Candy was sure of it.

What had happened then on the afternoon of Mod's death? What was it about the youngsters who had visited for a reading that afternoon? Candy wondered if the death had really been down to something medical – a colossal stroke as described on her husband's death certificate. Candy preferred to accept the real-world explanation – there was some comfort in that. There was, however, always a drift into believing in something occult. The house retained a presence. Oh yes, Mod was still here and despite all of her attempts to disinfect the place she could, in the quiet hours or the dark of night hear him breathe, smell his toxic odour of hate.

Candy remembered the horrid day when Kelly had been taken out of the family home. A girl, that's all she was, but her looks put her as someone who was much older. So much water had passed under the bridge by then and the family home had been deemed as unfit for an adolescent child. She was not being protected by her parents – well, that was the official line. Candy had been thankful that her daughter had been taken away from bad influences, but she had been devastated by the loss too.

For the authorities, everything was a bad influence in this place, Candy included. While Candy knew a covert relationship would continue between father and daughter the relationship between Kelly and her was lost forever. Kelly had spat in her mother's face, threatened her mother using vile obscene language as the police and social worker had dragged the girl out from the house.

Candy had expected Kelly to have attended her father's funeral. Indeed, she had expected Tom there too. The latter had declined, had preferred to remain in custody after the murder. From the former, there had been nothing, an eerie silence then and ever since. Candy had expected her daughter to visit. Candy had dreamed of some reconciliation, but this was a dream, nothing more. The years were passing by; time marched on with no communication and perhaps now, if Kelly still lived, she was lost, was no more to her mother.

* * *

Carmarthen AD 1990

June

Anya had been talked into joining a rescue excavation at the end of the summer semester. A new carpark for a supermarket meant some serious infrastructure changes for this sleepy South Wales town and the civil engineering work would impact on possible archaeological layers. The work was believed to be outside what would have been the Roman town of MORIDUNUM. A rescue excavation was felt necessary to identify the course of the Roman road out and to confirm the existence of post Roman Medieval ribbon development along the old Roman road.

Philomena had been in her element and had used all manner of flattery to persuade Anya to spend a little more time in Carmarthen to help out.

'As a *mature* student you'll be good for the morale of our final year who most definitely need to be taking an active role in what might be an exciting excavation,' she had wheedled.

'Less of the mature please,' Anya had responded but Anya had capitulated, somewhat out of guilt, and had joined the excavation for a week.

The summer had started with some good weather for a change, an escape from the rain and damp of the spring. As the air had warmed, Anya thought more about her future and, if the summer season went well at the old antique shop in Denbigh, she would ask Huw about staying on permanently. That, in turn, meant that she would not come back to Carmarthen to finish off the degree. Anya felt that she had failed the first time around and having completed a first year for the second time, perhaps this wasn't for her. She did feel like a 'mature' student, out of place and that her time to be a student had passed. A big decision, and in truth she should have talked this through with someone as it meant wasting an opportunity, limiting her chances and choices for the future. Anya knew, however, that her personal tutor wasn't up to understanding or talking through anything much and if she had dared mentioned her plans to Philomena, the outcome might be quite different.

Walking down Jobswell Road to the dig site, her small backpack which was slung over her right shoulder pulled down heavily. Last night she'd packed Tim's notebook and stone into bubble wrap and then tough brown wrapping paper. This being her last day on the dig, her intention was to hand the package over to Philomena so she could keep it safe. These items could go with the others in Philomena's box of artefacts.

The small, designated area for exploration at the excavation site had been well chosen. Disturbed modern layers quickly gave way to those very much more ancient. The first graves yielded well-preserved non-Christian remains. Layered, in context finds identified the inhumations as Roman. Urns for cremations were also present. The team had identified one of the graveyards for the Roman town.

Anya had arrived early this morning. She wouldn't be staying for the whole day but wanted to take the opportunity to say goodbye to Philomena who had been off site for the previous few days. Anya now knew a little bit more about Philomena and guessed that after a couple of days away, she would be in early, checking out the progress and what she'd missed. It would be a good chance to catch her. The thing was, and this troubled Anya, was she going to be able to make it clear that the goodbye was something more final?

Walking onto the site was a little bit of a thrill in the early morning. The sun, low down in the sky, cast long, strong shadows on the ground. She was anxious too as she followed her own shadow that

277

stretched out before her. The ground was dry and hard. Walking on she noticed that some of the graves were now empty. The bodies were leaving, and she was leaving too. The remains had been marked up and placed in brown paper bags. They'd be shipped off to some research facility where the pathology would be investigated and discussed in reports yet to be written. No doubt there would be a lot of boring statistics eking out the stories that might be shared from what was left of these people and the lives they had led in the past. Anya detested statistics despite being more than competent with them. The first degree that she had started was all about maths and economics, but she had crashed out of the course and the university after that first year.

Noises at the site gate indicated that some of the other volunteers were also arriving. They were making their way to the site hut and the first mug of tea for the day. There was nothing better than a cup of tea outside. The others would have a good chat about this or that – the latest film which a few of them had been down to the Lyric to see the night before. Anya smiled to herself and wondered if they'd enjoyed themselves.

Anya discovered Philomena along with one of the dig leads, a Ken someone with cool, well-weathered jeans and the trademark trowel in his back pocket, deep in discussion in a shallow depression. Another grave. This particular feature had caused a little bit of a sensation when it had been discovered some days before. Anya looked down on the two and listened in to the discussion for a few seconds. Ken was then up off his knees, and, barely acknowledging her, he headed off on some errand. His absence gave Anya a chance to speak to Philomena.

'We'll have to tent this up today,' Philomena said in greeting. 'Can't leave this open to the elements, or any nosey snoops for that matter either. This grave, it's a little special Anya.'

The chance to explain was lost in the other girl's enthusiasm.

Anya nodded and looked into the grave scene, trying to seem interested whilst searching for an excuse in her mind for not saying what needed to be said. A plastic tarpaulin cover for the night had been peeled off leaving a fairly well-preserved skeleton beneath.

Anya had come to know Philomena quite well through this first year. They'd met regarding their shared matter now on a number of occasions. They actually got on quite well – they were even friends perhaps. Anya allowed herself a little smile. If the establishment only knew – here was an archaeologist who truly believed she was part of a reincarnation, but she'd never be sharing this. It was their secret.

Anya found herself bending down to view the finds more closely and this put her at the same level as Philomena. Despite Philomena being so young, Anya fully accepted her as more than competent in her profession. Now, once again, there was a chance to explain, but Anya just couldn't bring herself around to it – couldn't quite get the timing or find the words and her mind was working harder at finding another way round the problem. She could explain in one of her nice handwritten letters – that was the answer.

'OK, it was a woman, fairly tall.' Philomena looked her way. 'It's the dish, only small but even now, before the lab, that dish has come a long way.' Philomena pointed at a small greenish disc with the point of her trowel. The object had been placed on the right-hand side of the skeleton.

'Even without cleaning up you can see that dish has travelled some distance in antiquity for it to be here in Carmarthen.'

Anya could see that too as she knelt in to take a closer look. The decoration, it wasn't Roman, but contemporary.

'Persian?' Anya ventured and Philomena nodded. There was a smile broadening across the archaeologist's face.

'I think you're right Anya and that makes this find more than a little surprising.'

There were voices, people coming their way – the volunteer diggers were all coming over and Anya stood. Philomena rose too – perhaps she sensed something.

'I've just popped in to catch you – to say goodbye,' Anya said nervously.

'Right,' Philomena responded, and Anya was aware that Philomena was observing her closely now.

'Are you coming back over the summer then?' Philomena questioned.

'No, I'm going to spend a bit more time up north. I'll do a bit of work for old Huw. Get a bit of money together.'

'Why? You could get a summer job here? He'll start to depend on you.'

'It's only for the summer Philomena.' Now she'd lied to get away from Philomena's well-meaning interrogation. Anya knew she was being observed still, but she couldn't look the other back in the eye.

The pair were being met at the graveside, the team had descended on the two of them, deflecting Philomena's attention. Anya took the opportunity to slip back into the group and evade any further questioning.

Odd, through the corner of her eye, Anya took in Philomena's shadow, it moved but Philomena was stood still in one spot. Anya dismissed the image, there were more people crowding in at the grave now and the shadows could get muddled up, couldn't they? Still, as she walked quietly away, she noted that her shadow was clear. The shadows from the other diggers too, they were cast behind their owners where they had blocked out the early morning sun.

Anya looked back once more. 'No,' she said to herself when she noted how Philomena's shadow was behaving in the same way as everyone else's. She frowned with the thought, however, a little unsettled. She had seen what she had seen.

* * *

Anya made her way up to Trinity College, still feeling guilty. Checking her watch, she upped her pace. Time was going to be tight. The

281

TrawsCambria bus would be arriving at the bus station at 10.30 a.m. Her kit was packed and ready to collect from the student house but there wouldn't be any time spare. She had a package in her backpack which she'd labelled clearly last night.

FAO

Philomena Hutchinson

Archaeology Department, Trinity College

The deception now bothered her. Clearly it was always in her mind not to say goodbye properly. When handing the package over to the porter the deed was emphasised when he challenged her.

'Oh, she's down at the excavation love. You should pop it over yourself.'

'No,' Anya responded, 'I'm catching my bus home this morning. Please, just make sure she gets it.'

The porter shrugged. 'I'll pop it over to archaeology for you.' He went up on tip toes to place the package on the top mail shelf. '*Hwyl fawr* love!' the porter called after her as she made her way out of the college entrance.

21. Hades Calls to Persephone

The Ancient Greeks believed that Persephone was allowed back out from the underworld for but half a year. In that time, she brought with her the new growth and life in spring and the warmth of summer. Come autumn she was to return to her husband in his underworld lair of dark shadows, and the living world above would die through the winter that followed.

You can't cheat death; you can't come back from the dead, can you? There is sadly only ever one chance at life.

Denbigh AD 1990

August

Anya had been back in Denbigh now for several weeks, back at the old antique shop. The place had gone a little feral in her absence and clearly Huw had not been coping. Perhaps towards the end when his mother was failing, he just hadn't been able to face the shop. She suspected, however, that he had not wanted to keep things going since her departure the previous September.

Anya was now starting to make a difference and some of the old clientele had dropped in upon hearing that she was back and that the old place was sorting itself out again.

283

Of Denbigh town she had at first been wary when walking some of her old haunts. Passing the old mid link house on Love Lane she noticed a for sale sign. The place had been renovated and actually looked appealing. Walking on she headed up the steep metaled track through the Burgess Gate and up onto the castle green. She kind of wanted to go into the castle, just to show that old museum custodian that she had moved on, that things had turned around and that she was making a success of her life at last. Entering the little museum kiosk, she held back a moment, remembering her experience of being in this place last.

'If you're thinking of visiting the castle, we're closing in half an hour,' came the voice of an older woman from behind the till.

'Err... I've been around the castle before,' Anya responded.

'So, you won't want to look around again will you. I'm locking up in half an hour.'

'I was looking for the old custodian,' Anya continued. 'Is he about?'

'What old custodian? Are you paying or are you going?' The woman had clearly had enough for the day.

Anya smiled. 'I'm going,' she replied.

* * *

The old antique shop had been busy this morning. Denbigh seemed to be quite crowded for a Thursday. There had been several sales and a number of people had made requests for items. Anya was busy at the desk, scribbling down some notes – Huw could look out for some of these items when he was out and about at house sales or in the auction room.

Distracted by the paperwork, Anya was unaware that someone had entered the shop. When she looked up there was a young woman standing before her.

'Hello, can I help you with something?' Anya asked by way of welcome.

The young woman returned a weak smile and replied, 'I've found what I'm looking for.'

'Oh, well done,' Anya responded. 'Would you like to show me? I can gift wrap it for you if you like. Depending on what's taken your fancy.'

Again, there was that weak smile and the woman replied, 'You've not been here for a while, have you? I've visited more than once. I wondered if perhaps you'd be here today, on the anniversary.'

'Anniversary? I'm sorry, I don't understand.'

There were some other customers at the door. They seemed to be struggling with the handle.

'I'll just go and let these others in and I'll come back to you,' she said, puzzled.

'No, no you won't,' the other woman said, and Anya turned to look at her. There was a command in this young woman's voice and a cold stare in her eyes that stopped Anya in her tracks.

'Excuse me?'

Her visitor flashed her another smile, the smile of a hyena. Anya was starting to become nervous, and she cast a quick glance towards the shop door.

'They've already gone,' the visitor replied, 'and now I have you all to myself.' The woman took several steps closer.

Anya held her ground.

'How long ago was it now? I've been in once or twice, as I said. Old Goggy's been in. That's what they call him isn't it? Huw Gog, useless bugger. I've missed your pretty face mind because you're a bit different, aren't you?'

Anya didn't know the woman before her but she was already coming to some conclusions about her character. The words volatile, aggressive, and sinister came to mind. Anya had met individuals like this more than once when she lived on Love Lane. Such people were unpredictable. Anya wondered if there was a connection with some of the lowlife types that she'd had the unfortunate experience of meeting in her past.

'You're wondering, aren't you? You're wondering who I am? Should I share some more clues with you? Would you like that?'

Anya, in as calm a voice as she could muster, said, 'I'm sorry, but I don't know you and I'd like you to leave now.'

The visitor smiled once again. 'You're right, we don't know each other. Yet we're connected. That anniversary I mentioned – my brother lost his liberty on this day five years ago, and you? You lost someone special.'

Anya was suddenly putting the parts of this ridiculous guessing game together and was becoming increasingly fearful for what was going to happen next.

The visitor was now right up close and in her personal space.

'Surprise,' the visitor whispered, and, turning to look through the shop window, she added, 'Here he comes, just like the cavalry. I'll be seeing you around Richards.' And with that, the visitor calmly walked up to the front shop door. She slid the top bolt before pulling the door open. Stopping briefly, she turned to fix Anya one final look and then she was gone.

Anya stood, transfixed, frightened silly and it wasn't until the bell on the door clanged that she came to.

'What was she doing in here?' Huw demanded.

Anya looked at him but had lost her voice to answer.

'She's been in once or twice,' Huw grumbled, unaware of the state Anya was in. 'She's the sort of woman you want to watch in case she steals something. Common skank, her kind are real trouble. Gutter girl into drink, drugs and…' He seemed to catch himself before he said any more. Anya could feal the tears welling up in her eyes

'I'm sorry… I'm too quick to judge,' he added.

She rushed up and put her arms around him. She was shaking now with fear.

'I'm frightened. I'm frightened,' she repeated.

* * *

Ruthin AD 547

St Meugan's Ministry to the Northern Cymru

It had taken just two weeks to travel down to Illtud's college but some twenty years or more slipped by before Meugan made it back up to the village of his birth. He had strong, vivid memories of his father Llyr the headman and his mother, but his expectations of a great reunion, of seeing his parents again, were just dreams. They had long since passed on and his memories of this habitation were not as he found it today.

The village was a quieter place on his return and few now lived within the village hub. His recollection of a more crowded town, with houses, barns and some more majestic buildings were no more. Rebuilding trade, the pulse of commerce through the town, proved too much of a dream. The Kingdom of Gwynedd had dropped several steps behind what Roman Britannia had was once achieved, trapped as it was in an enduring struggle with the English. The world and the opportunities it afforded in the past were no longer.

Here he was, a learned man, trying to capture the imaginations of those with whom he had once lived among. He came bringing God's mission and the voice of the Christian founders. Following in the footsteps of the good shepherd, his task was to draw in the flock and establish a house of God in each of the communities through which he passed. Here at the red fort, links to the Christian faith had all been washed away by the tides of time.

Reaching the village centre, he climbed up to stand on the large erratic limestone block that sat in a small clearing. Villages all across the land had such stones – calling places for announcements and travelling preachers. There were, however, dark connotations with this particular stone. Had it not once been an executioner's block where Huail, brother of his good friend Gildas had met a sudden and shocking end?

The people of Cymru grew vegetables and tended livestock for their own consumption. Little, if anything, was brought to market and few travelled far. As Meugan explored this landscape once again, he contemplated the events he had lived through. There were visual pictures in his mind, his father and mother, the arrival of the lords of Gwynedd and the English before them. Of all, he thought about those who had come first. How, as young boys, they had caught sight of Gwenllian; he had strong visual memories of her.

Then there was Arth, the bear of Britannia to whom Gwenllian was promised. Try as he might, Meugan remembered little of what Arth actually looked like in life. There was the day that he had persuaded his father Llyr, to take the canoe out onto the marsh and there on the tumulus they had found bones and relics. These, Father had never identified to Meugan but the sword, this he knew had belonged to Arth and so, were not the bones the lost remains of the last lord of Britannia?

Meugan looked for the paths of his youth, the connections between the low hills that stood proud of the mere waters. The place had changed, and he could not quite identify now where events had once taken place.

A meeting ground from ancient times where old gods were revered, this he found, for people still met in this place. It was here where he would catch up with the locals and here where he laid the foundations for God's house, the first in this vicinity.

The people took well to the scriptures, enjoyed the stories, and looked to Meugan when of guidance they were in need. It was from here that he, Meugan, would talk about the events and the leaders who had once been amongst them as travellers in time.

'We should bring them to the house of God,' Meugan announced. 'We must find what remains and return them to God our Father.'

There were nods of confirmation from the congregation and so began the search for restitution.

Of all the landmarks to be identified, the tumulus in the mere was known and remembered and so, in high summer, a party, with Meugan at the lead, landed on this rise of the ground to search earnestly for what remained. Overgrown, this was now an island of dense blackthorn and undergrowth. Clearance was no easy task and time at the effort produced little but shards of old bone. The villagers had put together a small wooden box for they had expected that little would remain after so many years.

In this way some bones were brought to rest in the grounds around Meugan's house of God. The ossuary was placed west-east in a shaft pit, but the bone preservation was poor, and no one knew quite which bone was which. Heads bowed in solemnity; the congregation wished the deceased on to the next world.

Of Gwenllian there had been much talk and rumour. Meugan remembered somethings of her capture by the English and how the elders had told the children that she had been taken away by Cynric so as to be his bride. This was the story that was shared but there had been a deep sadness and shock in the community soon after the English had departed. To this day Meugan suspected that there was something more, that unsettling dark truths had been omitted from the story of Gwenllian's last days.

Meugan tried to locate the young oak where local tradition had placed Arth and Gwenllian together, meeting as lovers. Today there were many oaks and the villagers claimed each one as 'the oak'. As he stood considering, he experienced a feeling of loss. Where was this beautiful woman of his memories laid to rest? Was she here or did she lie cold and lonely in dark English earth? There was no one here who knew, no one left who remembered.

22. Elysium

Elysium

He had promised her Elysium but if this world was Paradise, then she cared not to discover the dark underworld realm of Hyades. A life with Hyades, however, was what she deserved.

The old gods had a long reach and their desires had seeped through the tapestry of time. They did not want to be forgotten and as she had grown from childhood through puberty, so their demands had become more audible, a lust for revenge not yet satiated.

Childhood had been an agony. There were things that she could see but not understand and through her the demons expressed their will. As she had grown so a balance had developed and today, she could read and feel beyond the edge to exercise her own needs and desires. Time, however, had not played fair and through circumstance she had missed what she had sought to find and take for herself. Her half-wit of a half-brother, a monstrosity of mistakes, had murdered what might have been most precious and yet she felt that a link between light and dark still endured somewhere, just beyond her touch.

* * *

Denbigh AD 1990

Late August

Huw engaged his key into the Yale lock and pushed his front door open.

'Hello!' he called out. 'I'm home!'

He was greeted by a deathly silence – too quiet.

'She must be out in the back,' he said to himself and, putting down his bags, he made for the back door and the rear garden. A still, empty silence greeted him there too. He retreated back into the house, believing perhaps that she'd gone out, that she'd be back at any minute, but he headed for Anya's room just to check, pulling at the ungainly knot of his gaudy tie. Pushing the door, it came to an early stop and would not open further. He stretched his head round to identify the obstruction beyond.

* * *

Carmarthen AD 1990

August

Philomena came out of the bunker, a term that was now affectionately afforded to describe the archaeology department. On leaving the dark access corridor she was dazzled by the bright light of the outside. Trinity was quiet on a Sunday morning, nothing very much happened then.

On the path in front of her, almost denying her ongoing access, was a large, glossy magpie. The creature made her stop in her tracks. Out of habit she looked around for another.

'Where's your mate then?' she enquired of the bird. It made no move to fly off, instead it tilted its head to observe her; it was almost studying her, carefully, considering.

Philomena was not generally superstitious, but she did have a thing about magpies. Most of the time she was happy to see four, but if you saw just one, then the day would go downhill from there on. In fact, Philomena considered it meant even worse than that – something quite unpleasant would occur and the rest of the time would be spent waiting for the nasty event.

It had been several seconds now, and the pioden wasn't going anywhere.

'What have you seen? What are you after?' As Philomena addressed the bird it hopped towards her.

'That's enough,' Philomena spoke her thoughts and she stamped out at the bird and threatened it with her fist just to show she meant real business. The thing took flight up and onto the fence that ran alongside the path. There it remained, chattering loudly at her, defiant.

'What? You're pushing your luck mate!' she said in response and then suddenly felt a bit stupid. *Oh, for goodness' sake get a grip Philomena, take no notice. It's only a stupid bird.*

Philomena continued on her way down the path. The pioden hopped along the fence alongside, chattering. Chattering at her! Philomena turned again to face the bird.

'I'm going to throw something at you in a minute mate because you're really starting to bug me!'

At this the bird flew straight down towards her head. Philomena ducked as black feathers clipped the top of her hair and the damn thing passed over and perched up in one of the magnolia trees, out of sight.

'Good riddance to you, nasty sod!' she called out at the bird, but she didn't hang about outside for a response. She crossed through the ornate courtyard garden and bolted into the science block, somewhat shaken by the encounter.

* * *

Denbigh AD 1990

Late August

'Has she taken anything?' the paramedic was now addressing him. 'Mr Roberts? Do you know if she's taken anything?'

Huw shrugged his shoulders. The flashing blue lights, the seriousness of the situation, this was all now catching up with him.

'Err…' Huw started to reply.

'If she has taken something, we need to know Mr Roberts. If we know we'll be able to treat her more effectively.'

'I, err… as far as I'm aware she's taken nothing,' Huw returned but his mind was now on overtime. Had she, was she still taking drugs? A strong feeling of betrayal surged into his mind and then almost as quickly as the idea had formed, he quashed it. No, no, there had been no evidence. No, he could not have deceived him. No, he was sure she was clean – had been clean in all the time that he had known her, and he felt a pang of guilt now for the disloyalty in his thoughts towards her.

The stretcher was clicked up to height and was pushed out along his drive to the awaiting ambulance, doors open, a silent cacophony of lights and drama. The neighbours would all be aware. They'd all know, be pointing the fingers of accusation. 'That woman he's taken in. The addict, the prostitute.' Huw's mind was in a whorl, a blind panic, as he climbed up to join Anya and the stretcher in the ambulance.

'You're going to accompany her Mr Roberts?' the paramedic questioned.

'Yes, yes,' he replied automatically as the two professionals calmly set about their tasks, clicking things, securing and closing, checking the patient. Anya's left arm dropped, exposed, and the scars screamed out at everyone present.

'She's clean, she's not been a user for years,' Huw said, defending her. The paramedic responded only with a nod as Huw took her hand in his. The door was slammed behind and all the world now was confined to the ambulance cabin. The stretcher was clipped into place, and the vehicle moved off. In all this there was such an activity, of lights, of sounds, of the bump, bump of the road, and of the wild swings from side to side as the vehicle made its way. A vehicle for the seriously ill? It was the most uncomfortable ride Huw had ever taken.

Anya had not been responsive in all this time – a tepid corpse – and now suddenly, a return of pressure on his hand. The paramedic, standing up by her head, reaching out fiddling with some plastic tubing, was unaware, lost in the vehicle sound. Huw leaned over as he was sure, in all the noise, the discord of this vile transport, he was sure she was speaking.

'Huw.'

'Yes, yes, Anya – good girl. Stay with us,' he responded.

'Huw, when I go, when I pass on, put me to rest next to Timothy.'

'Don't be daft. You're not going anywhere young lady,' he said reassuringly. 'We'll have you back up and ship shape by the end of the night you'll see.'

'No,' came a weak reply and Huw had to lean in very closely to catch near silent words.

'I've seen my pasts,' Anya continued.

He squeezed her hand. 'No love, no. Look to the future…'

* * *

She flipped over in the cool aqua, the pool lane lines stretching out in dark blue tiles deep below. She was strong, powerful. She kicked out, the whoosh through the water effortless in her black one-piece swimsuit. He would not miss her now, he could not, for he would be the next in on her lane, the next for the relay swim.

And she was strong, so strong, like never before, and she swam and swam – she could keep going forever, cutting through the black ripples and on into a band of deep cold. The dark purple clouds overhead tore open, allowing shafts of pure white light to cascade down from the heavens, lighting up the bottomless lake waters, the dark brooding mountains behind. Then ahead on the bank – a figure, waving her on. He was there, he had waited for her. Now he called, he called her name – Gwenllian, Gwenllian!

Have you been called to the quest?
Is your soul prepared?

Postscript

Hannah had brought a bag with her tonight and had been potching about upstairs. Dan guessed that she might be staying the night but hadn't questioned her. She was the one that he didn't want to let slip by and so he was inclined to let her make her own decisions. He'd wanted her to move in a long time ago but had kept this to himself – he didn't want to push. Hannah only lived around the corner and had the habit of calling round in the evening and staying until quite late and then he'd walk her back round. Perhaps she didn't want to upset anyone in her family, but everyone knew they were a couple in every sense of the word. Dan liked Hannah being around and had the confidence that any decisions she made would work well for them both.

This evening, like most mid-week, was all about catching up with work and work was going very well. He'd sold and registered thirty vans this month – that was totally unheard of for this part of the world and the dealership was wondering how best to keep hold of their young protégée. Still, there were downsides. With such good business there came a shed load of bloody paperwork. Dan was switched on enough to know that the Devil was in the detail – the paperwork counted for success, so he needed to go through things carefully. This was a tedious job and Dan didn't much like tedious tasks, so he kept them for home where he had peace and quiet and generally not so many interruptions.

Hannah bounded back downstairs to join him. She was positive and upbeat.

'That's all sorted,' she announced.

'You're staying the night then?' Dan enquired.

'Yeah, no point in keeping up the pretence anymore is there,' she responded.

'I guess not – it's cool with me. Your parents OK with this?'

'Why wouldn't they be? It's not like we've rushed into things and been bloody stupid teenagers, is it?'

'No. I put some stuff in your fridge too. I'll make us something nice to eat and tomorrow I fancy doing some baking. What time will you be back from work?'

Dan grinned. Hannah would sort this place out and he was all for some creature comforts.

The doorbell went, giving them both a start.

'It's your dad, come to drag you back home,' Dan joked, making for the front door. Hannah followed in his direction – just in case.

At the door was a large man who Dan didn't recognise.

'Err, so sorry to interrupt you both, it's Mr Roberts,' the large gentleman said by way of introduction.

'Yes and…?' Dan responded.

'Huw Guto Roberts.' Dan made the name connection and nodded.

'Might I come in Daniel?'

Hannah shot Dan a puzzled look.

301

'Err, yes, this way Mr Roberts.' Dan ushered the large gent into the living room. Hannah made to close the front door behind them both.

'Take a seat.' Dan motioned for him to sit on the orange settee in the living room. 'So, Mr Roberts, what can I do for you this evening?'

'Thank you, Daniel. I'll come straight to the point of my visit if I may.'

'Sure, you go straight to it,' Dan Jones responded.

'You were a friend of Anya, Anya Richards yes?' Huw gave Dan an earnest look.

'Yes, I know Anya, but you're speaking of her very much in the past tense here Mr Roberts.'

Hannah, who had been standing awkwardly in the doorway up to this point, walked over to the settee and squeezed into the corner, before saying, 'Hi.'

Mr Roberts nodded, and Dan remembered to introduce her.

'Sorry, Mr Roberts, this is my girlfriend, Hannah.'

'Hi,' Huw responded in turn. Continuing their previous conversation, he said, 'I am. I am speaking in the past tense here, yes Daniel.' Huw nodded his head several times in quick succession before breathing in deeply. 'I've got bad news.'

'Oh,' Dan responded.

'She's passed on, my Anya, I mean Miss Richards, she's passed on,' Huw managed to get out before breaking down into tears.

'Ah, right OK – I'll do us all a cup of tea,' Dan announced, leaving Hannah to pick up the pieces. Dan was hopeless with things like this, and he made a swift exit to the kitchen, clicked the kettle on and pottered about with some cups and things. An excuse to get out of the situation. When he returned, a tray with three mugs of tea between both hands, Hannah was consoling the large gent with an arm around his shoulders. She lifted her head and if looks could kill, Huw wouldn't be the only one grieving over a lost loved one tonight.

'Ah, Mr Roberts, a *paned* for you. I wasn't sure whether you took milk, but I've put some in and some sugar, might perk you up a bit. Give you a chance to tell us what's happened, yes?'

Huw set about getting back some of his self-control.

'I'm so sorry,' he said. He turned to Hannah beside him. 'Thank you, I'll be alright now, I'm sure.' He accepted the cup of tea from Dan.

Dan sat down opposite Hannah and Huw.

'So,' Dan began, 'are you ready to tell us what's happened?'

'Well, you knew Anya and you were great friends with a Tim, Timothy, yes?' Huw began.

'Tim was my best mate. He had a real crush on Anya, and she liked him too. It had gone on for ages, but they were both too shy, too starstruck to even talk to each other. Then, when they finally got around to meeting, well, I suppose you know the story?'

'No not really,' Hannah interjected.

303

Jones looked at his girlfriend. 'OK, well I guess it's complicated and I'm only on the edge of it. I helped to bring them both together and now Anya's dead too? How has that happened Mr Roberts?'

'I don't really know how.' Huw shook his head. 'Anya had come back from college to live with me and help out in the shop over the summer break. I had the feeling she was going to stay. Then Anya had this confrontation with another woman in the shop. I'd seen this person before; she would call in randomly from time to time. There was something about her – rough, like I noticed her because she looked like trouble. I don't think Anya had met her in the shop before but maybe she was somebody from Anya's past when Anya was living in the squat. I had a bad feeling about this woman – not a nice person.'

'The confrontation, Mr Roberts; what was it about? Dan asked.

'I don't know because Anya wouldn't say, but she was frightened by it. Anya wasn't the same after and a couple of days later I found her just lying there unconscious on the floor in the house. So I called for an ambulance.'

'Have you spoken to the police about the woman in the shop?' Hannah questioned.

Huw lowered his head. 'Yes, I rang and went to the police station and gave a description of the woman but what had she done?'

'She'd threatened Anya, frightened her,' Dan chipped in.

'Yes, sure but I don't know what was said and the police said they couldn't do anything based on what I'd told them.'

'Did the police know of the woman, you know, from your description?' Hannah added.

Huw sighed, 'They didn't say as much but I think maybe. Anya was involved with some unpleasant types when she was doing drugs and things. It's part of life when you choose to live like that, so the police reckoned.'

Dan shrugged. 'They were helpful then, and you don't know any more Mr Roberts?'

'No, but briefly, just once, Anya came to and spoke to me in the ambulance during the journey into hospital. They kept her alive for days, but she wasn't really there anymore. There's been a lot, you know, *a lot of a to do*. Coroner's inquest and all such manner of things. The police came and searched my house. The paramedics questioned whether it was drugs.'

'Anya looked really rough when we saw her, didn't she Dan? She could have been taking heroin or something?' Hannah added.

'They did all these tests, toxicology or something, and there was nothing like that, but initially I think there was a question of a poison, organic or something.'

'A poison?' Dan asked, 'Like somebody killed her?'

'I don't know, the police did some snooping and of course there was that woman in the shop. They came back to ask me about her again but quickly dropped the whole thing. After a full post-mortem, the coroner's enquiry recorded an open verdict – some of the drug abuse in

305

the past had damaged Anya's internal organs. Lots of things in her past, you know.'

'Who was that woman in the shop Mr Roberts?' Dan asked.

'I don't know.'

There was a sudden cold sensation running down Dan's neck and back. All this was connected to that afternoon in Prestatyn and that vile family. God only knew what underworld networks they had and what they got up to. Hannah was looking at him, she could see he was troubled. Huw, however, pushed on with the main reason for his call. He wanted to do something for Anya, and he knew that Daniel would be able to help.

'When Anya spoke to me, you know, the last time in the ambulance she asked to be put next to Tim when she'd gone. I didn't know Tim, but she had mentioned you and your work in the past, so I looked you up. That's why I'm here. She didn't have anybody left – just me and you Daniel. They're going to release her body so I've a funeral to arrange. I'll get something in the paper. She'll have had school friends – they'll come to pay their respects even though, well, she'd lost contact because of the drugs and that. They would come don't you think Daniel?'

'I'm sure they would Mr Roberts,' Dan reassured.

'And you'll know where this Timothy is lying won't you?' Huw continued.

'Aren't there rules about where you can be buried in a church yard?' Hannah asked. 'I'm sure you'd have to ask Tim's relatives. They might not want Anya being buried next to their son.'

'If I can't bury her body then I could spread her ashes,' Huw responded. 'Perhaps we should go for a cremation anyway, but she will lie next to her Timothy, I'll see to that.'

'You're taking a lot on Mr Roberts, what about her family, her next of kin?' Hannah was concerned and showing some maturity in all of this.

'I don't know of any family, the stepmother and sister – they've moved away. The father well, he's another reason for the police coming down to the conclusions that they have. He's no longer with us of course.'

'Grandparents, cousins or something?' Hannah persisted.

Huw shook his head. 'Not that I know of. Besides,' Huw continued, 'where have they all been? When she needed someone, where were they?'

'I'll contact Tim's family,' Dan confirmed. 'I'll help out too. I think Tim would have liked Anya to be next to him, sure he would.'

'Yes, yes but once the body is released, I'll have to make the arrangements, contact the vicar for the church where Tim lies. I'll need to know what I can do so I can plan things properly.' Huw spoke with great feeling and intent. He was going to do his best for Anya. They were all in agreement.

Dan stood up and walked over to the patio doors at the other end of the room beyond the black IKEA dining table. There was a view from the back garden to the mountains beyond.

'This woman that threatened Anya, you're sure there's nothing more?' Dan turned to face Huw.

'What is it Daniel?' Hannah questioned.

'Ah, it's just that Anya felt there was much more to Tim's murder. There was a reason, we'd upset the apple cart and the killer, and that he was seeking revenge.'

'What are you saying – he might be out, released and coming to get us?' Hannah asked, sounding concerned.

'No, but just briefly, Anya described someone else and maybe there's a different kind of danger. Some things frightened me a bit when this all kicked off that summer – could never explain it.'

Hannah stood up. 'Mr Roberts, it's getting on.'

'Yes, yes its time I was on my way,' Huw replied.

'I'll take your details for Dan before you go and well, we'll be in touch, yes?' Hannah added. 'If we can do anything to help – you'll ask, won't you? You'll keep us involved?'

Huw nodded and she led him out to the front door.

After seeing Huw out, Hannah came to stand next to Dan at the patio doors and put her arm over his shoulder.

'Were you quite close to Anya?' she asked.

'No,' Dan responded. 'She was pretty and really nice; shy really. Her mother died when she'd just started in the comprehensive school, and we all felt for her then. I hadn't realised that her father had started to abuse her after. You don't know, do you?' He turned to face Hannah 'She just seemed like one of the cool girls in school, bright and everything going for her. Fun to tease a bit but you just don't know what's in the background. I've been really lucky.'

'And me,' Hannah added putting her arm around his waist now and holding him tighter. 'Perhaps we can do something for her now and help old Huw out too?'

'Anya mentioned the name of a detective inspector – what was his name?'

'Did she? When was this, Dan?'

'I met her again last summer. She was all excited and had found some things to follow from Tim's notebook. She'd met that DI who was interested – oh God what was his name?' Dan rubbed his temples between finger and thumb. For the first time in ages, he was having a mega headache.

'I'm going to take tomorrow morning off work. I'll ring in first thing. They'll be OK with it because I've done really well for them this month. Then I'm going to go down to the Police Station to see if I can make contact with this detective inspector.'

'Do you want me to come with you Dan?' Hannah asked.

'No, you shouldn't go taking time off too, but I'll meet you after. We could have a quick lunch together. What do you think?'

Hannah nodded. 'Sounds a good plan.'

Jones clicked the room lights off and they both looked out through the patio windows. The Clwydian hills were clearly silhouetted against the night sky. Dan Jones had the strong feeling that the malevolent presence was not at rest; there was something out there, just beyond the edge, watching, waiting. Of this he was quite sure and the whole thing made him feel very, very uncomfortable.

About this Book

The Maen Huail

Gildas wrote the only contemporary accounts of Britain from AD 500–AD 570. In his writings he states that he was born in the same year as the Battle of Badon Hill (Mons Badonicus) in which the Britons vanquished the Angles and Saxons. Legend has it that Gildas had a brother, Huail, who was executed by beheading on the Maen Huail (a large rough limestone block) which now sits on a plinth beside Exmewe Hall on St Peter's Square in Ruthin. Gildas was tutored by St Illtud in

Llantwit Major in South Wales. He was among a number of famous students who included St Patrick, St David, St Samson and St Meugan. Gildas was the only pupil of St Illtud from whom any written accounts survive.

Interestingly, the oldest church in Ruthin is dedicated to St Meugan and is one of very few that take his name. Is it possible that Meugan and Gildas met whilst being tutored at Illtud's college in South Wales?

Might they have both originated in North Wales?

St David is sometimes referred to as David Aquaticus. He is thought to have stood in cold water for long periods of time in the belief that the waters would wash away his sins. Such feats of personal discomfort were later remembered and inspired his followers across Wales.

Terms used in A Banner of Dark Shadows

English	German & Danish Settlers – Angles, Jutes and Saxons
paned	a heart-warming cup of tea
Sais	a *derogatory* Welsh term for an English person
Y Ceffyl Du	the Black Horse Public House (now closed and boarded up)
Cer! Shiw!	Go Away!
Hwyl Fawr	Goodbye

Books in the Series

On Badon Field

A Banner of Dark Shadows

The Fallen and the Fled

On Badon Field

The sun is finally setting on Britannia, Rome's most Westerly province. The central administration has collapsed, and the country begins to fracture into many individual kingdoms. Arth, the second son of the Votadani, is sent by his father to the great gathering at ISCA; this a last call to arms for all those with Roman sympathies, to make a stand and fight for Britannia.

Whilst at ISCA, Arth meets a mysterious Roman girl, a traveller from the East, who has crossed the vastness of the Roman World. As a gift this Roman girl presents Arth with an ancient artefact, a small and much damaged wooden goblet. This he keeps for her, and the fortune it brings favours the bold, for on Badon Field, Britannia will vanquish her enemies.

Now a survivor and a respected leader, Arth is included on a magic charm. Cut into stone on the eve of battle this charm is to bring eternal protection for those who share blood over its engraved circles.

While out walking early one morning, in the summer of 1985, Tim picks up a stone carved with strange markings – whispers from a forgotten time. From this point on, Tim's destiny today will be connected to the man he once was long, long ago.

Praise for On Badon Field ISBN: 978-1-7399754-0-1

'On Badon Field is a compelling, fascinating story that moves seamlessly between the final days of the Roman Empire and modern-day North Wales. A transition like that is something which is difficult to manage but Martin Kaye spans the gap with ease. Both elements of the story are gripping in their ability to grab and hold the reader with equal intensity. Quite simply, it is exceptionally well done.'
Phil Carradice Author and Broadcaster

'A very thought-provoking adventure which raises deep questions about the meaning of life, and the possibilities of reincarnation: a very readable mixture of mystery and history. We recommend it thoroughly.'

Mrs Patricia and Rev. Lionel Fanthorpe, BA, FCP, FRSA, FCIM, Cert.Ed.

Author's Website:
www.fachlwyd.co.uk